The Spyglass and the Cherry Tree

Also by Matt Beighton

Monstacademy Series
The Halloween Parade
The Magic Knight
The Egyptian Treasure

For Younger Readers
Spot The Dot

MATT BEIGHTON

THE SPYGLASS AND THE CHERRY TREE

THE SPYGLASS AND THE CHERRY TREE

Printed in the United Kingdom
First printed 2017

A CIP catalogue record for this book is available from
the British Library.

Hardcover ISBN: 978-1-9997244-6-7
Perfect Bound ISBN: 978-1-9997244-0-5

www.mattbeighton.co.uk
www.greenmonkeypress.co.uk

For Phoebe and Willow

Toni, you are my rock. Without your endless
patience and support, none of this would be possible.
Thank you, now and forever.
Love you x

The North Wood

North Bay

Balzor's Strait

Kobold

The Hidden Well

Glen of Tears

Port Escrildor

Theandre

Landragog

Tor

Druidmotte

Dune

Golmankin Range

The Silver River

Wizened Peaks

The Wandering Place

Alastor

The Gloom

Fenhar

Loritas

The Shadowlands
(where the spirits roam)

Hillmoss

Galadah

Lisrath's Peak

Tenlef

Scirien Mountains

y of
ouls

Carak Tak

Melagan's Folly

Kevidar's Pass

Beilmor

Orcwood

Crazak D'Ur

Orccleith Range

Phoenix
Falls

The Longman Trail

Bay of
Sorrow

Westport

The Solar

The Kraken Dwell

Kanthor
(The lost realm of the Elves)

Hartann
(The realm of men)

Eragar
(Walled city)

Harangar
(The Burnt Fort)

Milsander
(The Royal City)

Realm of
Milsandith

Prologue

Sparks leapt into the air as the metal blades of heavy axes fought against unyielding stone. Endless rain poured down the mountainside sweeping through the valleys and picking up speed and volume as it flooded rivers and lakes and scythed through the forests before rushing into the ever-widening quarries that erupted like boils on the landscape. The crack of whips echoed around the hills as hideous creatures, twisted and warped like demons from a nightmare, bent double under the urgent force of their masters driving them deeper and deeper into the ground. Many drowned, dragged under the rising water by their heavy clothes but still they were driven on. Their masters were frenzied in their desire for that which history had long foretold was hidden out of sight.

Scurrying amongst the slaves, leather-clad shamans were protected from the worst of the rain but were soaked through nonetheless by their insistence on dropping to the bottom of each new hole and listening intently to the rocks and tree roots that were being unearthed. Each one would pull out a bone horn and place it to the wall and listen intently whilst all digging around them stopped and the workers fell quiet. Only the sound of falling rain and distant thunder interrupted the silence. Inevitably, they'd shake their heads and look to the sky in anguish, and the digging would resume.

As days blurred into months into years and eventually into centuries, the race known as the Shrunken dug deeper into the bowels of their world scarring its landscape forever. Rivers were dammed and diverted and forests plundered for their timber. Not a hill went untouched nor a valley left unmined in their insatiable quest. Until one day a shaman, crouched on his knees at the foot of a deep well hidden in the shadows of an ancient oak tree, his horn pressed firmly to the sodden clay wall, sighed and closed his eyes. Silently, he stood tall, and this time he didn't shake his head. Instead, he nodded almost imperceptibly to the solitary young miner who stood alone as the only other witness to what was about to happen. The miner lay down his axe and reached into his belt for a smaller, more delicate trowel. He took to his knees and slowly, painstakingly teased away the mud ignoring the muddy water and nervous sweat that ran down his face. Eventually, he took a step back and, along with the shaman, looked down upon the oily black glass that shimmered even in the half-light of the storm.

The shaman turned and walked slowly away, stopping only to whisper a message to one of the guards at the entrance to the hole. Behind him, the swish of a sword followed by a deep moan and wet thud reassured him that the only witness to the discovery had been taken care of. It had been found.

Skye Thistle

The army of goblins stretched away to the horizon. They were scrambling forwards, climbing over each other in their eagerness to rush the waiting army of men. The frosted grass underfoot was soon turned to mud as their clawed feet churned and kicked away at it. Their quarry was still small on the horizon, but the foul creatures were doing all they could to cover the distance quickly.

Waiting for their attack were a vast army of men fronted by hundreds of mounted cavalry and backed by thousands more foot soldiers stretching to the rear. Row upon row of men stood to attention beneath banners of every colour and design. Each one was waiting, ready for the command from the tall girl sat proudly in the saddle of her strong warhorse that paced to and fro in front of her soldiers. She was no more than a teenager, and her wiry frame didn't seem strong enough to support the heavy armour that she wore. Long ginger hair flowed from under her helmet and danced in the fierce wind that swirled around the battlefield.

Around her, snow started to fall with a softness that seemed alien against the raging noise of the oncoming goblins. Where it settled on the warm hides of the horses, it melted with a soft hiss, but it was starting to settle in drifts against the trees at the edge to the woodland that flanked the battlefield on both sides. The woodlands that were to be their refuge if all went wrong. They were being cut off from their only salvation by the failing weather.

Thousands of men at her side. Thousands of men rapidly called to arms from all corners of her empire. How many could she rely upon if the fight went south? How many would flock back to the darkness if her plan failed? She knew that she had some good men around her, men that she had fought with for years. For the rest, she knew she could do nothing but hope.

The goblins were close. A pallid mist hung above their steaming bodies as they tore through the icy air. The goblins didn't feel the cold, the girl had been told. It was one of many things that she knew about goblins, information that the village women had passed down to her when she was younger and raids on the village more common. As she flexed her fingers to take the edge off the chill, she wished she could stay as warm as they were.

The enemy were close enough now to see the hate in their eyes. She knew it was time. The girl screamed her defiance at the oncoming wave of darkness and allowed her spear to drop into her saddle. Her call to charge echoed through the legions at her command. With a mighty roar, she led the cavalry forwards at a gallop.

A wall of green rose up as they drew closer, each goblin climbing on to the backs of those in front in a desperate bid to wrench the mounted soldiers from their saddles. The goblin weapons were largely old and worn, but they still looked sharp in the dawn light. From this distance, their chattering cries and unholy screams merged into one incoherent noise. She knew there was only one way this could end. These demons needed sending back to the hell from which they came.

The ground vibrated to the pounding of horseshoes hammering into the earth. The girl felt her horse slip on the frozen turf and strain every muscle to keep its balance. Suddenly, they were on top of the goblins, and the girl thrust her spear forwards and straight through the chests of the first of the enemies to reach her. She cast the spear aside, weighed down by the spiked bodies, and drew her sword. It shone in what little light there was, and she felt the power course through her arms.

A goblin came at her from the side. The girl managed to drop her shield in time to take the blow, and she felt the dull throb reverberate through her arm before she removed the goblin's head with her sword. She felt a thud against her calf as a goblin on the ground hacked at her with a blunted blade. She hacked down and rewarded it for its trouble by piercing it with the tip of her blade as it jumped upwards, screaming, towards her face.

Enemy after enemy fell beneath her until, from nowhere, a crossbow bolt smacked into the neck of her horse. She felt it tense and thrash around beneath her, its muscles moving like a sack of thick snakes. With a loud whinny, it fell to the ground throwing the girl clear at the last minute. She slipped as she tried to scramble to her feet, but that split second was all it took for her enemies to fall upon her. She heard their claws and teeth scratching against her armour before her helmet was pulled from her head.

Looking up through her forest of matted red hair, the girl saw two pools of emerald green punctuated by deepest darkness. She saw the eyes blink slowly and the head pull back from hers. She saw the goblin raise a rusty sickle high above its head before bringing it swinging down towards her neck.

The blow never came.

Just as the blade should have been making its terminal mark, Skye Thistle found herself jolted from her dream and flung onto her bedroom floor, her hands groping at her neck. She was sweating again and completely tangled up in her quilt. These dreams were becoming more common. She was having them practically every other day now.

Skye glanced across at her bedside table and looked at the alarm clock. It read 5:00 a.m. Still too early to get up. She shook her head clear and allowed herself to drift back to sleep.

In many ways, Skye wasn't a typical fourteen-year-old, but she did like her sleep. The chaos of her bedroom and the feeling of control that it allowed her made her feel more comfortable there than anywhere else in the world. The walls had originally been painted white but were now hung with scraps of old notebook paper covered in scribbled handwriting and half-finished designs for contraptions and inventions. Skye preferred to write things down before they flew from her head forever.

Books were scattered across her floor, but, unlike

many of her peers, Skye had no interest in biographies of famous singers or the love stories of the latest boy bands. Skye had no time for fairy tales of either the romantic or imaginary kind.

Here Be Goblins!

Those were the words scrawled in faded marker onto a cheap wooden plaque that had been nailed to her door by her mother. That had been Skye's only concession to the *hobbies* that her mother forced upon the family.

Goblins featured heavily in Skye's life. Her mother was what she called a *believer*. She believed in goblins, fairies and all manner of other woodland folk. If ever a family member ventured further than the local village, they were expected to bring back some sort of ornament that featured a hideous goblin or fabulous fairy. As a result, the house was littered with cheap, tacky models. Skye had relented to the sign on her door simply to avoid yet another argument. She definitely wasn't a believer. This made her dreams all the more worrying, never mind that her classmates at school might find out about her mother and make her life even more miserable. She didn't have many friends as it was.

She didn't have to worry about not having friends for a while, though. Skye breathed a huge sigh of relief.

Today was Saturday. Not only that, it was the best Saturday in the whole year. Except maybe Christmas. It was the first Saturday of the summer holidays and that meant that it was the longest possible time until she had to think about that dreaded school again.

Or at least it was *normally* the best Saturday of the year. This year was different. As soon as she'd arrived home after the last day at school, Skye's mother had met her at the door with a wide-eyed grin that Skye had instantly recognised as trouble. She'd had a bad enough day as it was, getting into yet another fight with the school bully Keith Boggart. She didn't need any more bad news.

"You're going on holiday!" her mother clucked as she grabbed Skye around her shoulder and directed her straight up to her room to pack. "To see Ron and Wilma!"

Skye's stomach sank. Ron and Wilma – they'd said it made them feel too old to be called Grandma and Grandpa – were Skye's mother's parents and were eternally dull. What was worse was that she was being shipped off for three weeks! Half of her summer holiday had been wiped away just like that. She felt like crying. Instead, she'd stormed to her room and packed her bags. As she fled up the stairs, a pair of bright green eyes watched her from behind the laundry basket.

Skye turned curiously towards the glow, but there was nothing there. She shook her head and carried on to her room.

In the end, it hadn't taken her long at all to pack, and she'd spent the rest of the night sulking under her quilt. Other than a few basic clothes, the only thing she'd bothered to pack was her trusty Swiss Army knife. It had been a present from her grandpa Hank and her grandma Sophia, her father's parents, for her eighth birthday. Her grandpa had passed away soon after that and her grandmother not long after him, and Skye considered it one of her most treasured possessions in the world.

The only other thing that Skye really treasured was an old silver ring that had been given to her by her mother two summers ago. At the time, her mother had told her that it had been passed down through the family for many generations and that Skye should treasure it.

The band was dented and grey with age and the large stone that once sat on top had long since been lost. The six pronged, claw-shaped setting now sat empty, but Skye treasured it nonetheless and wore it constantly on her left middle finger. She had developed the habit of turning it over and over until her finger was rubbed sore whenever she felt nervous. She never cared, though. It helped her to feel safe in some strange, unexplainable way. It reminded her of her childhood, of picnics in the garden with her mother and walks through the park with Hank and Sophia. Her grandmother always used to joke that the ring made her a princess and would grant her any magic wish that she could think of. It hadn't been able to stop her grandparents from getting ill, no matter how hard she'd rubbed it.

When it was eventually time for Skye to wake up, it was to the clangs and bangs of her parents preparing the car to leave.

After noisily racing up the stairs, her mother whipped the quilt back from Skye's head. With a groan as her eyes adjusted to the light, Skye stared up into her muddy, smiling face. She let out another, longer groan as her eyes wandered down and rested on the fake pink wings that her mother was wearing on her back.

She knew that her mother had been out into the garden digging around and trying to communicate with the Elder goblin who, her mother said, was very distrustful of human beings and would only talk to other fairies or goblins, hence the wings.

Skye knew better than to argue as it would just lead to a long conversation that would leave her brain itching as she tried to persuade her mother to adopt a more appropriate and acceptable hobby. Instead, she picked up her suitcase and followed her mother downstairs and to the car.

Eventually, after her father had finally found the keys, the engine spluttered into life and they were on their way. As the car pulled away from the house, a pair of bright green eyes burnt briefly in the thick privet hedge that bordered the driveway. Skye caught the glow reflected in the rear-view mirror, but by the time she had turned around, there was nothing more sinister than the neighbour's cat sat watching her.

The journey passed quickly and soon they arrived at Ron and Wilma's house, Shutterly Manor. The grand house sat in a perfect location right on the coastline. A path to the side of the house led down to a shingle beach and a gravel road to the rear led to a long-abandoned lighthouse.

As soon as Skye exited the car and saw her grandparents waiting on their drive, her mood clouded even more. Wilma was wrapped head to toe in a long piece of vivid cerise material, bringing to mind a Roman emperor who had accidentally left his pink pants in the washing machine with his toga. This did nothing to hide her massive frame and enormous bust. She was nearly as wide as she was tall. It just made her look like a giant cranberry. Resting on her fat nose were a pair of stunning white-rimmed glasses speckled with sparkling rhinestones. She had clearly painted her lips a dark plum colour earlier in the day, though by now most of it was spread across her teeth and upper lip. To finish it all off, Wilma had teased and pulled her pepper-coloured hair up into a tall bun that sat nearly a foot above her head.

Skye snapped her gaze away from her grandma and saw that her grandpa Ron was steadfastly waiting his turn to speak. He was little more than a stick with shoes. He was tall, just over six feet, but Skye was prepared to bet that he didn't weigh much more than Skye herself.

Unlike his wife, Ron didn't sport glasses, in fact his only facial adornment was a supremely bushy moustache. Skye suspected that it was dyed midnight black as Ron's close-cropped hair had long ago turned white. His moustache easily stretched from one ear to the next. When Ron was excited or angry, it would bristle and shake until it hung lower than his bottom lip.

Her parents had soon made a hasty greeting to her grandparents before racing away to enjoy their few weeks alone. Skye had tried to be polite but had made her way to her room as quickly as possible shaking her head every step of the way. She couldn't believe that she'd have to spend most of her summer holiday with two people who, if they stood side by side, looked like the number ten. She wouldn't even have the chance to laugh about it with her best friend Arthur. He was going on holiday to Cyprus with his parents for the first week and wasn't allowed to take his mobile phone. Skye was all alone, stranded! The very least she could do would be to spend the time alone in her room as she had planned at home.

Her bedroom at Shutterly Manor was large but sparsely furnished. A king-sized four-poster bed sat alone in the middle of the floor with an old wooden chest of drawers and matching wardrobe pushed against the far wall. On the other two opposing walls, large windows were bordered by heavy red curtains that had been opened to allow the sun to flood the room with light.

By the time Skye had unpacked all of her clothes and books, it was starting to get dark outside. One of the windows looked out across the bay to the back of the house. In the distance, Skye could see the dim lights of ships passing over the dark sea. In the sky, the clouds were rolling and promised a summer storm. Sure enough, as she stared across the darkness, thick raindrops started to fall against the glass.

Something felt wrong. Skye didn't know what, but something was causing her stomach to churn and her hair to stand on end. She looked across at the abandoned lighthouse. From here, it was only a few hundred yards across the gravel road, but the darkness hid any details. In the distance, she could hear angry waves crashing against the rocks at the base of the cliff.

As she looked, a small green light flickered inside the lantern room before disappearing just as suddenly. Skye blinked, convinced that she'd imagined it, but, sure enough, it flashed again.

Nobody had been inside the lighthouse for years. Skye had tried herself but had found that the only door in had rusted shut. She had to investigate. This might be the only excitement she'd get all summer.

Grabbing a jacket from her suitcase, Skye stuffed a torch into her pocket and her trusty penknife into her sock and made her way to the back door of the house.

It didn't take Skye long to run the short distance to the lighthouse, battling every step against the growing wind and rain. Worryingly, the once-rusted door now hung open and swung loudly in the storm.

Not knowing what she might find, Skye made her way slowly through the door and up the winding steps.

The lantern room was dark and damp, most of the windows had been broken and the wind and rain blew freely around her. Skye stood and stared. Playing with the ring on her finger and unsure of what to expect, she made her way through the forgotten maps and star charts towards the other side of the room. Rested against the wall and tilted towards the sea was an old brass spyglass that had once been used to spot ships stranded on the rocks in the bay.

Skye placed her eye against the eyepiece. As she scanned the sky, she was caught off guard when a bright red light filled her view. Before she could focus on it, however, she had moved the telescope away.

It took her a few seconds to register that she had seen anything at all, and a few more to readjust back to the same location. What she saw made her jaw drop. Through the eyepiece, Skye saw a small, planet, about half the size of the moon and covered in what could only be forests and seas.

The more Skye stared, the more her eye was drawn into the eyepiece until she had to pull away before she bruised herself.

Skye was bemused. When she took her eye away, there was no planet in the sky, but there it had been as real as anything through the telescope. It was clearly big enough for her to see unaided. She could see the moon hanging there in the sky almost mocking her. It was as though the planet only existed inside the telescope.

Tentatively, Skye placed her eye back against the eyepiece and stared hard at the new world. Without warning, Skye's mother's face filled the entire view for the briefest of seconds before vanishing as quickly as it had appeared. Skye stumbled back from the telescope and half expected to see her mother standing there playing a practical joke. Worryingly though, Skye was still alone.

"Get a hold of yourself, Skye," she said, pulling herself upright and straightening her T-shirt. "You are a scientist. You don't believe in nonsense, and you may just have discovered a new planet. After all," she reasoned, "one little look can't hurt."

Breathing heavily, Skye placed her eye carefully to the cold metal. As she looked upon the planet again, she felt herself once more being drawn into the eyepiece. At first, she thought that she was just being too eager and pushing her eye into the scope, but the more the pressure increased, the more she became convinced that she was being pulled, rather than pushed.

This time, she didn't fight back. It felt like a fishing hook had been cast through the telescope and had hooked on to the back of her eyes, though there was no pain. Somebody was reeling in the hook, and her eyes felt like they were being pulled straight through the eyepiece.

Skye panicked and gripped the telescope and tried to pull her face free, but she couldn't. She was stuck. Her eyes were actually being pulled into the telescope. Grabbing at her head, Skye soon realised that it wasn't just her eyes, her whole head was being stretched long and thin and was being drawn further and further in.

She was filled with the very strange sensation of being thinner and longer than she had ever been before. In the end, she gave up and decided to stop fighting. The moment she did, Skye felt her whole body stretch, shrink and disappear into the telescope.

Hidden in the rubbish behind where Skye had so recently stood, two bright green eyes faded into the darkness.

New World

Like a cork from a bottle, Skye was catapulted across an infinite black space. All around her was nothingness. She had the feeling that she was travelling at great speed, but there was no rushing wind or feeling of falling. It would have been peaceful if it hadn't been so unreal. Skye had no idea how long she had been travelling for. It felt like she was floating for either a matter of seconds or a lifetime. It reminded Skye of the times spent on wet, boring Sunday afternoons, endless minutes shaving away the long, endless hours.

With a suddenness that startled Skye, she burst through the darkness and was blinded by a bright light as she slowed and came to a stop, lying on her face in a heavily wooded area.

Skye's head spun as she sat up.

Where am I?

The air felt different, thin almost, like there was less oxygen. Skye was finding breathing difficult.

You know where you are!

The voice may have been her own, but Skye didn't like the mocking tone.

You travelled through the spyglass! Whether it is magic or something else, you travelled right through to the other side!

Skye started to panic. Her breath came in short gulps and she struggled to stay conscious.

Either this is the most real of your dreams yet, the voice in her head continued to reason and mock, *or you really have travelled to somewhere else entirely.*

All around Skye were trees and bushes similar to those back home. Had she not just had a rather bizarre journey, Skye could have believed she was in a forest in the middle of England. Wherever she was, she had to pull herself together and make the most of the situation.

"One look!" she muttered to herself. "One look, you said. What harm could it do? Pah!"

Taking her time and trying hard to remain calm, Skye sat down between two tall trees and allowed the setting sun to warm her slightly. Without thinking, her right hand started to play with the ring on her left middle finger. A sharp pang of pain shot through her chest as she thought of home. Wherever she was, there was no way to get back home straight away, if at all. For all that she had with her, she could be stranded on the other side of Earth and still have no way to get back.

Arthur would help her; he always knew what to do. He was the rock that kept Skye grounded. Everyone at school mocked them and sang songs about them loving each other. Skye did love Arthur, possibly more than anybody else in the world, but not in the way that they meant. She'd known him since she was born, they'd grown up together, had chicken pox together, and even had *baths* together when they were really young. They'd learned to ignore the others, though. And for that Skye loved Arthur even more. She was awkward and weird and caused more trouble for Arthur than he deserved and yet he ignored all of the other children and allowed her to be his friend no matter how many late-night text messages she sent him asking him for the answers to yet another piece of homework that she'd left until the last minute.

Text messaging. That was the answer. Skye leapt to her feet and started feeling the pockets of her trousers. She always had her mobile phone with her. She could just text Arthur, and he'd know what to do! Hopefully he hadn't left for his holiday yet. It wasn't there, though. Her pockets were empty. She fell to her knees and started rooting around amongst the leaves on the ground. She found her pocket knife lying at her feet where it had fallen from her sock and pushed it back in, but it took her a while longer to find her mobile phone. When she picked it up, she saw that the screen had smashed. A spider's web of cracks danced across the surface. The screen was on though the image was faint and showed that she had no signal. Even as she watched, the image flickered and died and the battery fell, leaking fluid, to the ground.

Skye felt the darkness rise inside her, and her fingers started to tingle. A loud scream caused birds to cascade from the treetops and Skye to cover her ears. She realised that it was her own voice screaming over and over, incoherent and without meaning other than to shout down the universe for doing this to her. For casting her into whatever pit she now found herself. All of her emotions bubbled to the surface, and she started to weep as she screamed. She sobbed until she had no energy left, and only then did she slip into a dark, dream-filled sleep.

In the distance, mountains like dragon's teeth rose to meet the grey sky. A thick, oily mist was pouring down from the sharp peaks and cast a silvery pallor over the desolate landscape that filled the foreground.

The air was chilled but not cold enough to be uncomfortable. It smelt faintly of heather and gorse and a wild wind whipped in from the mountains. Though it raged and swirled amongst the long-dead tree trunks, it did little to the temperature of the air and made no impact on the fog. It was as though the wind was of another world.

Skye sensed instinctively that nothing lived here and yet there was still movement. The mist had a life of sorts, and, if Skye stood and watched carefully, it slowly took on the form of people that she knew or had known but also of creatures that she knew all too well from her dreams. They were smaller than Skye, maybe chest-height, and wiry. They were stooped at the shoulders and wore a look of resigned misery on their grey-green faces. They were made all the more grey by the fact that they were nothing more than mist twisted into their form, and yet their eyes burned fiercely with an emerald green glow. Skye recognised them as goblins. Not the cartoonish figures from her mother's drawings or the smiling pottery Hobgoblins in the garden. These were the fierce if broken goblins of her dreams.

Skye dared to take a step closer and moved amongst the eerie shapes. All around her were familiar faces, her grandparents who had passed away recently, not Ron and Wilma but her father's parents. Her more caring, treasured grandparents. There was her old music teacher, Miss Cleff, and many more who she recognised from her life. They walked across the rolling hills like actors in a silent movie, never turning to look at Skye but seemingly focussed on a point somewhere on the horizon.

Suddenly, the goblins turned as one and locked their gaze directly at Skye. They knew she was there. This was their place, and she was an intruder. She turned to run, panicking at what they might do to her. She couldn't move. Her legs were pumping as hard as they could, but her feet felt as though they were moving through treacle. Each step she took forwards only seemed to drag her further back amongst the ghosts of the goblins that she had slain in her sleep.

She stopped and collapsed to the ground, out of breath and devoid of the willpower to keep running. She twisted and looked up into the steely green eyes that bore down upon her from a thousand ghostly faces.

"Welcome to the Shadowlands!" The voice poured down into the valley from the mountaintops and filled every nook and cranny. It was at once a whisper and a bellow louder than the wind. "We are the fallen, the forgotten and the foredoomed!"

"Why am I here?" Skye screamed. The gale raged on around them, and yet her voice seemed too loud and sharp for such a place. When she spoke next it was with a softer tone, reverential. "Where is this place?"

"This is the Shadowlands, Skye Thistle! This is where we come after we have given all that we have to give. We are the few, the lucky few, who have given of ourselves all that we can and may now live forever in this place of eternal rest."

"So, it isn't real? This is just another dream?"

"This is a dream, Skye Thistle, but it is very real. One day you will see. All of this will make sense to you. We may be beyond the living, Skye Thistle, but never forget that we live on here in the Shadowlands. We will always be at your service, and you will need us come the end. Go in peace, Skye Thistle!"

The wind picked up its pace and the mist started to blow away, pouring back over the razor-edged mountains leaving nothing but a cracked and barren salt plain devoid of any sound or movement.

Skye closed her eyes and stepped backwards into darkness.

When Skye woke, she realised that she hadn't been dreaming for long. The sun was still setting on the horizon. In the distance, animals called out to one another but remained out of sight. Soft, feathery leaves floated down from the canopy, but Skye ignored them as she started to look more desperately for a way out. She was surrounded on all sides by tall trees and scrambling bushes, and the enormity of the fact that she was no longer on Earth suddenly made her feel very small and claustrophobic.

Panicking, Skye started to breathe harder and harder in the thin air until she was overcome with tiredness and felt her eyes becoming heavier and heavier. The leaves on the ground rustled underneath her as she rolled on to her back. Before she fell into a deep sleep, she looked up into the branches above and saw a small creature clambering clumsily closer and closer. A creature with green eyes.

When Skye awoke sometime later, the sun had started to set over the horizon and she was shrouded in a subtle pink half-light that gave every shadow a dark, foreboding feeling and made Skye feel uneasy. She shivered despite the warm air. She propped herself up on her elbows and immediately felt a sharp pain in the side of her head. When she raised a hand to feel it, her fingers came back covered in blood where she'd struck her head against the tree when she had landed.

"That won't do," she muttered to herself as she tore a square of fabric from her T-shirt and held it to the wound.

After her head had stopped swimming from the pain, Skye stood up and tried again to take in her surroundings. Around her, Skye could see a small clearing no bigger than her bedroom on Earth that was surrounded by thick, tall trees crowned with gloriously golden foliage.

The leaf litter crunched underfoot as Skye moved around. Clinging to the sides of the trees was an eerie silver moss that waved in what little breeze managed to break through the forest wall. Brightly coloured mushrooms clung to rocks and crevices in the trees and formed beautiful rings underfoot. They bulged and quivered in the soft breeze and occasionally exploded in a puff of delicate spores. A small, furry creature with large, bright eyes, not too dissimilar to a rabbit took fright at Skye's approach and raced away through such a group of exploding mushrooms. It hadn't reached the edge of the ring before it fell dead, choking on the toxic dust. Skye covered her mouth and sprinted in the opposite direction desperate not to succumb to a similar fate.

Above, the sky was turning dark blue, and, just touching the horizon, two moons hovered in mid-air. One was bright silver and the same size as her moon back home. The other was half as big but shone more brightly with an emerald-green glow. For a minute, Skye was certain that she saw a shadow fly across the surface. Before she could be sure, she was distracted by a sudden crack of a stick in the trees immediately behind her.

Skye spun round on her heels and looked hard between two tall silver trees. There was nothing there. Slowly, she stepped closer, her breath shallow and her heart beating ever louder in her chest. She felt sure that if anything was out there, they would surely hear it echoing against her ribs.

She crept closer, and still she saw nothing. Her heart echoed louder. In the distance, the pained scream of a dying animal was cut short.

Skye was now standing in front of the two trees. Her breath was thin, and she struggled to breathe deeply.

She moved closer still. She stepped carefully between the two trees, lifting her feet high to avoid tripping on the twisted roots and used one of the lower branches to support her weight. The bark was cold to touch and smooth like marble.

Skye stopped breathing.

Something was watching her. She could see a pair of green eyes in the distance.

Above her, a branch snapped from the tree and

fell at her feet. Her eyes snapped upwards in time to see something small and dark leap from the tree and head off at speed into the forest. Skye shot forwards and almost immediately something grabbed at her ankle. She tripped and fell, face down, into a patch of bright green mushrooms that glowed faintly against the growing darkness. Remembering the poor creature from before, Skye pushed her hands into the yielding mud and tried to push herself to her feet.

Panicking, she felt her mother's ring slip from her finger and disappear into the undergrowth. Skye scrambled around in the leaves for what felt like hours, but, no matter how hard she looked, she couldn't find the ring.

Tears came suddenly, flooding down Skye's cheek as the magnitude of her situation sunk in once again.

Lost. Alone. And now her mother's ring was gone, the one anchor that she had to her old life.

It took all of her willpower to force herself to stand up. When Skye looked back down at her feet, she was stunned to find a brown, tattered shoulder bag wrapped around her ankles. It was woven from a fibre that she had never seen before. It was inlaid with a dark blue thread set in a swirling pattern that looked almost organic.

As Skye lay there and watched, the pattern moved

and flowed easily across the fabric like moonlight on the sea. The bag was small enough to be carried on her back, but, when Skye picked it up, it was surprisingly heavy.

Staggering back to her feet, Skye opened the catch and loosened the drawstring holding the bag closed. Inside was a large piece of thick green canvas, several pieces of rope, and several berries wrapped in a piece of thin silk.

Skye suddenly realised that she was hungrier than she had ever been before. She reasoned that since she didn't know if anything else here was edible, she might as well make the most of the gift. Somebody, or some*thing*, was clearly looking out for her. It wouldn't make sense to send her a pack of useful items only to then poison her.

As soon as she bit in to the first berry, Skye knew she had made the correct choice. Sweet, sticky juice ran down her tongue, and she could feel herself filling up from deep inside. By the time she had finished a handful, she was as full as she had ever been and so she wrapped the others back up and placed them back in to the bag.

By now, the light had almost completely drained from the sky and the effort of chasing after the hidden creature had left her out of breath again. Figuring that she should find somewhere safe to sleep, Skye set off into the forest.

It wasn't a friendly forest by night.

"I doubt I'll find bluebirds and gingerbread cottages in here," Skye whispered, afraid to make too much noise.

Every step that Skye took was hindered by roots and binding weeds that snaked along the ground and ran from tree to tree. Occasionally, Skye saw strange symbols etched into the bark that glowed with a light that seemed to come from within. Strange vines hung down from the branches with leaves that glowed purple each time Skye brushed against them.

Other than the sound of her own breath and the crunching of her feet, there were few sounds in the forest. No sound of animals in the distance or birds in the sky. Nevertheless, Skye knew better than to think that she was alone. Every so often, Skye would hear a low rustling sound as if leaves were slowly being pushed apart. Overhead, long shadows slithered through the treetops releasing leaves that parachuted slowly to the ground.

The deeper Skye penetrated into the forest, the higher she got as the land sloped gently at first and then ever more steeply towards the summit of a hill. Before long, the weight of the pack on her bag and her tiredness began to take their toll, and Skye started to struggle to breathe again.

Finally, as one moon chased the other below the horizon and plunged her into complete darkness, Skye climbed a small tree and pulled out the thick green canvas from the bag. She tied it between two branches to form a basic tent in the canopy.

Once she had pulled herself inside, she nestled down into a crease between a branch and the trunk and tried to close her mind to the fact that she was alone and unprepared on an alien world.

Amongst the branches that hung closely to her own, Skye could make out deeper shadows. Each time she convinced herself that something was there, she'd look closer and realised that it was just a trick of the light or her mind deceiving her. She tried to ignore the fact that whenever she made a move towards the darker shadows, she'd hear a soft whisper of something moving swiftly and easily in the opposite direction.

Before long, she fell into another dreamless sleep.

By morning light, the forest was much more welcoming. In fact, it was almost pleasant to wake up to. What had seemed to be evil arms reaching out to grab her by night, now became convenient places to hang her pack. Her mood was made all the lighter by the re-appearance of her mother's ring. When she woke, she found it lying by her side on the ground.

It must have got tangled in my clothes when I panicked, she thought to herself. Either way, she was happy to have it back.

Skye's night-time walk had managed to take her to the peak of a moderately sized hill but, as the hill was covered in tall, shadowy trees, she was none-the-wiser as to where she was.

"I can't hope to make a good decision about where to go if I don't know where I am," she muttered under her breath. "Though this was surely not the best way to go about it," she continued as she struggled to climb up a tree.

By the time she finally broke through the canopy and into the dazzling sunshine above, Skye was hot, sweaty and more than ready for some breakfast. All of that washed away as her eyes adjusted to the light and she was able to focus on what lay around her. In each direction, the forest extended for countless miles, punctuated here and there with green glens such as the one she had landed in last night.

To the east of Skye and beyond the trees lay an ocean that glinted so brightly in the sunlight that she struggled to let her gaze rest on it. Here and there it was pierced by towering rocks that gave the impression of sharp teeth ready to bite into ships foolish enough to try to sail too close to the shore.

To the north, the forest continued to the horizon, far beyond anything else Skye could make out. About halfway to the horizon, the forest appeared to dip, almost as though a crater had been dug out long before the forest had claimed the land. From out of the dip spiralled a thin wisp of smoke, barely visible in the sunlight.

Skye made a note to check the area out later, though she imagined it was a few days' walk through the thick forest.

To the west lay yet more forest that eventually gave way to a dry savannah that ran almost as far as the eye could see, before giving way to an almighty range of mountains, taller than anything Skye had ever seen. In the sunlight, the mountains glistened and shimmered, first purple, then green, then blue and so on. It was as though they were covered in an oil slick, though the haze that shimmered in front of them gave Skye an uncomfortable feeling.

The mountains were not somewhere that she hoped to go. The south, however, was the most foreboding of all. The trees gave way much sooner in that direction and soon yielded to an arid wasteland of cracked, dry soil punctuated by large, sharp rocks. Occasionally, a large, stone city would grow out of the ground like a mushroom but largely the land was crisscrossed with dry roads and nothing more.

Out there, Skye knew, she would have little protection from the sun or from any predators that happened to be on the hunt. So far, Skye had seen very little life moving amongst the trees. Though Skye sensed they didn't mean to harm her, the laws of nature suggested that most things had their predators. Skye just hoped she wouldn't have to meet one just yet. She'd had enough of predators with her run-in with Keith Boggart earlier in the week. On this strange world, that seemed like a long time ago, far longer than it actually was.

The wasteland to the south seemed to run forever. But, far in the distance, past the rocks and the carcasses of long dead trees, there sat a tower of rock that defied gravity. Smaller at the base than at the top, it looked like a monolithic pint glass. Thick grooves were gouged out of the sides.

Into the north side of the rock, a dark, grinning face had been carved that resembled the goblins in Skye's childhood stories.

From this distance, Skye couldn't guess how high the top was, but she could tell that it towered over everything below it. The top of the rock had been worn flat over the years to form a platform. From there, Skye could just make out spirals of smoke rising from a fire.

Unlike the smoke to the north, this smoke was black and thick and blocked the sun where it rose in front of it. Somebody, or something as Skye kept correcting herself, lived on top of that rock. Whatever it was, it scared her.

Shuddering, Skye scrambled down the tree and packed her makeshift tent back into the canvas bag. The blue swirls continued to dance across the fabric, vivid even in the harsh sunlight that broke through the canopy. Every time Skye tried to touch them though, they recoiled away from her finger, reforming around it and flowing on regardless. Not wanting to damage it, Skye soon left it well alone and decided to head out towards the smoking crater in the north to investigate just where she was and, if possible, how she could get back home.

Lost

Almost as soon as Skye had set off, she started struggling for breath. She took a seat on a rounded boulder and decided to have a closer look at the detritus that littered the ground around her. For the first time since she arrived, Skye saw clearly that there was life on this planet. The ground hummed with movement. Tiny insects crawled over the leaves and under fallen trees and rotten wood. At first glance, it looked very much like any woodland back home on Earth.

After recovering her breath, Skye set off again towards the smoke, this time with more of a spring in her step and an inquisitive eye taking in the forest around her. Now that she was focussing, she couldn't just hear the birds twittering in the distance but could see them darting between trees or high up in the sky. Most were very small and darted around like hummingbirds, but occasionally Skye would see something much larger hovering in the distance looking for something to eat far below.

It didn't take long before she was out of breath again and was forced to have a rest. This pattern of walking short distances before resting continued throughout the day. Not long after midday, Skye knew that she was hopelessly off-track. Everywhere she turned, the trees looked eerily familiar.

"I just want to go home. I don't want to be here anymore," repeated Skye under her breath until it became a mantra repeated hour after hour as the day drew on seemingly forever. "Somebody help me, please," she prayed in her weaker moments.

Throughout the day, Skye kept a close eye on the forest for anything that might be considered edible or that might safely be drunk to quench her growing thirst. The air under the trees was oppressive and hot, and her clothes hung wet from her body. She passed a few small streams that managed to run a course through the hard earth, but the water looked cloudy and full of small, wriggling creatures. It wasn't until early evening that Skye finally found herself at the edge of something large enough to be called a river. The water was flowing more rapidly here and seemed clear enough. In desperation, Skye had no choice but to fill her hands and drink deeply because she knew that she would die if she didn't drink something soon. She also took the opportunity to eat another small handful of berries from the satchel to take the edge off her growing hunger.

Once it became apparent that the water had no immediate ill effects, Skye set off further into the forest. Eventually, she knew that she would have to stop wandering and set up camp for the night, but without knowing where she was heading, she didn't have a clue how much distance she still had to cover and so was determined to make the most of whatever light was left. Every time she stopped for breath, she made a decision to continue pressing on until eventually she was out of light and energy and surrendered to the inevitable.

That night, Skye made another bed atop a tree with the intention of scouting another view in the morning. It took her a while to find a perfect tree where she could get high enough above the ground to be safe, but eventually Skye climbed one to find a perfect nook against the trunk already filled with soft, warm leaves, some of which had been pressed together into a serviceable blanket. As she lay back she reflected that it seemed so long ago that she had first landed on this strange new world. She wasn't sure if the days were longer here than on Earth or if she just had to work harder than she had ever done before. Her body ached in places that she never even knew she had, and her head was clouded with fatigue.

Despite her tiredness, sleep didn't come easily to Skye. It wasn't until the light had completely left the sky that she finally fell into a restless sleep. Her dreams were filled with two-headed insects and a fog that rose up to choke her as she walked lost and alone through a dark forest.

Part of this fear, Skye knew, was that back home her family wouldn't have any idea where she was. If she became stuck here, there would be no body for them to find, no explanation to give them closure. She woke from this dream several times with a start and found that each time she had been crying softly in her sleep, her cheeks wet with tears and her eyes puffy and moist. Each time that she woke she slipped uncontrollably back into the same nightmare.

She missed her bedroom with her comfortable bed and all of her books.

She missed school and classes and everything normal.

She missed her father, and she even longed to hear the crazy ramblings of her mother.

Above all else, she missed Arthur. He would be perfectly fine here. He would know what to do. Skye wanted to go home so badly that it hurt, but she knew she'd have to earn it. She couldn't just tap her heels together and wish. She'd have to get proactive.

Tomorrow morning, she thought each time that she woke throughout the night *Tomorrow morning I'll find a way home.*

It wasn't long after one of these waking moments that Skye was jolted awake desperate for breath. No matter how hard she tried, she couldn't take in any air. It took a second to realise that something was being held over her mouth. She tried to claw it away, but her arms were pinned tightly to her sides with a thick, pulsing rope.

Colours swam across her vision, and her ears popped as she struggled to breathe. Her fingernails cut and scratched her own face as she desperately tried to tear the tendrils away from her aching throat. She felt a dull pain as her nose was broken as whatever was attacking her tightened its grip.

Harder and harder she pulled until, with one last, draining push, the tentacle gave way and she was able to rip a thick, matted mess of leaves away from her mouth.

Noisily, Skye gulped down air as she clawed at the

other thick vines holding her in place in the tree. Her eyes were open, but she couldn't see anything. It was too dark even with the starlight above.

All around her, she could hear a slithering sound as though something wet was sliding through the trees. Maybe the vines were attacking her? It didn't matter what it was, she needed to get down from the tree and fast. She knew she was too high to jump, but she couldn't find her way to the trunk to scramble down, either.

Without warning, something long and easily as thick as her arm, wrapped itself around her ankles and dragged her screaming from the branch. With a loud thud, she swung into the rough bark of the tree trunk and bounced off onto a thick branch below. A sharp branch cut into her side, and she felt a stab of pain as it tore open her skin.

As the emerald moon came out from behind a cloud, Skye blinked quickly, her eyes adjusting to the darkness. She strained to see clearly everything that was going on around her.

Skye spun suddenly as she heard a low, rumbling whisper come from somewhere in the trees.

"Stop squirming, little thing."

"Who are you? Let me go!" Skye cried, thrashing against the rope that still held her leg. All it did was grip her ankle tighter and start to rub sore through her socks.

"We are the ones who own the trees!" the voice wailed. "We are the ones who slither sightless through the night!"

Skye pressed on, "Let me go. I haven't done anything to hurt you!"

"Hurt us? No, you couldn't hurt us! The insect doesn't hurt the bird, but the bird has to eat. You are food, little thing, nothing more."

The cold unfairness of it all struck Skye through the heart. She wasn't used to being part of the food chain, let alone near the bottom. In her head, she was screaming for help, begging to be released, but every time she opened her mouth, nothing came out. Her heart raced so fast that Skye felt sure that she could hear the beats echoing around the canopy. Her mind spun, and she felt despair and anger start to well up inside her; her anger at being so weak and easily caught, her frustration at never daring to do things that might draw attention to herself, and her anger at what a pitiful end this would be. As her rage grew behind her eyes, she felt her brain start to tingle as though it had been bathed in a pool of sherbet. She felt her fingers start to tense and she swore that her mother's ring started to glow in the darkness.

Scared of her powerlessness and yet curious by how so very powerful she suddenly felt, Skye shook her head and felt the feelings drift away. Not forever, she sensed, but hidden away ready for when she next decided to look for them.

"Well, at least let me know who you are. Who is so cowardly to attack in the darkness to prey on the sleeping? Show yourself!" She finally found her voice and screamed so loud that it made her throat sting.

There was no reply.

She waited, hanging upside down high up in the alien tree. She started to feel faint from all the blood rushing to her head. She felt her mother's ring slipping along her finger. If she didn't know better, she would have guessed it was trying to escape. She clenched her fist to pull it back down to the base of her finger.

"Who are you?" she screamed over and over again until her voice ran dry.

"We are the glibberig!" echoed the deep voice as Skye's attackers revealed themselves from all around her. Instead of the one attacker Skye had thought she faced, there were four or five entwined with each other.

Skye took a moment to take in their full forms. Each one moved through the trees like a snake, but instead of shiny scales, the glibberig had a pale, translucent skin much more similar to earthworms.

Beneath their skin, Skye could make out thick purple veins pulsing along their enormous length and in the middle the dark outline of their stomachs as big as her fist. Each worm was easily twice as long as Skye was tall and twice as thick around as her leg. At each end, the glibberig ended in a fat stump. Whilst there were no eyes, each end had a large mouth that was filled with sharp, filthy teeth.

When they spoke, they did so without moving their mouths. Instead, they undulated their bodies until air was pushed out of a set of gills on top of each head which produced the sound.

"So, little thing, now that you know what *we* are, we are going to find out what *you* are. You needn't tell us, though. We will know by your taste," spluttered a glibberig underneath Skye.

"Wait!" pleaded Skye. She suddenly remembered the Swiss Army knife pushed inside her sock and tried to buy herself some time. "If you put me down, I will lead you to some more food. Better food."

"We know where all of the food is in this forest, little liar. Our traps catch bigger things than you." Each sentence trailed off with a whisper until it was barely audible.

"Traps? What traps?" stuttered Skye, desperately trying to reach up to her ankle to remove the knife.

Each time she got close, the glibberig would swing her round and she'd crack her head on the tree trunk or become sickeningly disorientated. She felt the creature increase its grip on her ankle and felt the bones creak and rub against each other under the sheer force. A warm pain shot through her leg, and stars swam across her vision. She had to escape before her bones were crushed and broken.

The voice in the darkness took on a mocking tone with a shrill edge that suggested that patience was being worn very thin.

"Do you think your bed just fell like that in the tree? Do you think leaves just weave themselves into nests like that? We build the nests and tired little animals find them too hard to resist. You are not so smart, little thing. You are not so clever!"

Skye had stopped listening. She had finally managed to reach her ankle. With a final grunt and push, she grabbed the knife from her sock. With a quick flick, she pulled out the blade and thrust it deep into the worm that was wrapped around her ankle. It was as easy as stabbing into air and the knife passed through the worm and out the other side into her own ankle cutting deep into the flesh, but Skye twisted it until she felt the glibberig shudder and start to unravel.

Before she had time to react, Skye felt the grip loosen

and the sudden, jarring sensation of being weightless for a split second before her stomach lurched and she started to fall towards the ground.

Skye felt branches lash against her as she fell and felt her arm break when it smashed against the trunk, but the branches served to slow her descent. When she finally hit the ground, it only knocked the wind from her, instead of killing her.

As the warm, throbbing pain in her arm overcame her entire body, and she felt her consciousness slipping away, Skye looked up and saw the glibberig start to slither down through the trees to complete their meal. Skye flexed her fingers and was dismayed to realised that her mother's ring had once again fallen from her finger. She knew there was no chance of finding it again in the fading light. It was lost to her. Out of nowhere, a sharp scream pierced the still air, though Skye paid it little attention. Above and around her, Skye heard the sounds of an almighty fight erupt and closed her eyes, ready to accept the inevitable death that she knew was slithering down the trees towards her.

Healed

When she was six years old, Skye had been involved in an accident whilst riding her scooter. She'd ridden too fast along a path and hadn't stopped in time. According to those who saw what happened, she'd clipped the edge of the curb and rammed into the side of a parked car.

Skye didn't remember much of what happened next, but she was immediately taken into surgery where the surgeons operated to set her broken leg.

It was at this point, whenever Skye told the story in the years since, that her memory started to clear a bit, though she wished that it didn't. She could remember a sensation of hovering above her body whilst she was being operated on, something she had read about in books before but never believed. She was a scientist after all, and unexplained phenomenon didn't interest her.

But Skye knew what she had experienced, and it had haunted her ever since.

All of this came back to Skye as she experienced a similar feeling, only this time she was hovering above her body as it lay on a wooden pallet resting on the dusty floor of a ramshackle hut.

As Skye watched, a small, strange creature danced around her body, gently swinging a metal amulet that was releasing a pale green smoke into the air.

Skye couldn't hear anything, but the creature appeared to be singing loudly.

Skye was glad that she'd listened to her mother and worn clean underwear every day as her dirty clothes had been removed and hung from a crude washing line strung from the walls. Skye's body was wrapped in linen robes but was otherwise uncovered.

With what felt like a tug on her soul, Skye found herself floating back down towards her body. With barely a flicker she was looking out of her own eyes again as she slowly regained consciousness.

After a while, her mind started to clear, and she could make out a slow droning sound, as though a wasp was stuck inside her skull. Panicking, Skye immediately felt for her mother's ring on her finger, and a deep sense of loss and sadness descended over her as she felt bare skin.

"Looking for this?" came a whisper from the strange creature. It held the ring between two of its fingers.

Skye tried to shout but nothing came out and she felt herself slump back against the bed.

"Do not worry, my dear. It is safe with me. After all, I returned it to you once before." Skye thought back to the morning she woke in the forest with the ring by her side. Anger rose inside her at the thought that whoever this creature was might have woken her and saved her from her night-time attack. She had no strength to say any of this though. "You may have it once you are ready. In fact, I'm beginning to think I may as well keep it considering how intent on losing it you seem!" The creature was smiling to itself at its joke.

Lifting her head slightly from the pillow to speak, Skye saw that her host was humming a simple, repetitive chant under its breath. The sheer effort of lifting her head exhausted her again, and she soon slumped back onto the hard mattress.

"Rest easy, little human. Rest for a while. You are not yet healed." The voice floated easily through the air and seemed to register in Skye's brain without even touching her ears.

"But—" she started before being interrupted.

"Listen to me, little human. You were mortally wounded. Your arm was badly broken, as was your nose and your ankle was sprained and infected with the venom of the glibberig, a powerful toxin that few survive. When you slid your knife through the creature, it transferred the toxin from its flesh yours. I set your arm and nose and used more than a little magic to help them along their way. I expect them both to heal in the coming days. You may still feel a little pain but they shouldn't hold you back. The herbs that I have used will heal your ankle before long and, luckily, I managed to remove the poison before it reached your heart, but it will not be without cost, I fear."

The healer must have noticed Skye trying to open her eyes and get up for she was pushed gently but irresistibly back down on to the bed.

Skye gave up and felt herself drifting back into unconsciousness.

Just before she passed out, she heard the healer say, "You have a long journey ahead, I fear. You will need every bit of strength and even more luck. For now, I can only give one of these but you must rest. I will see you again when you wake."

After that, there was no sound but the strange, foreign chanting.

Many times Skye drifted in and out of consciousness,

and each time she heard the same rambling chanting.

Sometimes when she woke, she felt as though she was burning with a fever inside her chest, like her heart was on fire.

Other times, it felt like a thousand ants were biting every inch of skin on her body.

Occasionally, she woke and felt at ease, as though the worst was over, but those times were especially cruel as they just made the others more unexpected and harder to take.

At no time was she able see properly when she awoke. She couldn't feel a blindfold over her eyes, but then the rest of her pain was so severe that she scarcely felt able to feel much else anyway.

Skye had no idea how much time had passed before she was able to open her eyes fully, but it was with a great relief when she was finally able to unstick her eyelids and blink in the unfamiliar light. Her vision was still blurry, and it took another long while before she was able to properly focus and distinguish anything other than fuzzy shapes around her. She reached up and felt a thick bandage pressed against her nose and realised that her arm had been strapped up with gauze. She was relieved that neither felt anywhere near as painful as they had when she had injured them.

As soon as she was able, she started to take stock of

her surroundings.

The hut was small and wooden, and her pallet was no bigger than a normal bed yet it took up half of the floor space.

Most of the remaining space was taken up with a roaring open fire that filled the air with warmth and the pungent aromas of smoke and spices. It wasn't unpleasant, but it did make Skye feel rather foggy. It reminded her of her grandparents' open fire that they lit during Christmas visits and that burnt with the scent of oranges and cloves.

The same, strange creature as before was bent over the fire stirring a bubbling pot.

Despite her better instincts, Skye wasn't scared or frightened by the situation. She felt pangs of loneliness and isolation and so far away from everything that she loved that it hurt, but not fear.

Instead, she found herself becoming extremely curious. Here was an alien creature that clearly meant her no immediate harm. Skye found herself looking more closely. She could only make out the back, but her captor was slightly shorter than her, about four feet high, and very wiry. It was humanoid in form with two arms and legs and, reassuringly after the incident with the glibberig, only had one head.

As the creature turned, Skye saw that it was dressed

in a blue robe that flowed past its feet and that was emblazoned with a silver handprint over the left breast that seemed to glow in the firelight. Around the waist was tied a simple rope belt from which hung a series of silver amulets and small glass jars. Inside some of the jars a thick smoke swirled against the glass. Skye was sure that she could see images flashing across the surface though she couldn't make out what they were.

Looking back to her rescuer, Skye noticed that thin white hair clung to the creature's head and hung past its shoulders in a tight plait. Its loose skin was a deep green with dark spots and that it had the softer features of a female. The eyes were bright green circling a deepest black pupil. The green iris seemed to pulse and glow with a burning desire that slightly unnerved Skye.

Skye was stunned. For all the world, this creature looked just like the goblins that her mother placed so much faith in.

The creature spoke softly to Skye, "I am Weard. I am a healer. You are lucky to be alive, human. You need not thank me."

Skye thanked her anyway.

"I'm Skye. Are you...," she faltered, nervous, "are you a goblin?" She was embarrassed to even entertain the idea. She was scared, though. Goblins were evil little creatures that were always up to no good. That's what the few books that she had read had taught her, anyway.

"Hello, Skye. What I am is of little importance right now, but you will find out in time. Where you are, is perhaps more prudent for you know."

"Where am I then?"

"I cannot tell you that, either," chuckled the goblin apologetically. "Rest assured that you are no longer on Earth, though I suspect you may have guessed that already." Skye nodded but said nothing. Even though she had suspected it, the enormity of being told it outright still felt like a punch to the stomach.

"I must warn you. Your appearance here is not welcome by some," the goblin continued. Her voice was informative rather than harsh.

"Me? Why?" Skye tried to get up but found that she couldn't move below her neck.

"That conversation is not for now, either."

Skye found herself growing impatient with the lack of answers.

"For now, you still need to rest, though we may talk awhile," Weard continued. "I am sure that you have many other questions? For example, why you cannot move properly?"

"Am I paralysed? From the fall. I mean, I know it

was a long way down, and I fell hard."

"Paralysed? Yes, that would be a good way to describe it." Weard saw Skye's shocked reaction and spoke quickly to interrupt her. "Paralysed but not permanently, and not from the fall. The glibberig like to neutralise their prey before they eat them, and their venom is designed to do just that. I managed to remove it from your system before it paralysed your heart or your brain but it was not easy."

Weard held up her hand and showed Skye a hideous black wound that ran the length of her palm.

"I doubt I shall be able to use it for a long time, not properly," she said.

"I am so sorry," Skye mumbled. "I had no idea. I mean, I didn't want this to happen. Thank you," she trailed off, feeling horrendous. She had no idea what had happened, but she certainly knew that she didn't want anybody else to be hurt on her behalf.

"Like I said before," Weard offered, "I don't want your thanks. Before this is over, we will owe you a greater debt of gratitude than you owe me. At least I hope that we will." She seemed to stop and think. "Otherwise, I have made a grave mistake," she finished, mostly to herself.

Skye didn't know what to say. She was having trouble processing all of the new information, so she simply asked, "If you don't mind me asking, what are you? I know you told me that now is not the time to discuss it, but I have no idea what anything is on this planet and I don't know what I might or might not trust to harm me."

"Well, I certainly mean you no harm, though others of my kind are not so welcoming. I belong to a tribe called the G'Oräk. We are indeed what your people call goblins."

"But," Skye interrupted, "Goblins are horrible little creatures that run around stealing things and killing farm animals."

"Are we?" Weard seemed amused at the suggestion, "Nobody told us that. It seems that we have been missing out on a lot of fun! It is rather unfortunate when other people seem to know more about you than you know about yourself, don't you think? Having spent some time in your world, I must say that we are very seriously misrepresented. We are not as sneaky and devilish as your stories would have us be. Well, most of us aren't. Unlike you humans, many of which commit far worse acts that you accuse us of, I might add!

"Nevertheless, I am indeed a goblin. Be careful, however. We find the term somewhat unhelpful. Not all goblins are G'Oräk, you see, and not all G'Oräk are goblins. Mostly they are, but from time to time we find it prudent to allow outsiders into our little tribe," she finished with a nod towards Skye.

"Like me?"

"Indeed."

"Why me? What have I done?"

"It is not what you have done, little one," her guardian whispered, "but more what you have yet to do. Your arrival has been foretold. The prophecy is very clear. You have been expected for many generations."

"I don't understand," Skye snapped, exasperated. She was more confused than ever.

"You will do, eventually," the goblin reassured her as she turned her back to Skye to check a boiling cauldron.

Skye was stunned. Goblins! Her mother had been right all along. How had Skye ever doubted her? Here she was face to face with an actual goblin.

G'Oräk, she corrected herself.

"We don't have the time now for a history of my people," Weard continued, "though you will need to know soon enough. For now, all that you need to know is that we are, on the whole, a peaceful race who have been wronged by a lot of other people in our time. We are the guardians of this forest, the North Wood, and see to it that it is as safe a place to travel as can be.

"You arrived in a place called the Glen of Tears. It's not a nice place. I have been tracking you since then. That is my bag that you carry with you. I am glad that it proved to be of assistance."

Skye listened intently and once more thanked Weard for her help with the bag.

"I cannot tell you why, Skye, but your arrival here is essential and was arranged. I was sent to your world to help your passage. I am only sorry that I wasn't able to better escort you here."

"Our world?" Skye stammered, unsure what this meant.

"I was there when you were attacked by an ogre not long ago. I made sure that he knew that you were untouchable."

"An ogre?" Skye had no idea what the goblin was talking about until a thought struck her. "Do you mean Keith Boggart? He wouldn't have killed me, just hurt me." Skye thought back to the last day of school when Keith had fought her to the ground. "It was you in the bushes? You were what he saw and the reason he stopped?"

"Indeed, it was. I couldn't take that risk. You really are very important to some people here, Skye. You very nearly didn't make it. The portal to our world has been locked away for too long. I almost missed my chance to help you find it."

"You were in the lighthouse, weren't you? It was you who broke open the door, wasn't it?"

"Yes, that was me. I've been following you for a while now, though you haven't noticed. I must admit, when you arrived here it took me longer than I'd hoped to find you, and then you managed to slip away in the morning," the goblin finished, somewhat embarrassed by this error on her part.

Weard continued, "Though we try hard, there are some things in this forest that are not welcome but that we cannot rid ourselves of. The unfortunate creatures that you encountered in the treetops, the glibberig, are a terrible spirit creature that has no place amongst friendly folk. They are blind but have a tremendous sense of smell and can hear a leaf fall on the other side of the forest.

"They do not track their prey. Instead, they set up traps in the treetops to ensnare weary folk looking for somewhere to sleep. They are slow and prefer to wait for their victim to fall asleep before attacking. You were very lucky that you woke up before they had time to finish you off."

"How long will I be paralysed for? I need to get home. People will be missing me." Skye considered the chances that Ron and Wilma would even notice her absence and continued, unabashed, "Arthur will miss me if I don't make it back before he returns from his holiday, anyway."

Remembering Ron and Wilma and particularly Arthur hammered home Skye's isolation once more, and she felt her heart sink. She doubted now that she would ever see them again, but she was determined to try everything that she could.

"Glibberig venom is hard to predict. You have made good progress since you have been here, but there is awhile to go yet. I think another week or so and you may be able to slowly move around. Until then, you must rest here. For now, let us be happy with removing the bandages from your arm and nose."

Weard tenderly removed the bandages and Skye moved her arm gratefully. It still ached and felt weaker than before, but it didn't hurt unduly and Skye felt reassured that the pain would ease over the coming days. The goblin stood up and turned a spit cooking over the fire. As she slowly sprinkled a pale silver herb over the food, she spoke just loudly enough for Skye to hear, "As for going home, I think that is possible. But not yet. You are here for a reason, Skye, though what that reason is, is not for me to say. When you are ready, I will take you to see our leader. He will tell you what you need to know."

Skye lay back down and thought hard about everything that she had heard, relieved that going home was a possibility. If she had to help the G'Oräk for a while, then so be it. Something wasn't quite right though, something that Weard had said was playing on Skye's mind, and she couldn't shake a terrible feeling.

"Weard," Skye started, tentatively, "you called me a 'little human' during one of my waking dreams. Then again today, you said I was lucky to be alive and called me a human. I never told you I was a human? How did you know where to come and find me? How do you know about my world?"

"No, you didn't tell me."

"Then how?"

"You are not the first human to arrive here, Skye, though I pray you are the last. There have been a few before you, and none have left with goodwill. There are many here who would prefer that your arrival be kept a secret through any means necessary. There are some of us who would agree with them, though for less...nefarious...purposes. We would prefer to keep you a secret, so that those who wish you harm do not know where to find you.

"For now though, do not trouble yourself with thoughts of this. You must rest and rest well. You have a long journey ahead of you if you wish to return home. I will leave you in peace now and return later with nourishment."

Weard stood up and left the hut, closing the door carefully behind her. Skye's head was spinning. Not only were goblins real, but she wasn't the first human to arrive on this world.

Skye knew that she would not find answers to all of her questions here, but until she was able to move again she had no choice but to rest. Feeling uneasy and with her head swimming in unanswered riddles, Skye closed her eyes and once more fell into a deep sleep full of unwanted dreams.

History Lesson

O ver the next few days, Skye learnt a little more about where she was. The planet on which she had landed was called Ithilmir and had a dark history. Weard was reluctant to reveal too much to Skye, instead she reassured her that their Elder would tell her all in due course.

It was close to midnight on the eleventh day since Skye had first woken when the G'Oräk entered the hut with a grim look on her face. By now Skye had recovered a fair amount of movement. She lifted herself up from the bed and watched Weard fumble and clatter around the hut. She appeared to be trying to avoid talking to Skye, and Skye was surprised to see that the goblin was crying. Not an uncontrollable sob, but tears were running down her cheeks and her eyes were puffy. She grabbed Skye's clothes from the washing line and threw them onto the bed.

"Weard?"

The goblin tossed Skye's ring onto the bed and interrupted before she could speak further.

"Snudge, our Elder, will see you. Now! We must leave now. Get dressed!"

Suddenly, Weard had a sense of urgency and started to drag Skye from her bed. "He didn't want to. Too much time in the company of deceitful humans already, so he said. But his hand has been forced. Bad times, indeed. Bad times."

Skye got the impression that Weard was rambling and talking mainly to herself. She scrambled to her feet and quickly put on her clothes and tied her shoelaces as the goblin dragged her towards the door.

Weard continued, "We must leave now. You must be seen. Come with me."

With that, Weard left the hut and didn't wait for Skye to follow.

Skye hobbled after Weard as quickly as her tired muscles would allow and made her way out into the darkness. She caught up with the goblin just as she was entering the treeline and made sure to keep a tight grip on her robe lest she find herself lost and alone again in the forest.

For many hours, they wound their way between

tall, dark trees, stepping around areas that looked perfectly similar to any other in Skye's eyes. Whenever she threatened to stray even slightly from the path, Weard would grab hold of Skye's hand and pull her closer.

"Do not get lost, little human. Not here. There are worse things than glibberig that haunt the North Wood, and they'll do worse than kill you."

Skye shuddered and made sure that she stayed as close to her guide as possible. After a while she started to tire, and her legs started to give way beneath her. Her breath started to come in a rasping choke, and she struggled to fight for every lungful of air.

"Our atmosphere has less oxygen than you are used to, Skye. Just breathe slowly, and take your time. Panic is the worst thing for you now."

There was no possibility of the G'Oräk carrying her, and so she allowed Skye to rest her weight on her shoulder and they pressed on. This slowed them down considerably, and the sun was starting to rise when they finally made it to a towering outer wall.

Skye had never seen anything quite so deflating as the wall in front of her. "You shall not get past me!" it seemed to scream. Made from entire tree trunks trussed together side by side, it rose high into the canopy and continued in both directions as far as the eye could see.

Above them, large birds floated easily in the air. Each one cast a large shadow on the ground. Skye couldn't help but notice their terrifyingly large talons and hooked beaks.

"Phoenix," muttered Weard. "That's not a good sign."

"What do you mean?" asked Skye nervously, "I thought phoenix were supposed to be good? Don't they live forever by being constantly reborn?"

"There are many legends of the phoenix, both here on Ithilmir and in your own world. I believe that some of them have lost the true meaning of the phoenix.

"The phoenix is not a welcome creature. It is a carrion beast, feeding on the flesh of the dead and dying. Here on Ithilmir, phoenix only resurrect in times of war when the battlefields run thick with blood and rotting corpses. Phoenix haven't graced our skies for many lifetimes. It is a sign of terrible things to come that they have risen again."

Skye stood stunned, not quite sure how much of what Weard was saying she believed. Even though these things were staring her in the face, so to speak, Skye still couldn't bring herself to believe that it was all real. She still expected to be woken up at any moment to find that this was all a dream.

Why would so many things that existed only in myth and legend back on Earth become real here on Ithilmir? It was all too much like a story for Skye. She tried to change the subject back to something that she felt readier to believe in.

"What is this giant wall, Weard?" she asked. "Why does it need to be so big?"

"The Holden Wall, built beyond living memory to keep the G'Oräk safe," the goblin replied as they started walking again. They headed east, following the wall as it curved.

After a short walk, they stopped in front of a low gate cut out of the wall. It was guarded by two G'Oräk who were dressed in battle gear. Instead of cloth robes like Weard's, they wore sturdy leather tunics and loose leather trousers. On their heads were leather helmets that pinched into a thin strip to separate their eyes. Embossed on their left breasts was the same silver handprint that adorned Weard's. They stared at Skye with the same black eyes with green pupils that she saw when she looked at Weard.

The guards were sat down at a table playing cards. Skye saw a pile of foreign money in the middle of the table. These were not guards who were expecting trouble.

Seeing their approach, the guards got up and stood

at either side of the gate. Both of them were carrying spears. One of them lowered his across the entrance.

"Halt!" he ordered. "Weard, why are you here at this time with this *thing*?" The last word was spat.

"I have brought her to see Snudge, on his orders. Go and take it up with him if you must, Brabble, but it will be the last thing you do. I know you only took this job for an easy life, so let us in and go back to your game." Weard indicated their table with her eyes and pressed for the gate.

Neither of the guards made any further effort to stop them, and soon Skye and Weard were inside the wall.

"I'm sorry, Skye, but Snudge doesn't like anybody who isn't a G'Oräk seeing inside the wall. I'll have to put this hood over your eyes."

Everything went black as Skye felt a rough sack drop over her head. At some point in the past, the sack had been used to store old fish, and Skye had to fight back the urge to gag every time she breathed in. In the end, she tried only to breathe through her mouth.

Skye felt her heart racing again, and her hands started to shake. Idly, she played with the ring on her finger, gladder than ever to have it back.

After entering the gate, they took a long, meandering route over what felt like well-worn cobbles until they reached a set of steps. Taking their time, Skye was led up them until a change in the air told her that they were inside.

Skye recoiled as her hood was removed and she was bathed in the light of a thousand candles flickering around a giant hallway, larger than any room Skye had even seen.

Above her, the ceiling disappeared into the darkness where old wooden eaves bent out of sight. The dark, stone walls were covered in floor to ceiling tapestries painted in dark reds and blues and adorned with the repeating motif of a silver handprint.

The only punctuation in the otherwise solid walls were magnificent stained-glass windows picked out with rich colours. Whereas the windows in the churches that Skye had visited depicted saints and scenes from the Bible, these showed great battles and goblin leaders.

Underneath each window sat a pale marble plinth on which was set an ornament. Some were bejewelled cups or necklaces, some more mundane wooden boxes. Each was inlaid with a small silver plate engraved with writing that was too small for Skye to make out.

In the middle of the cavernous hall stood a tall stone throne on which was sat another G'Oräk. The seat was hewn from a single slab of marble and was topped with ornate, twisting spikes. It left those who looked upon it in no doubt that the G'Oräk who sat upon it was more important than the rest.

The robes of the goblin currently occupying the throne were woven from the finest material that Skye had ever seen and floated on the air like a whisper. Never settling on one colour, it appeared to Skye to take on colours that she had never seen before but that she desperately hoped to see again.

Again, Skye noticed that the left breast was adorned with a silver handprint. Without any thought whatsoever, she fell to her knees in awe and fear.

"I am Snudge, the Elder of the G'Oräk," boomed a voice from above her bowed head. "You are Skye, this I know, of the humans. I have met some of your kind before, and I shall tell you now that I do not relish the thought of meeting another. Many times have I trusted humans, and many times have I been betrayed. You are weak as a species and your weakness is a curse that threatens my people. Do you have anything to say?"

The question caught Skye by surprise and snapped her out of her fascination with the robe. She was too nervous to speak. Instead, she muttered something unintelligible.

"Well?" the goblin probed, "What do you have to

say? Anything?"

"No, sir, nothing," she managed, choking back her fear.

"Why are you so nervous, little one?" he asked, not unkindly. "Is there something that you are hiding?"

Why was she nervous? Skye didn't know where to start. She wanted to say that she had been flung across space to a strange world, that she was in the presence of creatures that she knew were sneaky and nasty and dangerous, that despite everything else, she was worried that none of this was real and that she was dreaming. None of that seemed right, though.

"I am scared of you all," she pointed to the gathered goblins, "I don't know who you are or whether you mean to harm me or steal from me or who knows what else."

"Ah yes," laughed Snudge, though there was no humour in it. "We are the feared goblins. Isn't it always the way that the enemies in any war are painted as villains? Do you know how many soldiers did terrible things in the last war?"

Skye shrugged that she didn't.

"Every single one. They all killed, maimed and stole. And you know what? So did those we were fighting. People always think they are fighting for a just cause, otherwise they stop fighting. It doesn't make them bad people, Skye. It makes them followers. Do you have war on your world, Skye?"

"Yes," she whispered. "More than many of us would like. My great-granddad fought in a great war on my world. He was lucky to live, he said."

"And those people that he fought? What do you think of them?"

"They were awful people. They killed people just because of their beliefs."

"Did you ever take the time to ask your great-granddad what he thought of those that he fought?"

"No." Skye looked awkward. "He died before I was born. My granddad always said that he had forgiven them, though."

"Your great-granddad was a wise man, it seems. What do you think the men that he fought would think of your great-granddad?"

"He was a nice man, apparently."

"And yet he was still trying to kill them? You don't need to answer me, Skye. Just remember that not everyone is who we think they are just because they are painted that way. You may have your ideas about what goblins are because of tales and legends, but here we are in front of you yet to steal a penny from your pocket or cause you any pain. Isn't that interesting?"

Skye didn't know what to say. Instead, she looked

to her feet and stayed quiet.

"Why are you here, Skye? We didn't ask for you to come."

"I came here by accident, but now it seems that I am stuck. All I want is to go home. I promise. I mean you no harm."

"Harm?" Snudge seemed amused. "You couldn't harm me, *girl*." The last word was filled with mocking, all warmth lost from his voice. "No, you couldn't harm me, but you may be of use. In fact, your return home depends on you being useful to me."

"My return home? Do you really think you can return me to where I belong?" Skye allowed a glimmer of excitement to grow inside her.

"That remains to be seen. As I said, a lot depends on your fulfilling your usefulness to us here."

"I don't know how I could be of any use to you, sir. My ankle is still very sore despite Weard's herbs and I can barely walk." Skye didn't like where the conversation was heading. She was suddenly aware of the rest of the occupants of the room and of just how vulnerable she was.

All around her, the walls were lined with thousands upon thousands of G'Oräk. Each one was armed and had their full attention focussed on the conversation happening in front of the throne.

"Your ankle will heal with time. Your courage, I am not so sure about."

Skye had never considered herself to have any courage in the first place, but this didn't seem the time to say so. Instead she asked, "What do you need me to do?"

"First, I must tell you a little bit of history. Weard tells me that you are most curious." He shot a look at Weard that told her that she had already revealed more than she should have. "So, let me satisfy that curiosity."

Skye was offered a stool carved from the twisted trunk of a tree. She sat, attentive and ready to listen. To the side of Snudge's throne a small, wizened goblin with threads of thin blond hair sat uncomfortably as the leader started his story.

"The story of our world began a long time ago, during a period of time we call the Before Time. Our whole world was still being created and everything that you see now was just a never-ending landscape of molten lava and boiling seas. In the beginning, there was nothing living, no plants, animals or creatures. There were only the Spirit Voices. In the early Before Time, there were only two Spirit Voices, Good and Evil.

"For thousands of years, Good and Evil roamed

the land, watching as the seas and lava fought for supremacy. Eventually, Good and Evil couldn't avoid each other and so began centuries of endless battles, battles that have scarred the world to this day. Good created trees to provide shelter from Evil, so Evil retaliated by creating fire to destroy them. Good threw up mountains and dug out valleys, so Evil flooded them with water. We believe that everything that you see now, including the G'Oräks, were created as a result of the feud between Good and Evil.

"With time, the Spirit Voices grew weak and retreated to their own corners of our world. But neither rested peacefully. Each one became more and more suspicious of what the other was planning and so, over time, each Spirit Voice fractured itself into smaller, less conspicuous Spirits that could be sent out in to the world to keep track of the others.

"Good split itself off into Courage, Humility and Bravery whilst Evil created Fear, Envy and Spite.

"For millennia, the Spirit Voices roamed the world almost alone. The constant wars took their toll on the spirits, though. Every wound leaked life force into the world. It was this excess life force that enabled the very first plants, animals and early beings to begin to rise from the dirt."

"Enough!" The blond-haired goblin had started to

his feet and was banging his walking stick onto the slabs for attention. "You have gone far enough, Snudge. She need know no more. She isn't *one of us!* Even you admitted that humans are not welcome here, that they can't be trusted. Would you so quickly turn your back on your beliefs?" he hissed. To Skye's dismay, several of the gathered goblins nodded their agreement at the blond goblin's words.

"Elflock, you are neither the Elder here nor the invited speaker and so you will sit down and be quiet. I will not listen to any more of your spiteful drivel or warmongering. Do you understand me?"

Elflock didn't answer his leader but reluctantly took his seat again and sardonically bade Snudge to continue.

"After many eons, the world became full and the Spirit Voices were forced further and further into hiding until, thousands of years ago, they finally left for good and retreated into the Shadowlands. We believe to this day that the souls of our dead join those original spirits in their eternal journey through the Shadowlands."

"The Shadowlands?" Skye asked, suddenly interested. "Is that a real place or a place away from this world for the souls to travel to?"

"It is very real," Snudge replied, intrigued by Skye's

curiosity. "The Shadowlands lie to the west of Ithilmir, a desolate valley ringed by towering mountains. Nothing living remains and even though it was once lush and fertile it is now nothing more than a scar etched onto the landscape. There, the souls of those who have died wander freely for eternity. It is said that a constant mist swirls down from the peaks and covers the dead in a silver shroud. The Shadowlands are very real, but they are not somewhere that the living should ever tread. Those that have dared to venture there have returned changed or not at all. There were once mystic seers who were able to seek advice from those who had passed beyond the mountains through the use of dark magic or prayer but our kind hasn't seen such a seer in many generations. "Why do you ask, Skye?"

"No reason," she mumbled. "I was just curious."

Snudge frowned his disbelief but continued with his original tale.

"When the original Spirit Voices left, they did so with great haste. In their haste to leave, they left behind a relic of their original war.

"In the beginning, Good and Evil were still trying to keep watch on the other, and so they each created an orb, moulded from a ball of molten rock, into which they poured part of themselves. As they looked into the sphere, each one could see the other and could rest assured that they were far, far away.

"When the Spirit Voices left our world, they left the orbs behind, buried deep within the mountains. But, as these things have a habit of doing, they didn't remain buried forever.

"The first race of intelligent creatures to walk on this world were small, not dissimilar to ourselves; they would eventually evolve to become a race known as the Shrunken that still skulk in the dark places to this day.

"When they first settled into simple villages, towards the end of the Before Time, they started to mine stone in a quantity that has not been seen since. For centuries, they chipped away at the mountains. It was only a matter of time before they stumbled upon one of the Spirit Orbs.

"Had fate been kinder on that day, they would have found the Orb of Good and the world would be a very different place. Unfortunately, they found the Orb of Evil and were instantly drawn to the darkness that they sensed lurked within.

"They took the stone and named it Akeldama in honour of their first god. The stone sat for a dozen centuries within a stone tower built solely to contain their most precious treasure. However, within a few generations, the Shrunken had changed from quiet creatures who worked and lived peacefully with the land into a race controlled by darkness and evil and from which all the dark forces have since grown."

"I really must insist…" Elflock was on his feet again and striding towards Skye. She backed away, unsure what to do as he continued to rant and rave to the audience who tried to look away awkwardly. "Guards, seize this imposter and throw her into the forest. We do not need her here. We can do this job ourselves!" The guards that lined the room didn't budge.

"Elflock, you are a long-time servant of the G'Oräk and in *some* circles are respected and for that I will give you *one more chance.* However, it really will only be one more. I shan't ask if I've made myself clear because, quite frankly, I heard myself speak and know just how clear I was. *Sit down!*" The last command was issued with a raised voice and stopped Elflock in his tracks. Once again, the outspoken goblin made for his chair all the time grumbling under his breath.

Snudge settled himself and rubbed at his eyes. Skye could tell that there was more but had the good sense not to press the G'Oräk Elder any more than was necessary. She knew that anything she learned now might help her to survive, and so she sat and waited as the goblin ate slowly from a loaf of bread and drank from a heavy flagon. He glanced across at Elflock and ensured that the goblin was seated before continuing once again.

"For many years, the Shrunken remained isolated beyond the forest known as the Gloom as other races grew and prospered around the world. In fact, it took another race entirely to burst the bubble that had kept the evil pegged back. A race of small, evil creatures, the Nelapsi, had begun to advance across the plains to the north of the Tall Pine Mountains with the aim of finding a purer source of water than that on the coast where they had settled.

"The Nelapsi were and still are a species of the night, travelling great distances to feed on those that they attack. They swarm like locusts, and their small armies can reduce a city to ghosts in a night.

"Few people know what happened next, and even fewer have ever written it down, but it is often told that the leader of the Nelapsi, Liorath, broke through to Alastor, the capital city of the Shrunken realm. It is written that he was so taken with the power bestowed up them by Akeldama that Liorath immediately took a Shrunken princess named Malgas for a bride and spawned a child that would shape the very world itself."

"The Nelapsi," Skye whispered. "They sound like vampires. Creatures of the night that feed on the blood of their victims. There are stories of them back home, though I've never believed them."

"There is much you don't believe in, little one. Is that not so?" asked Snudge as Skye felt her cheeks redden, "Yes, they are vampires of a sort. They don't turn into bats like those in your nightmares, but they do move quickly through the night. So quickly, in fact, that they may as well fly."

As Skye listened she could feel the temperature drop inside the hall. The worried looks around her told her that this story was all too familiar to the other G'Oräks and was not something that they relished hearing. It didn't matter, though. Skye needed to know. Skye indicated for Snudge to continue, and, reluctantly, he returned to his tale.

"For thousands of years, different tribes came and went and fought endless wars with each other. For a very long time, goblins fought as one tribe. There were far fewer of us back then. Eventually, too many of us wanted command and so we broke off into different villages under different leaders. It was a day that weakened the power of goblin-kind.

"The G'Oräk settled here in the North Wood and built our village, Kobold, named after one of the first of the G'Oräk. For the longest time, we stayed clear of the worst of the fighting, though many more of the goblin tribes threw themselves deep into the war and even started to fight amongst themselves. We wear the silver hand of peace, though," Snudge held his hand to his chest where the silver mark rested.

"We did not seek war, Skye. It is important that you know that. Instead, we retreated further and further into the North Wood and built the Holden Wall to keep the invading hordes at bay.

"We prayed, Skye. We prayed to our gods for help, and we found them lacking. Do you know how it feels to believe in something so hard only to have it ripped from under you when you need it most?"

Skye didn't want to say that this was exactly how she felt at that moment. All her life she'd believed in science. It was more than belief, in fact. It wasn't a believe or not believe situation, it just *was* and always would be. And now here she was talking to a goblin.

"I think I have an idea," she muttered.

"Hmm?" Snudge didn't appear to have been listening, so he went on. "This time, instead of praying, we sent a healer out into the Wandering Place to the Druidmotte, a place where goblin druids had started to form their own society away from the politics of the tribes. Once there, he spoke to the gathering of the druids, and they sent him forth with a prophecy."

At this point, everyone in the hall started to speak

at the same time echoing Snudge's voice until their voices sang in unison and echoed into every corner of the great hall.

"A dark shadow will fall in the south. Those who seek to fight shadows shall be delivered a warrior from the skies to combine the forces of old and chase into the Shadowland those who came before."

As the echoes of the prophecy fell silent around the hall, a loud indignant harrumph drew everyone's attention back to the blond-haired goblin sat with his arms firmly closed across his lap and his back to Snudge. Once he was sure that he had everyone's attention, he turned his head towards his leader and mocked surprise at the waiting audience.

"Well," he said, "why don't you just give her the key to the throne? You have given her just about everything else!" He was almost wailing by this point like a child whose favourite toy had been taken away. "You have no right to do this, Snudge! To share the secrets of our tribe, of your family, with this little filthy human!"

"That is enough!" roared Snudge over the rising commotion. "You really do insist on pushing as far as you can, Elflock, but right now we have business to attend to and you are a burden to that. Guards!" He summoned the well-armed guards from around the room and directed them to seize Elflock. "Take him to the cells and give him a night to think about his behaviour. Tomorrow, maybe he will see a more diplomatic way to air his many, many grievances about my leadership."

When the erstwhile disrupter had been removed and some form of order had been restored to the restless audience, Skye muttered, more statement than question, "And you think that the one that the prophecy mentions is me."

"No," sighed Snudge as he relaxed on his throne. "The prophecy was believed for a long time, but we were never sent our saviour.

"Over time, it fell into folklore until eventually it was just something that you told the children. Eventually, the fighting died down as tribe after tribe ran out of men, money or desire, and a tense peace fell over the world. We had no need for prophecy anymore, but still some held on. They believed."

A G'Oräk appeared behind Skye and handed her a goblet of cold water. Another was passed to the Elder, and he drank deeply before continuing his story.

"Peace is hard won and ill-kept, and soon small battles started to be fought again. My parents were killed in the first attack to make it past the Holden Wall.

"Goblins, Skye. Can you imagine that? Killed by

their own kind." He spat with disgust and placed his cup down. Skye saw that his hand was shaking.

"Before I could be killed, I escaped into the North Wood. That first night I ran and cried and mourned until I was sure I would die from grief.

"Somehow I survived until morning, and that was when I resolved to return to my tribe one day and lead them to the victory that we deserved, a victory over all evil.

"I stumbled through the forest, lost and alone, for many weeks. I grew weak and tired but soon learnt what it meant to have courage. To keep going when everything seemed lost. One night, whilst I was looking for somewhere to sleep, I stumbled through a hole in a tree and found myself falling head first into a dark tunnel. There I met my saviours.

"From that point on, I was raised by a tribe of tree trolls. We lived within the trees, and they taught me to be brave, to have courage in what I believed in and to follow it through, no matter what the cost. They taught me that not everything I held true was real and that I needed to learn to deal with things as they are. Does that sound familiar, Skye?"

Not for the first time, Skye was sure that Snudge knew more about her than he was letting on. Either that or he could see right into her soul. She didn't answer.

"When I came of age, I returned to the River Gate and asked to be taken to the Elder. His name was Goldwine, and he was old…far too old to be ruling in such a perilous time. I spoke to him long into the night. He must have seen something that he liked for it was agreed that I would assist him in his leadership with the aim of taking over when he finally moved to the Shadowlands.

"Goldwine lived for only a few months more before handing me the throne and passing on. I mourned him as a brother, as was right, but inside I was yearning to fight, to lead my people to victory.

"Not long into my reign, a human child was delivered to us. She was picked up in the Shadow Glen and brought before me. I must admit, Skye, her journey to me was less adventurous than yours, and she arrived in better condition."

Skye blushed and dropped her head a little. She knew that it wasn't her fault, but she hadn't exactly shown a lot of courage so far.

"Her name was Carmine, and I spoke to her as I am speaking to you now. I told her of our fate, of the prophecy and of the part she was surely to play. She spoke all the right words and broke bread with us and then disappeared into the night, never to be heard from again. Some say she roams the Wandering Place, a lost spirit. Fanciful, I say, but let them have their fancies.

"Then there was Gregor, a strong man but weak of heart. He set out with three of our finest warriors only to slay them as they slept and turn his back to fight with the Nelapsi. Luckily, they are even less trusting of humans than us, and they slit his throat as soon as he arrived.

"Two others have arrived between then and now, and none have proved to be worthy of fulfilling the prophecy. So I ask you now, Skye, why are you any different?" This last question was whispered so quietly that Skye had to strain to hear it.

Skye never knew if she drew courage from knowing that the goblins needed her or if she was just desperate for friends whilst Arthur was so far away. Maybe she just knew that she must try to show even the smallest amount of courage if she was ever to leave Ithilmir. Whatever the reason, Skye got to her feet and looked Snudge straight in the eyes.

"I don't know the task that lies before me, and I don't know how I can help your people, but I will not shy away from it. I will be here in the morning, and the morning after and I will not slay your people whilst they sleep or wake. I am not strong, but I am clever. You say the tree trolls taught you courage? Then teach me. You may not believe that I am the one that the prophecy mentions, but I could still help. I'm here right now, aren't I? There is nobody else to help. Teach me and let me do whatever I can."

She turned to the collected G'Oräk gathered around her and tried her hardest to look strong and brave. She would try her best to help them, after all she didn't seem to have much choice, but she needed them to know that there was one thing she wanted more than anything else. Something that she had yearned for since she had arrived.

"Then, let me go home."

Mission

There was a lot more to be done before Skye was allowed to leave the great hall. There were songs that needed to be sung and prayers and incantations to be said and followed. By the time she was led hungry and weak to a table laid with strange meats and breads, she could barely hold a thought in her head.

Skye was sat at the foot of a long, wooden table, at the head of which sat Snudge. Around the sides over a hundred G'Oräk were squashed, all desperate to eat with their Elder. Skye noticed that many of them were having hushed conversations between themselves and occasionally overheard snippets that didn't fill her with confidence.

"She's an outsider, after all. Not even a woman grown"

"Look what happened last time. Never again, Snudge said."

"She'll never last anyway. She'll disappear before she starts if Elflock has his way!"

The last one jolted Skye awake. Clearly somebody wasn't happy that Skye was here. Weard had warned her about that much in the hut in the forest. Why had Snudge changed his mind and agreed to see her? When Weard had come to collect her, she had seemed distant and distracted, shaking with nervous energy. She said herself that Snudge didn't want to see Skye but had changed his mind.

Skye had never been very good at judging social moods, something that had often landed her in trouble with teachers or bullies at school as she often spoke her mind regardless of other people's emotional state. But even Skye could sense that there was an undercurrent of tension in the room. There was too much conversation along the lines of "It'll be all right. It has to be all right, right? Snudge wouldn't let it happen again, would he?" for Skye to be comfortable.

She ate the rest of the meal in silence, making sure to enjoy it while she could. There were large slabs of bloody meat that Skye didn't recognise along with pale white vegetables that tasted a lot like swede. It was all served in a giant bread trencher which Skye used to wipe up the gravy and washed it all down with a mug of sweet mint tea.

When the meal finally came to an end, Skye was collected by a young goblin.

"I'm Jargogle, so I am. I'm the G'Oräk that takes things to and fro, so to speak. That I am."

Her guide had an ungainly walk that suggested he had suffered an injury to one of his legs sometime in past and his shoulders were stooped low over his chest. Like most G'Oräk, he had no hair on his head. Instead of the silken robes of his kin, he wore a simple loincloth to hide his modesty. His body was covered in a spider's web of scars that criss-crossed across his back and chest. Some of the wounds were still open and slowly wept with blue blood.

"What happened to you?" Skye asked, trying to put an arm on Jargogle's shoulder.

The goblin recoiled and gripped Skye's wrist more tightly, "Nothing happened. No, it didn't. Skye mustn't ask those questions. No, she shouldn't. She'll find out soon enough. Yes, she will."

Skye knew better that to press anymore and allowed herself to be led gently to a bed at the rear of the hall, away from the warriors and priests that lined the rest of the walls. Her bed was little more than a scattering of blankets and cushions on the hard mud floor, but it was more comfortable than anything she had experienced since arriving on Ithilmir, and so she settled down to try to make the most of a good night's sleep.

"Jargogle," she asked as the crippled goblin started to leave, "what will I find out? What can you tell me?"

The goblin stopped and turned back to face Skye. For a moment, he appeared indecisive.

"'It's okay," she reassured him. "I don't mean to scare you."

Eventually, the goblin spoke, trying hard to whisper but he soon slipped into his erratic shouting. Skye found herself trying to insert a breath on the goblin's behalf.

"Mustn't be here, you shouldn't. You're not wanted by goblins. Going to war is what goblins want. No, not silly humans sneaking and stealing from *her*…"

The goblin trailed off and slapped a hand to his mouth.

"Who are you talking about, Jargogle?" Skye asked, "Who is the lady you mentioned?"

The goblin recoiled from Skye's words and tried to slink away. Skye reached out instinctively and touched his shoulder to reassure him. She felt his thin bones move under her grip as though he were at the end of a long fast. As she guided him closer, she felt him collapse to his knees and bow his head. This was a goblin who was used to being beaten hard.

Skye reflected that not all goblins would be equal here. There were those who floated to the top, like Snudge and Weard, and there were those who would just sink and skulk around the bottom. Jargogle was lower than most, and Skye found herself taking pity on him. She doubted he'd be able to tell her anything useful. It would just be dregs of information that he had picked up elsewhere. But she was desperate for any kind of control over her situation. She decided to try to push harder.

"Jargogle, I need you to tell me why I am here. Who were you talking about? Who is so important to you?"

To Skye's horror, the goblin didn't reply. Instead, he screamed as loudly as he could and started to hiss and spit at her. Shocked, she let go of his wrist and tried desperately to calm him down. The last thing she needed was for the other goblins to think that she had harmed one of their friends. She needn't have worried though, as soon as she let go of his arm, Jargogle fell to the floor and scrambled away. Skye had never seen anything so wretched.

As he disappeared into the darkness, Skye heard him screaming to all who would hear "Do not trust the human! Do not trust the human!".

Luckily, Jargogle's outburst hadn't attracted the attention of any of the other goblins, and so, once her heart had stopped racing, Skye lay down on her bed and tried her best to get to sleep.

Skye must have finally fallen asleep as, whilst it was still dark, she was gently shaken awake by a rough hand and a whispered hush. Opening her eyes, Skye was surprised to find the intense gaze of Snudge looking back at her from only a few inches away. Stretching her arms out slowly, Skye made an effort to sit up and moved some of the blankets to pad out the hard wall behind her.

"Snudge?" she asked, her voice echoing more loudly than she had intended around the hall.

"Be quiet, girl," Snudge hissed. "I am here to speak to you and you alone. We cannot speak here. Follow me."

Snudge stood up and headed for the large wooden doors at the front of the hall. Skye followed silently making sure not to wake the sleeping G'Oräk. In the darkness, she saw pinpoints of green light and knew that they were being watched as they made their way out. She knew instinctively that the watchers were not friends of hers.

Skye knew that there would be talk tomorrow, but

for now she had no choice but to follow Snudge out into the warm evening air.

There was a strong smell of night flowers on the breeze as Skye stepped outside. In the distance, a bird called longingly to a mate. Skye found Snudge pensively smoking a wooden pipe and stood next to him, looking into the distance, not wanting to disturb whatever it was that the Elder was thinking about.

"I assume you are no longer having trouble breathing?" Snudge asked after a long while, tapping his pipe out onto the ground.

"Yes, thank you."

"There is a creature, strange and evasive, that lives at the bottom of our lakes. It is a tiny fish, the lungfish, and it has an extraordinary ability to breathe almost any gas except for oxygen. This, it releases as a waste gas.

"We discovered when the first human arrived that allowing a lungfish to live inside the lungs of a human would allow them to breathe our atmosphere and use what little oxygen there was. Don't look like that," he continued, noticing Skye's horrified expression. "It is too small for you to see and is otherwise perfectly harmless. You will barely notice it is there."

"How does it get inside me?" Skye asked, nervously.

"It's already in you," Snudge answered calmly.

"When you drank the water in the great hall, Jargogle made sure that there was a lungfish in it. I gather you didn't notice."

Skye felt herself going pale, and her dinner threatened to make another appearance. She started to wretch at the thought of something living inside her.

"It was either that," stated Snudge bluntly, "or you slowly suffocated."

Skye reflected on this and decided that the best way to deal with this horrific information was to just pretend like it wasn't happening.

Snudge tapped out the contents of his pipe and reached into a small leather bag for more tobacco. He slowly pressed the dried leaves into the cup with the patience of a man who has all night before striking a thick match against a rock. He sucked deeply as he lit the pipe and blew a pink smoke ring over Skye's head. When he spoke, his voice was dark and serious.

"What I am about to tell you must never reach the ears of the other G'Oräk. They are far too delicate and could not handle knowing the threat that we face."

Skye assured the goblin that she would remain quiet about anything that she was told, and Snudge continued.

"We have been at an uneasy peace now for many generations, but it is a delicate peace, more easily broken than a teacup. Our world is always just one stupid action away from returning to war. For many moons, we have relaxed the guard on our wall until, nowadays, it is more of a token gesture than anything."

Skye reflected on the relaxed attitude of the guards that she had seen as she entered the Holden Wall. They hadn't seemed to be the most attentive, being more interested in their card game. She chose not to say anything.

"It appears that I have been remiss in my leadership. Yesterday, a band of Nelapsi scaled the Holden Wall on its western side and slaughtered a family of G'Oräk in their sleep. We managed to capture one of the group and disposed of the rest but not without cost.

"The Nelapsi were heavily armed with strong swords and arrows. They have never attacked this far north before or been this much of a threat. They normally carry flint weapons more suited for dark deeds in the shadows.

"When questioned, the Nelapsi appeared to be under the impression that the family were hiding Fréod, the sister stone of Akeldama, the stone that the Good Spirit forged. This is ridiculous on two fronts. First, we don't have the orb. We never have. Second, if we did have it, why would we leave it unguarded in the home of a common weaver?"

Skye asked curiously, "Does anyone have Fréod? The good orb?"

"Not that we know of. Many heroes have searched for it over the ages, but nobody has ever claimed to have found it. For all we know, it was destroyed in the first great battles."

"And Akeldama?"

"That, we know exists." Snudge shuddered. "It is that to which we must divert our attention now. An evil has been rising in the south. A dark fire has been lit on Liorath's Peak where the first evil built her tower.

"The first spawn of Liorath and Malgas were hideous half-breeds that possessed none of the good in the world but all of the greed and malice. For a while, they led an army of half-Nelapsi that spread darkness across our world, though they never made it as far north as the North Wood. Eventually, they were slain, and the tower fell into darkness."

Skye thought back to when she first arrived and climbed the tree. She was under no doubt that the dark fire that she had seen on top of the tall rock was Liorath's Peak. She said as much to Snudge.

"That is indeed troubling, young human. It is likely that a new evil is rising and has rediscovered Akeldama. We do not know what they intend to use it for, but rest assured that no good deed has ever been done under its influence. Come, we must stretch our legs."

Snudge led Skye away from the hall and beyond the edge of the trees, stopping beside a small brook than ran lazily between the thick, tangled roots.

"I'm not sure how I can help, sir. I am not a warrior." Skye aired the concern that had been playing on her mind.

"This much is true," Snudge conceded. "However, my little show earlier was entirely for the benefit of the people who doubt you. I still happen to believe in the prophecy. Whether or not it concerns you? I couldn't not say. You have certainly arrived from the skies. Indeed, your name is evidence enough of that. And you have arrived at a most fortuitous time. You may yet help us avoid a war. Do I believe that the one spoken of is you? Yes, I do. However, that may simple be that I *wish* it to be you. For now, let us just say that you are the best we have!" He said this with a soft smile on his face, and Skye relaxed slightly. "But it does no good for a leader to reveal too much fuzzy thinking in front of those who follow him, especially when so many of those followers are against any solution except war.

"Despite what eons of war have taught, indeed cost us, there are those who would still head straight back into another one and another age of darkness and fear. They feed on nights like tonight where they can use attacks like this to spread their hate and vitriol. But they don't think about the cost." Snudge paused and drew on his pipe. "Or they don't care. War will come to us in the end. That I am certain of. I am eager to keep it at bay as long as possible.

"Don't be fooled, Skye. Even though many believe in the prophecy, they were – indeed we all were – expecting somebody more..." He paused and waved his hands around Skye.

"Strong?" she offered.

Snudge sagged. "I suppose. Older, maybe, or wiser. Those that you will travel with will have their doubts, Skye, even if they don't show it. Prove yourself to them, Skye, as soon as you can. I believe in you."

Skye tried her best to digest this information. She had never lived through a war but had seen enough on the news at home to know that it was not something she could ever imagine a person wanting.

"But what do they hope to gain by going to war? Can this evil be defeated?" she asked.

"They believe so. I am not so sure. One of the warriors who fought for the spawn of Liorath was Carmine, the first human to arrive here. After the death of her lord, Carmine succumbed to a great rage and fled into the darkness with a Nelapsi captain. There they produced children that were closer to human than anything else, and within a few generations a new race of half-humans arose. Can you imagine a race of people with the anger and self-centred arrogance of humans with the guile and viciously murderous attitude of the Nelapsi? To most, they are indistinguishable from humans, slightly different in appearance perhaps but altogether too similar in their thirst for war and destruction.

"They were stronger and more evil than anything that had roamed this world before. Many of them learnt to channel the power of Akeldama and became mages and necromancers able to not only raise the dead but have them follow them into battle to die all over again.

"Dragons flew through the air and scorched the land below. Many of our forests were burnt, and the Wandering Place was destroyed beyond recognition.

"Our druid were no match for their magic, and for generations it looked like the race of men would rule the land under Carmine's reign."

Skye was beginning to understand more why Snudge had such a distrust of humans.

"The armies of Ithilmir united. Goblins fought alongside orcs, fairies, trolls and elves and drove these men back beyond the Wandering Place and beyond

Liorath's Tower, but we did not pursue them too far south for we knew little of that land and less of what lurked there.

"We considered them defeated, and for a long time that seemed to be the case. It seems that we were wrong. This new evil is not a coincidence. Whatever lurks on top of Liorath's Peak is descended from their line and will stop at nothing to continue the work of their Lady Carmine.

"Akeldama still has power beyond imagining and can still be used to view the world, though I am told the images are hazy. Whilst they hold Akeldama, there will be war," Snudge continued. "For now, they are weak and their army is small. We must remove the evil from that tower before they can grow any stronger. That is your task, Skye. To enter Liorath's Peak and steal Akeldama."

Allegiance

Skye knew that she had to get away to think. This wasn't a simple task that she had to do. This would put her life in danger.

No wonder the others had all left or deserted, she thought. She couldn't do it. She knew she couldn't, but all of these people seemed utterly convinced that she was their only hope. Skye had her doubts, but she also knew that her only hope of getting back home was currently to do as they asked. She feigned tiredness to Snudge and headed back to the hall and her bed, but she knew that she wouldn't be able to sleep. She doubted she'd ever be able to sleep again.

Green eyes pierced the darkness as she slowly made her way to back to her bed and did little to ease Skye's mind. For the next few hours, she lay quietly in her bed going over and over what Snudge had told her.

By the time the sun had risen above the trees, Skye was no clearer as to which course of action to take. Not many of the goblins were awake yet, but the few that were sat around making small talk or eating breakfast. She made her way to the long table and took the edge off her hunger with sweet porridge and the same sweet, filling berries that she'd first had in the forest.

With her stomach tied in knots and feeling sick with fear, Skye rose from the table and set off for the great wooden doors at the far end of the hall.

Something about the way that several G'Oräk were loitering by the archway made her uneasy. Deviating off course, Skye made for a smaller door leading out from the eastern wall. She ducked through and escaped without being harassed by any guards. She made her way quickly towards a wide-rutted track that led away from the hall as it threaded between the trees.

Before long, Skye found herself approaching a village, surrounded by a low wooden wall broken by an open gate. An old sign hung above the gate told Skye that this was the G'Oräk village, Kobold. By the looks of the hinges, the gate hadn't been closed in a long time.

As it entered the village, the road narrowed to the width of a small carriage and ran straight between double-storied wooden buildings. Each had a panelled wooden door that opened onto the road and was overhung with a first-floor balcony.

At irregular intervals, roads ran perpendicular to the main thoroughfare creating a rough grid system. Skye guessed that the entire village was a few miles across though less than half of that in width.

To the south of the village, Skye could see a square tower rising twice as tall as any house but only a few steps wide on each side and capped with a stone spire.

The first thing that struck Skye was the sheer number of people making their way along the streets. At times Skye found herself having to push herself through crowds to make any progress along the main road.

The second thing that she noticed was the diversity of people around her. The streets weren't just filled with goblins, though they outnumbered the other races significantly. Here and there, Skye noticed creatures that looked suspiciously like humans making their way through the throng, their heads towering high above the others. Weard had told Skye that she wasn't the first human to arrive here, but those walking around in front of her looked both familiar but at the same time very different. Snudge had been right, there were subtle differences. They were taller and far stockier than any men Skye had ever seen at home. Their jawlines more pronounced and their foreheads hung lower over their eyes. Such a contrast of something so eerily familiar yet so obviously foreign disorientated Skye for a moment, and she found herself rubbing her mother's ring for comfort.

At the other end of the spectrum, Skye had to make sure that she kept a close eye on her feet in case she trod on one of the numerous gnomes and pixies that bustled about no higher than her knees.

In front of her was everything that Skye had never believed in. Goblins, gnomes, pixies and even the occasional troll all made their way through the streets on missions of their own. Some were clearly traders whilst others were there to provide a service.

The trolls, Skye noticed, were exclusively used for heavy work. They were often tethered to the front of carts, and Skye was horrified to see that they were being whipped by the drivers to make them go faster. When Skye had seen this being done to horses back on Earth, she hadn't really given it any thought, but now that she saw it being used as a way to get more intelligent creatures to do as they were told, it seemed barbaric.

In fact, Skye realised as she stood and watched the scene unfold in front of her, there was a clear hierarchy in place in which most of the goblins were clearly at the top. The gnomes and pixies were not buying or trading goods. They were crawling around in the dirt collecting and cleaning up anything that the goblins dropped. They had the horrible jobs that goblins didn't want to do themselves.

Here and there were goblins who had found themselves somehow even lower than their smaller servants. Skye started to notice these urchins nearly always hidden from view down dark, damp alleyways. Occasionally, however, she noticed that they made their way onto the main street to beg for food or water. The other goblins treated them with contempt or ignored them completely, often kicking away their begging bowls or spitting on them as they passed.

Slowly, taking an interest in everything that she saw, Skye made her way through the crowded streets. Around her, the more successful goblins bustled to buy or sell their products, offering handfuls of gold coins or pressing items into Skye's hands. She noticed that shops were operating out of people's houses, mainly through the front windows. Some were selling fruit or bread, others spare parts for machines and carts. At each window purveyors were proffering free samples of their wares to try to entice customers closer.

On every street corner, there were performers vying for the attention and coins of the shoppers in the street.

Some were talented musicians playing instruments that Skye struggled to recognise. Others were dressed in brightly coloured costumes and juggled fire and swords. Street magicians made their way amongst the crowds offering high rewards for those brave enough to gamble on their card tricks.

Skye floated aimlessly through the throngs like an untethered balloon bouncing around in a breeze. She got lost amongst the colours and fragrances that wafted over the crowds. She allowed herself to relax for long enough to sample some of the small samples of foods being offered to her from the open windows and gave in to delicious morsels of strange breads and meats.

Every now and then, Skye would find herself thrown off balance by urchins begging her to give them coins or food. She brushed them off as best she could, but most were her own age or older and she soon started to grow claustrophobic in the crowds.

Looking up, she aimed for the tall spire and eventually found herself evicted from the mass of goblins into an open square lined on each side with small shops selling artisan items. In the middle, a tall stone fountain provided a place for the smaller goblins to splash and cool off in the rising heat.

In one corner of the square, Skye noticed that a

large crowd had gathered and had formed a noisy circle. She made her way over and used her elbows to push herself closer to the front of the mob.

At the centre of the circle, an old goblin was circling a terrified gnome. The goblin had one leg and a patch over one eye, but Skye was horrified to see that it held in its hand a short, sharp sword. The gnome was unarmed. Skye heard the goblins around her offering money to each other, betting on the outcome of the fight that was about to happen.

Sickened, Skye pulled herself away from the crowd and ran towards the other side of the square. She stopped by a drain and felt the sick rising in her throat. She was no longer sure what she knew or where she was and now she wasn't even sure what to think of the goblins. She knew that fights like that wouldn't be allowed to happen without Snudge's permission, and yet she couldn't believe that somebody as seemingly nice as him would allow it.

Disorientated, Skye made her way around the square trying to take her mind off what she had seen.

"Try my little secrets, little girl!" cried a hooded goblin, cowering behind a small wooden table in front of one of the houses to Skye's left. The voice was familiar, but Skye struggled to place it immediately.

Skye turned and looked into the hooded face. She

couldn't make out any features, but the eyes glowed greener than any Skye had seen so far. Cautiously, she made her way over to the table and examined the products on display. The table was covered with small glass jars, each filled with different coloured liquids.

"What are they?" Skye asked nervously.

"Potions, they are," answered the shrill voice from beneath the hood. "Druids make them all. Many magic uses."

"What does this one do?" Skye asked as she picked up a bright pink vial from the table.

"Good choice! Good choice! Good luck!"

Before Skye could object, the goblin had removed the glass stopper and thrust it under Skye's nose. She breathed in the heady smell of lavender before she had a chance to back away.

"Very nice," Skye said as she tried to move away from the table. As she stumbled, she found that she no longer had full control over her legs. She staggered forwards and fell against the goblin's table which folded under her weight and sent the glass containers smashing to the floor. Skye rolled onto her back and was overcome with the aromas of the spilled potions and her vision started to blur. Before she lost consciousness, she looked up into the hooded face of the trader. Horrified, she watched as he pulled back his hood slightly and revealed his scarred, weeping face.

"Jargogle?" she whispered as her tongue swelled in her mouth and her lips closed shut.

"I'm sorry. I had to follow you. They made me follow you. They listen to her, so they do. You need to learn the truth, *girl*," the goblin muttered as Skye finally passed out.

Capture

When Skye opened her eyes, she was in a dark room illuminated by a row of spluttering candles. Her arms and legs were tied to a wooden chair, and her head was swimming with pain.

A wet feeling trickling down her neck told her that her head was bleeding. She had obviously hit it on the stone ground of the village square but had been too numb to notice at the time. There was a pain behind her eyes, and she was struggling to focus through the blur.

The position of the candles meant that Skye was blinking in their light but that her captors were shrouded in darkness. Around her, the movement of the air and the slight echo to her voice as she screamed gave the impression of a large, bare room beyond the shadows.

"Filthy human mustn't struggle," rasped a familiar, horrible, high voice full of hatred. "There is no danger. Not yet. Oh no, no way!" Jargogle's words hung heavily in the air.

A second voice broke the silence. "You are perfectly safe with us. We wish you no harm beyond what you have already suffered." This voice was calm and deep. This was a voice that was not only used to giving commands but was used to them being carried out without question. Jargogle, Skye suspected, was more used to carrying out the instructions.

"Safe as houses! Safe as houses! Ha!" sang the first voice again. Skye didn't like the laugh at the end. It was far too unhinged. The voice was strangely familiar, though. She hoped that the second voice had a strong hold on the leash that held him back.

"We are the League of War." This was a third voice, equally calm as the second but far more feminine. Skye thought back to her teacher Miss Mimosa and how she would shower her with scorn in such a calm and measured manner that Skye would never know why she felt so awful afterwards. "We are here to make sure that the G'Oräk follow the…correct…path through these troubled times."

The second voice started, "We have no doubt that Snudge has told you of our history and where you fit into it. What we would like to know is what his plans are for you? What did you two discuss during your late-night walk last night?"

Skye knew she was in trouble. She kept quiet.

"Fair enough," said the third voice. "If you won't talk, let us. You have seen for yourself the poverty that our own people are living in here in Kobold. There are goblins begging in the streets for food whilst other species are allowed to come in and work.

"Snudge has allowed this to happen, and now when we need goblins to stand back to back and fight, our own people are weakened by famine. How can Snudge expect to raise an army when we have no strength and no loyalty left? "You are aware of what is happening in the south? That once more a dark evil is rising at Loriath's Peak?" The voice didn't wait for Skye to answer, instead pressing straight on. "We, that is, the League of War, think that the time for counsel has passed and that we must act with strength and aggression now before the enemy becomes too strong."

The second voice took up the story. "This is the time for heroes, Skye, not hecklers. We need swords, not words. Isn't it funny that one word is so similar to the other, yet the result is so often very different?

"The prophecy is true, Skye. We all accept that. A human will be sent to save us. This is beyond doubt, though Snudge and his legion would have you believe that we deny such a tale. Where we differ is on how that human will save us. Do you want to be a hero, Skye? Riding into battle to bask in the songs and prizes that come with victory?"

"A thief, she is! A sneak!" sang Jargogle, all angry and sharp and full of venom. "We know what we would rather be!"

"Oh, do be quiet, Jargogle. She isn't a threat to you," snapped the second voice. "Nobody would believe you were helping us or even care for that matter. You are not important."

Skye suspected that the scars that covered Jargogle's body had come at the hands of the other voices speaking to her. She wondered how the sneaky goblin had explained them away to Snudge. She wandered if Snudge knew that Jargogle was here? She wanted to feel sorry for the wretch, but she couldn't forget what he had done to her in the market square.

"Well, Skye, what is it that you want?"

"What do I want?" she asked mostly to herself. Suddenly, everything came in to focus again. "I want to go home. This isn't my war. I don't know any of you or what you've done. I just want to go home, back to where I belong."

"Ah yes, back to your own little world." The

commanding voice now had a gentler tone. Skye could almost let it reassure her that everything would be all right. "And let me guess. Snudge and his cronies have promised to send you home as soon as you've completed their fool's errand?"

Skye nodded.

"Well, Skye," the syrupy voice continued, "we will send you home right now."

Skye glanced up into the candlelight. She knew she would feel much more comfortable if she could just see their faces, look into their eyes and see if they were telling the truth.

"You could do that?" she asked, suspicion hanging on every word.

"We are incredibly powerful. Of course, we'd need something from you in return. Nothing nearly so dangerous or impossible as Snudge is asking, however."

Skye tried to fight back the growing excitement. Her chest felt on fire as her stomach churned. She glared into the candlelight, begging them to continue without saying so much as a word.

"All we ask," interjected the other, more controlling voice, "is that you tell us Snudge's plan. Where he is sending his little group of fools. What they plan to achieve. You don't owe him anything, Skye. As you said, you don't know any of us or what we have done.

For all you know, Snudge may be the most evil of all our race."

Skye's head was swimming. She'd thought she had a handle on the situation last night, but now she wasn't sure. What they were saying was true. Snudge's idea was a sneaky one with no honour, and she really didn't owe him anything. But then, Skye had never had any honour, preferring to stay out of the way of trouble altogether. However, she owed Weard everything. The healer had brought her back from death after her fight with the glibberig.

Skye doubted that she'd be any good in a battle. She hadn't handled Keith Boggart very well, had she? Where it not for Weard scaring him off, she would have been in even more trouble. And now one of the trusted G'Oräk was involved as well? It didn't make any sense.

The voice was right, though. Jargogle was a small cog in all of this. There were bigger players, and Skye sensed that two of them were sat in front of her right now.

"We will leave you to think on it, Skye," said possibly the second voice, "but don't think too long. We will be back soon. It would be terrible if we had to…take measures, shall we say, to ensure that you see things our way." Skye felt the air move as her captors left her alone in the room with her thoughts and her aching limbs. As they exited, Skye was sure she heard Jargogle's familiar giggle as he celebrated what he saw as a victory. He was quickly hushed into silence.

In the end, Skye did not have too much time to worry about her situation. Within an hour of her waking up inside the dark hall, Skye was being untied by two friendly, if rather gruff-looking, G'Oräk.

Her captors hadn't returned since leaving her, and the soldiers informed her that they had fled as soon as Snudge's guards had arrived.

Rubbing her sore wrists and ankles to get the blood flowing back into them, Skye made her way back, under armed escort, to Snudge.

She had initially expected to be taken back to the great hall where she had first met Snudge and subsequently spent the previous night. Instead, she was guided towards the western gate and out of the village. After a short walk through more thick forest, the pathway started to descent rapidly into a large crater, wider across than many small villages.

In the centre of the crater, cleared of trees on one side but nestling amongst them on the other three, stood a large house. Skye hadn't known what to expect from the G'Oräk Elder's home, but she wasn't disappointed. It was four stories high and wider than it was deep. On the front, there were a number of large glazed windows and a high wooden door painted red. Embossed upon it was the silver handprint of peace.

"Welcome to my home," announced Snudge when he finally opened the door to Skye and her guards. "Please, consider it yours whilst you are in our service."

It took Skye awhile to take in the grand entrance hallway. Ahead of her lay a large wooden staircase, wide enough to drive a car through. It wound off to the left towards a high-ceilinged hallway joined to several rooms via large, dark wood doors. The walls were panelled with a similar dark wood and were hung with painting of G'Oräk.

"My predecessors," described Snudge, clearly in awe. "Great goblins, each and every one of them, but all of them have presided over times of war. I would like to be the first to sit on the throne in peace. Is that too much to ask, do you think?"

Skye tried to dodge the question. As soon as they had entered the hallway, her guards had announced that they were going off to the kitchen to find food, and Skye wished wholeheartedly that she could follow. She found that her mealtimes had been all over the place at the moment, and her stomach was not forgiving her. Snudge seemed to notice her distress.

"But, of course, where are my manners, Skye?

Please, let us go eat. Then, we have much to discuss."

Skye happily allowed herself to be guided towards the kitchen were a large, overbearing G'Oräk introduced herself as Phroat and subsequently introduced Skye to some of the most wondrous food she had ever eaten. Skye made sure to fill herself to bursting point as she feared that she had a long night ahead.

She may have been saved from making a difficult decision about which side of the coin she wished to fight when she was rescued, but it had left a lot of unanswered questions in her mind, questions that the League of War would no doubt seek her out to help her answer.

Council

It was a few hours later when Skye found herself sat opposite Snudge at a round, heavy wooden table. Around the table were placed several ornately backed chairs that remained empty.

To one side, Snudge was involved in a deep conversation with one of his aides, and so Skye sat and stared out of the window at the night sky. Not for the first time, she thought longingly of home and wondered if one of the stars that were shining so brightly tonight might be Earth. It was not lost on Skye that the last time she had looked out onto a sky like this had been the night she reached for the spyglass in the lighthouse.

Skye was snapped out of her daydream by Snudge clicking his fingers. The main door in to the room opened with a soft thud and in strode a selection of warriors. At first, Skye thought that they were under attack and cowered away, but each soldier took his place peacefully at the table.

For the first time, Skye noticed that not all of the warriors were goblin. Two of them looked more like humans, though with far harder facial features and far sturdier builds. They caught Skye staring their way and gave a grunt and a nod, but that was the limit of their conversation.

"Welcome, everyone, and thank you for coming at such short notice," started Snudge as he stood to address his guests, his voice louder and more commanding than normal. "We do not have the time, nor I the inclination, to waste what little we do have by going over old history. You are all G'Oräk here, either by birth or invitation," he gave a nod to the two men and Skye, "and as such know what is at stake. We are here tonight to discuss what might be done. I will be honest with you all. I hope to receive counsel from each of you before the night is done."

The G'Oräk Elder drank heavily from a goblet placed in front of him and cleared his throat before continuing. "But first, introductions. This," he pointed at Skye, "is Skye. She is a human."

There was a whispered buzz around the room. Snudge had clearly succeeded in keeping Skye's arrival under wraps from most of the folk in the village after all.

"Are you saying…" started one of the men.

"Hush, brother. Let Snudge tell us what he is saying before you jump to childish conclusions," lambasted his partner.

"Thank you, Geldrig. But yes, Gondrag, I do believe that Skye is the one spoken of in the prophecy."

This time there was nothing whispered about the buzz. The room erupted into a cacophony of noise as every man and goblin at the table rose to speak at once. Skye stayed in her seat and noticed that Snudge had done the same.

After a while, Snudge rose and in a quiet yet firm voice ordered silence.

Everybody obeyed.

When order had finally been restored, Snudge continued, "As I said, we don't have time to waste, and so I fear you must take what I say on trust, for now at least. Skye has arrived at a most fortuitous time, and we would be unwise to dismiss her aid if she can be in the least bit useful. If I may, however, I would like to finish my introductions."

As Snudge introduced each member of the group, they took to their feet and bowed towards Skye.

"You have already met our honorary Felmir,

Geldrig and Gondrag. They are brothers from Lörieas in the south. If you are lucky, you may get to visit their homeland on your journey. They are descended on their father's side from Gorath, one of the first generation of half-humans that left the armies of Carmine and bred with the rock trolls in the mountains. Though the blood of humans runs through their veins, it is inherited from the most duplicitous and evil of creatures to arrive in our world. As I have already told you, the first humans to arrive here thought only of themselves and bred with creatures that they couldn't hope to tame. Their offspring were short-tempered enough before mixing with the rock trolls. But now? Just try not to anger them." They took their seats again with a grunt.

"Next is Curglaff," Snudge indicated a small, wiry G'Oräk with even more heavily weathered skin than the other goblins that Skye had seen so far, "captain of our river fleet and a brave soldier. His father, Carafan, fought and died in the battle of Keredor's Pass." Skye recognised Curglaff as one of the soldiers that had escorted her from the Legion of War earlier that day.

Another goblin was invited to stand. "Snowbroth, our most revered druid and eldest of our tribe. He may not be a strong soldier, but his knowledge of alchemy has been of assistance in many battles before."

Next to stand was Weard, Skye was glad that somebody she knew was sitting in on the meeting. The rest of the table were shortly introduced as Brabble, Brack, Corngaff, Longcraw and Yop. Skye recognised Brabble as the grumpy guard on the gate when she and Weard had first passed through the Holden Wall. She wasn't too happy to see him again and vowed to keep a close eye on him.

Most of those around the table were seasoned warriors of varying ages, and all bowed towards Skye. Yop even went so far as to pledge his sword to Skye's side. The exception was Brack who was the G'Oräk minstrel.

"A group of experienced warmongers and battlers plus you, Skye. We have enough experience here tonight for good counsel, if I'm not mistaken. So, what is our course of action to be? I know what the Legion of War would have us do as, I believe, would Skye?"

Skye had no idea how Snudge knew what had been said to her and even less how he knew that Skye had been agonising over it all night.

"I am undecided," she said. "They told me that they could send me home today, that I wouldn't need to do anything that you asked of me."

"And in exchange? You would simply have to give them information about what I had planned?" Snudge asked it as a question though Skye knew that it was entirely rhetorical. Once again, Skye realised that Snudge knew more than he should. She wondered whether Elflock was perhaps not the only one with spies. "Skye, they have no intention of sending you home. They already know my plans. They've known for quite some time. They were simply testing you to see where your allegiance lies."

Skye hung her head. What Snudge said made sense, of course, but she couldn't help mourn the chance to return home, no matter how unlikely it had been. Skye reasoned that if they had to kidnap somebody to make their point, it was probably not a good point to make.

Unsure of how to respond, Skye muttered, "The Legion of War tried to persuade me that war was the honourable course of action. That I would return a hero."

"And what do you make of that?" prompted Curglaff.

"Nothing and everything. What they say is true. Sneaking in to steal Akeldama does seem like the work of a thief and not something that would earn us a place on the wall downstairs."

"A hero rarely sets out to be a hero, Skye," whispered Snowbroth, his voice never rising much above the cusp of hearing. "A hero is created through their selfless actions. Is heroism what you seek?"

"I didn't arrive here wanting to be a hero. To be honest, I didn't intend to come here at all. It was a series of strange circumstances, and, begging your pardon, I just want to go home. I'm not cut out for any of this. Why can't you send me home right now? Why are you so sure that I am the one spoken of in the prophecy? It's been bugging me since I arrived. You are all so convinced that I am the hero you have waited so long for."

Skye almost missed the small wave of his hand as Snudge dismissed Brack. The goblin disappeared through a small side door and returned a few minutes later with a small tapestry. Skye recognised the style as one of the battle scenes depicted in the great hall.

"Look closely." Snudge's instruction was firm but gentle. Skye turned her eye to the scene enacted across the fabric. On one side was an army of goblins pouring over a snow-covered hill. They were racing towards a dark wizard dressed head to toe in black. Only when Skye looked more closely, she realised that they were the robes of a queen and atop her head was a silver tiara. In her hands, the queen held a small orb that had been picked out in blue and purple thread. Lines radiated from its centre showing the power emanating from within. The queen looked familiar, as though

Skye had seen her in a foggy dream many years ago. It wasn't the queen that drew her attention, though.

Skye stopped and looked at Snudge. The goblins were being led from the front by a mounted leader. The detail was quite vague but there was no mistaking the tall, slender frame and vivid red hair. For all the world, it looked like Skye.

Snudge spoke, "That tapestry is over a thousand years old, Skye."

Skye didn't know what to say, so she said nothing and waited, lost in her own shock. Eventually she mustered the courage to speak. Her voice was cracked and dry and strained with her nerves.

"I can't kill anybody. I'm not a murderer."

"Indeed, you are no killer. Hopefully, if all goes to plan, you won't need to be. "What they say is, as you pointed out, true, Skye." Snudge continued. "Stealing Akeldama is sneaky and sly. However, from what Weard has reported back to us, you are quite adept at avoiding trouble back on Earth, are you not? The monster who tries to slay you each day on the field? Most days, he never finds you, and he knows for certain that you are there. These skills will prove invaluable on such a sneaky mission, I'm sure! If you are able to sneak past the queen who, do not forget, doesn't even know that you are going to be attempting to do so, then you may complete the entire quest without spilling a drop of blood.

"However, there's no doubt that to ride in to battle to slay a thousand orcs would undoubtedly earn you a song or two from Brack. Maybe Brack would be so kind as to sing you one of his shorter verses right now?"

He gestured for the minstrel to stand. Brack did so and gently plucked the strings of a small violin to get a tune. He cleared his throat and started to sing in the most melodic voice that Skye had ever heard. The sadness was there for all to hear, and Skye felt herself drifting away on his soft words.

> *Through the hills and valleys deep*
> *Rode men that saviours could not keep.*
> *Back home, a house to tend*
> *The women mourn, no heart to mend.*
>
> *Though they rode and fell with grace*
> *Forever left, a lover's place.*
> *And yet what for, their village burns*
> *From Shadowlands, they shan't return.*

By the time that Brack laid down his violin, every head was bowed in silent thought and most were weeping.

"Brack wrote that after returning from the Battle of Coraka not too many moons ago. It is a song about true heroes, Skye. Yet all of us are weeping. Why would we weep for heroes?"

"I understand what you are saying," Skye whispered, humbled, "I apologise for my crassness. I shouldn't rush to put my life in danger like that."

"Did you not listen, girl?" Snudge snapped, "It wasn't just one hero that died. By courting war, the Legion and all those who follow are dooming all of the men who are sent to die. One man may become a hero for a great deed, but many more become forgotten heroes for just doing what they were sent to do." Snudge was standing now and banging his fists onto the table with each word that he hammered out. "I will not send goblins to die when there is another option, as sneaky or dishonourable as it may be. There is no honour in the evil that is rising in the south, no valour, no courage. It is pure darkness drawn from the dawn of time."

"Then it is decided, is it not? We must set forth immediately and reclaim Akeldama?" Brabble asked. "Though I don't see why we need the girl, prophecy or not. She is a bad omen, Snudge. We should be wary."

"You are an old friend, Brabble, and have fought by my side many times. Is this not so?"

"It is," Brabble agreed.

"How many times have I led you astray? Have I ever put you in harm's way more than was necessary?"

"You have not, my Elder."

"Then, trust me now. Skye is important, and you must do all that we can to protect her."

"This was not a council of war, was it, my Elder?" Snowbroth stated, "You intend for us to be the ones to bring forth Akeldama with Skye if I am not mistaken?"

Snudge sighed and sat down. His hands massaged his temples. "You are not too far from the truth, I admit. I had hoped that one of you might present a better option that was not yet exhausted, but alas it seems that we have but one course of action. You all know the stakes along with the risk. I will not think unfavourably of any who choose to leave now. You have my blessing."

Skye breathed a sigh of relief when nobody left the room. She had known that she would have a part to play in bringing back the orb, but she felt better now that she knew she would not be travelling alone.

The party broke up for drinks and more food. Skye took the time to take a walk outside the house to clear her head. Inside, the group were drinking sour wine and reliving stories of friends lost in battles long since ended. Skye reflected that, back home, she'd had that with Arthur. They'd shared so much over their short lives that they always had a story to tell the other if they needed cheering up. She looked to the stars for help. Back home, she had often used her own telescope to peer into the vastness of space and had often found that it made her feel reassuringly small and her problems insignificant. Here, she just felt so very far away from everything that she knew and loved.

She was about to face a very real danger and had no way of telling the people that she loved and that loved her. No way of escaping. Back home, she was never in any real danger. Most things could be solved by running away. Where would she run to here, though? She knew what the forest was filled with, and she knew what was lurking further south.

There was nowhere to run to and nobody to complain to. No Arthur to share her worries with.

Skye was jolted back to reality by Curglaff gently grabbing her wrist.

"Come on in, girl. Snudge owns this house and in there we are safe, but out here the forest rules and there are things that you do not want to meet. There will be enough danger once we get on to the road. Let's spend tonight in safety. Besides, Snudge is about to tell us everything he has gathered about our little adventure."

The group were soon all gathered back around the big table and Snudge was filling them in with information that his scouts had gathered.

"We now know that the new army is, in fact, led by a queen. She is calling herself Queen Camarina, and we believe she is descended from those first half-breed humans. She has no rightful claim to any throne in the land, and yet she is gaining support far and wide."

"Her army?" Skye interrupted, "How does she have so many fighting for her?"

"The large majority are being recruited from the surrounding villages. It is the same in any war. The leaders need bodies on the front line, and the villages provide."

"And they fight willingly for her?" Skye asked, shocked.

"Of course not, but they have no choice. Man and boy will be dragged away in the night to take their place at her side. If they refuse, they will be killed. And their families after that. They would rather surrender themselves in battle to save those that they love. You may be surprised to learn that even creatures such as goblins have feelings that you may relate to! You may find on your journey that you encounter such refugees from the queen's malice. Do well to remember that they have done no wrong. No matter how alien or bedraggled they may appear.

"Despite her growing army, at the moment the queen is weak. She has Akeldama in her possession but doesn't yet fully control it. It is giving her power, dark power drawn from the Spirit Voices. But it is at a cost. Each time she looks into the orb, she surrenders part of her being, a part of her soul. As she grows stronger, the part of her that makes her human gets weaker. Soon she will be nothing but evil. We must strike before then."

There were nods around the table as everyone took in this news.

Snudge continued, "Akeldama is capable of inferring magical ability onto those who wield it. We do not believe that Queen Camarina has this power yet, but we cannot be sure. We do know that hordes of goblin, Nelapsi and various races of trolls have been drawn to her side by the darkness. Her army numbers are in the thousands already. Another reason why all-out war would be folly. Beyond that, we know very little.

"You must first ride south on the Silver River. This will allow you to stay under the cover of the trees for further than you would on open ground. However, the river runs dry beyond Hillmoss. From there you must proceed on foot. If you can safely travel that far south, we have friends in the marble city of Lörieas and there you may rest and regroup. I am sure that Gondrag and Geldrig would be happy to share their homes with you.

"There will be few other villages and inns on the way. Those you find should be avoided. We cannot risk word of your presence getting back to the queen, Skye. However, once you are past the Wandering Place, you may stop at the Druidmotte to seek shelter and advice. Queen Camarina would not dare attack such a magical place yet.

"We rise early tomorrow, get some sleep."

Snudge rose to leave the table, and Skye watched the rest follow suit.

"Remember this, friends. A lot of the races who now fight for the queen used to be our allies and lived amongst us. We drove them out through fear, hatred and rumour, and their oppression has led them into the arms of those who appear to care.

"Once again," Snudge concluded, "the G'Oräk, indeed the world, are in your debt. You will leave at first light tomorrow. Sleep well tonight. You will not feel a bed like this again until you return, I fear."

The Beginning

Skye got little sleep that night and rose before dawn. She had been woken many times by disturbing dreams of goblins standing on the backs of dragons riding down through the sky to hack at her with swords. Each time she woke, she had rushed to the open window to be sick. It wouldn't do to let the others know how nervous she was, and so Skye gave herself a quick wash in the hand basin and lay awake in the bed until she was summoned.

Before they had retired to bed, Brabble had approached Skye in the corridor and thrust a package into her arms, wrapped in a red velvet. Inside was nestled a short sword that was sharpened so finely and polished so hard that it shone even in the half-light of a single candle.

"Her name is Burrower, and she belonged to my

son, Horrin. He fought valiantly with her before perishing during a cheap skirmish in the Gloom, outside Alastor. Now, I pass her to you. She will keep her edge even through the toughest of times."

As Skye took the blade, Brabble looked at her uncomfortably. Skye didn't know what to say. Brabble had made it clear that he disliked her, and yet here he was giving her a valued possession.

"Thank you," she managed after a few seconds of awkward silence recognising that it still probably wasn't enough.

"I don't like the fact that you are joining us on this quest, Skye. I cannot lie. However, if you are to join us, you may as well be armed."

At first, Skye had placed Burrower on the wooden chest in the corner of the room, but the sword had glowed so brightly that she hadn't been able to sleep, and so she had moved it under her pillow. She remembered reading in class that Medieval knights had done the same. Skye wondered if it had brought them good luck or just horrendous dreams like she had suffered.

As she lay awake in her bed, Skye reflected that she had spent a lot of her life in fear. When she was younger, she was afraid that her parents would die. Something that she knew all children feared.

Her fear of her teacher, Miss Mimosa, seemed

sensible to Skye. She was a monster.

Keith Boggart, of course, was a big fear, and the fact that, any day now, Arthur would realise that there were far less high-maintenance friends out there than her terrified her.

Today was different, though. All of those things that Skye was normally afraid of seemed so small now, so easily fixed. She could spend more time with her parents rather than alone in her room solving the world's problems. Arthur would always be there, but Skye knew that she could make more effort to be less annoying and less, well, Skye. Keith Boggart would always be a menace, but, sooner or later, his dim-witted approach would see Skye move ahead of him and away to college.

This quest, this *adventure*, as Curglaff insisted on calling it, wasn't the same. The fear Skye felt, the fear of her own mortality, was all consuming and made her hurt on the inside.

How could she march off knowing that she might never come back? All of her intelligence, all of her *cleverness*, meant nothing now. Skye knew that she couldn't argue her way out of trouble if she was captured by the enemy. By all accounts, she wouldn't even get the chance to open her mouth. The Nelapsi wouldn't care what she had to say, and the trolls wouldn't understand it even if she got it out.

There was a very real chance that she wouldn't be coming back from this. She really wished she had somebody to talk to, but she knew that she couldn't reveal her apprehensions to her companions. Skye was their saviour, their prophecy come to life. She was a coward.

Before dawn, Skye was woken by a gentle tap on her door. Opening it, she was greeted by Brabble who whispered to her to follow him and to bring Burrower. Not knowing where they were going, Skye grabbed up her sword and followed the goblin down the darkened corridors and out into the clearing in front of the house.

"Before we fight," he instructed her, "you must learn how to use that gift."

Skye held the sword out in front of her and tried her best to look like she knew what she was doing. She had been on a school trip last year where she had been given lessons in fencing. She had been the worst in the group, and Arthur had taken great delight in breaking her guard each time.

It hadn't seemed important. Come to think of it, a lot of things outside of maths and science hadn't seemed important before, but now that she was about to enter a battle for her life, she wished she had taken more time to enjoy the same things that her friends and parents enjoyed. She vowed that if she made it back, she would be a better friend and daughter.

"No," laughed Brabble. "Here, let me show you." The goblin reached over to her and lowered her arm to waist height. "If your sword is too high, the enemy will slice underneath it. If it is too low, they will stab you over it. Be ready to raise or lower it depending on where your enemy strikes."

"Should I not be striking them?" Skye asked, feeling very small.

"For now, let us practise defensive manoeuvres. Later, perhaps, you can attack."

For the next few hours, Brabble tried his hardest to teach Skye everything that she would need to know to be able to defend herself. After a while she started to feel more confident in herself and dared to risk an attack or two as he lunged in. Every time, though, he would flick her sword away and breach her guard.

"Not quite yet," he would laugh each time.

Skye found herself relaxing in the goblin's company and laughing for the first time in a while. She was still uneasy around Brabble. She couldn't forget how much he had been against her presence before. However, in the absence of Arthur, it was nice to have a friend that she could laugh with. Over the hours, she told him all about her family and Arthur, about Keith Boggart and how she could never stand up to him.

"Maybe now that you have a sword," Brabble

had winked, "you won't need to worry about him so much?" he finished as he knocked her sword to the ground yet again.

"Somehow, I don't think they'd like it if I took Burrower into school."

Eventually, Brabble lowered his sword and put his arm around Skye.

"To bed, I think," he said gently. "The sun will rise soon, and you must get what little sleep you can before we leave."

"Thank you, Brabble," she offered as she gave him an awkward hug.

"Everyone needs to know how to use their weapon." He shrugged.

"No," she muttered. "Thank you for being my friend."

Back in her room, Skye didn't have time to dwell on her thoughts for long before a second gentle knock on the door summoned her down for a light breakfast of eggs and some form of wild bird, possibly the previous owner of the eggs. Skye barely touched hers; her stomach was full of butterflies for what lay ahead.

Instead, she took to making idle conversation with Geldrig and Gondrag, but they had little to say and insisted on filling up on food and drink. Skye remembered what Snudge had warned her about the rest of the group. She knew that she still had to win over some of the other warriors.

After they had all had their fill, Snudge came round with heavy backpacks woven from a fine, strong leather. Inside, they were filled with hard non-perishable food, bottles of clear water, tents and spare clothing. Skye dragged hers to the doorway and returned to join the fellowship for a last meeting with Snudge before they departed.

"It is two leagues from here to the best launching spot on the Silver River," Snudge started. "Curglaff knows the way through the woods, and he knows the way down the river. Do as he says and you should arrive in one piece.

"Tonight, you will stop at the Wyvern's Wing Inn outside of Dune, just before the river splits east and west. In the morning, you will carry on to the east, past Lörieas and on to Hillmoss. There, you may rest again. Then, I am afraid, you are on your own into the Wandering Place. You will find no friends that far south. You must rely on each other for support and strength. Do not look for allies, and avoid those claiming to be such."

The rest of the crew nodded their heads in understanding, though Skye was forced to raise her hand in question.

"Yes, Skye?" Snudge asked, patiently.

"Are these towns, Lörieas, Hillmoss etcetera likely

to be friendly? Will we not risk bumping into Nelapsi or Felmir?" She looked at Geldrig and Gondrag. "Bad ones, that is," she finished, sheepishly.

"Nelapsi rarely step into the light, Skye, instead preferring to fight in the dark forests and shadows of the mountains. Felmir might be a threat, though they are quite conspicuous in their size. I'm sure you will be able to see them before you reveal any horrific secrets."

This got a laugh from the rest of the gang, and Skye felt a little foolish for asking such an obvious question.

"However, you raise a good point. Agents of the enemy will be everywhere, and they may possibly even be G'Oräk. Elflock may have spies feeding information to the queen as we sit here, though hopefully even he isn't that dim. We have seen ourselves how far north the Nelapsi have travelled with the murder within our walls. Do not be too loose with your tongues when you are in unfamiliar company.

"Above all, our aims must remain secret. If you are asked, you are simply travelling warriors on your way back to your homes beyond the Wandering Place. Do not be too specific, do not invite further questions and above all," Snudge's voice took on a sharper edge, "do not attract more attention to yourselves that you must."

"What are we to do if we fail or realise failure is inevitable?" This question came from Yop who, beyond offering Skye his sword at their initial meeting, had held his counsel so far and said very little to anybody.

Snudge looked uneasy. "We have our army ready, though it is small and no real match for that of the queen. If all hope seems lost, send a message to us here and I shall send forth the army to meet you outside her gates. Remember though, our intention is to be in and out without the queen noticing. We do not want a war whilst Akeldama is held within her fortress. Do I make myself clear on that matter?"

"Yes, sir," they all agreed.

Skye felt certain that their actions were the safest for all involved. Brack had promised to pen an ode to Skye and her part in the "sneaky theft" as he insisted on calling it, so long as Skye promised to come back alive.

Before they had chance to leave, Snudge pulled Skye to one side to give her a parting piece of advice.

"Remember," he said, "our prophecy speaks of you being victorious. We, indeed I, have faith that you are the chosen one to lead us to victory, Skye. Be brave, be strong, and, above all, be smart."

With that, the goblin gave her a hug and retreated to help the others finish their packing.

Final preparations were made for their departure. As the sun was rising above the treetops, Skye and the band of goblins and men stepped out and into the trees. There were no goodbyes to be said. Instead they busied themselves with final adjustments to items in their packs or to the direction in which they were to head.

As they disappeared into the forest's edge, Skye looked back at the Snudge's house and thought with a heavy sadness that it might be the last time she would see its warm, welcoming door.

The journey to the boat was passed under a pleasantly warm sunshine that was broken and dappled by the canopy overhead. The leaves were starting to turn brown, and Skye suspected that they would soon be heading into autumn.

There was little conversation on the track, instead most seemed lost in their own thoughts and on keeping a sure-footing over the twisted roots and warped ground underfoot. Occasionally, Brack would break the silence with a verse or two of a song, though he often sang alone and his pure voice was lost quickly amongst the trees.

Within the hour, they emerged into a clearing similar to the one that Skye had landed in. This one was bordered on its west side by a narrow, fast-flowing river. It was no deeper than Skye's ankles, and she was relieved to see that the boat was a flat-bottomed canoe designed to hold more passengers than they needed, meaning that there was still room to spread out once both the adventurers and their bags were on board.

Curglaff took immediate control of the ship and stood at the rear controlling the rudder. The flow of the river did most of the work. Other than an occasional shunt away from the bank, the group were content to just sit and relax in the warm air.

As they progressed down the slow-moving waterway, Skye noticed that the landscape changed subtly from one region to the next. Mostly the river was edged with dense forest but, every now and again, the trees had been cleared to make way for farmland. The produce started as simple corn and wheat products but, as they ventured further south, this gave way to small orchards and vineyards. On each of the plantations, Skye spotted small, scurrying figures moving in and out of the crops, picking fruit here, sowing seeds there.

"Gnomes," offered Brabble. "Goblin farmers hire them to work their farms."

"Are they slaves?" asked Skye, remembering what she had been taught about the American South in history lessons back at school.

"No, goblins do not take slaves. The gnomes are happy for the work, mostly. They have been driven from their homelands in the mountains and are often the first race to be thrown to the front when war comes. Nobody could blame them if they just took themselves south of these lands forever and made a new life. Instead, they have chosen to stay in their homeland and do what they can to survive."

"How sad," whispered Skye.

"It is what it is," mused the goblin, who returned to the front of the boat to take up an oar.

As the day passed, Skye took to leaning over the side to see what she could see in the water, but it wasn't until they finally moved into deeper water that she began to see some evidence of life below them. The river teemed with small, scaly fish.

"Try to catch one for lunch. Flockfish are delicious when grilled," chuckled Brabble, seemingly unfazed by their previous conversation.

Skye stuck her hand in to the water to try to grab one of the flockfish as they swam past. Instead of trying to swim away, they all turned and attacked her fingers. She managed to pull her hand out of the water quickly, but not before one of the fish had caught a deep bite on her middle finger.

Skye sat back in the boat in a huff and decided not to talk to the rest of the group again that day, much to their amusement. Brabble, for his part, didn't stop laughing until they were a mile downstream and he was out of voice.

As the river widened and grew deeper, their progress became much slower. By the time the sun was directly above them, Curglaff told them that they wouldn't reach the Wyvern's Wing by nightfall and that they would need to spend the night in the forest. This didn't fill Skye with confidence. She was surprised when a few of the more seasoned adventurers agreed with her.

A vote was taken. It was decided that after a quick lunch they would continue as quickly as they could and stop only when the sun sank below the trees. Then, they would build a camp and a fire on the ground and station watchmen throughout the night.

Their plan made Skye feel a little better, but she was still not looking forward to another night amongst the trees. As she sat back in the boat, her ankle throbbed with memory of the glibberig attack and even though Weard's magic and herbs had healed her arm quickly and effectively, it still ached whenever she worked it too hard.

Discomfort

B y the time they had found a suitable place to moor the boat and set up camp, the light was fading rapidly from the sky and the shadows were long beneath the trees. Any remaining warmth had disappeared, and Skye realised that the journey they were heading on was going to happen during a bitterly cold season.

After landing, whilst Curglaff busied himself tying up the boat, Brack and Brabble went to fetch wood. When they returned, they lit a small fire in the middle of a cleared space and they all set up hammocks in the trees.

After a feast on shellfish caught fresh from the bank of the river, Skye retired to her hammock and listened to the rest of the fellowship sing and tell stories of their past glories. Again, she thought of Arthur. A few years before they had been on a camping holiday with Arthur's parents to the Lake District. As they had sat around a campfire with a dozen other families who they had never met, Arthur had jumped to his feet and urged everybody to join in a verse of "Swing Low, Sweet Chariot." It hadn't been long before the whole campfire was singing and swaying along. Arthur had self-confidence that Skye could only dream of. She envied him and missed him in equal measure at that point.

Eventually, Corngaff turned to Skye. "I think it's about time we gave you a history of what we are up against, Skye. Though I'm sure it's not the history that Snudge would want us to tell you."

As Skye listened intently, Brabble wandered over to her with another bowl of broth and covered her with a thick woollen blanket.

"On our side, or as near as we can call it, are the G'Oräk. Or at least most of us are. We have allies in the east and west with the wood pixies. They are far taller than the pixies that your kind celebrate on your planet. They are nearly as tall as you, Skye, and far stronger and faster. Devilishly clever as well, your average Wood Pixie. They are not particularly vicious fighters, but they are generous with their magic and use it to the greater good. We also have the support of some of the tribes of half-humans. How many of each could we count on in an all-out war, though? Not many more than a few thousand, I'd guess.

"Our enemies are far more numerous, I'm afraid. There are the turned goblin tribes, of course, and the Nelapsi. Some of the Felmir have turned as well from what we hear. The cave pixies and the river nymphs have always been dark and have pledged to fight for the queen. They are not vast in number but are small and quick and do not suffer from a conscience."

Corngaff took a long pull of his drink, and Weard took up the story, her softer female voice not making the enemy sound any less foreboding to Skye. "Normally, the trolls don't fall into either side. They prefer to stay in their own territory and defend it against everyone else. However, we have troubling news that the queen has been raising a new race of dark trolls, bred from the rock trolls of the deep south and the orcs that once roamed the world. If she has managed that, then it suggests that not only is there a new dark force to deal with but that there must somewhere remain a tribe of orc, something we thought had been extinct for generations.

"The majority of the beasts of the world pledge no allegiance to anyone. The glibberig that you met, for instance, fight only for themselves. That is also true of a race of creatures whom I expect you shall meet very soon, the tree trolls."

"The tree trolls that raised Snudge?" remembered Skye.

"The very same, as he tells it anyway," replied Weard.

"Why will we meet them soon?" whispered Skye, noticing a drop in the conversation.

"Because there is one stood above you on that branch," muttered Brack calmly.

Skye flicked her head upwards and came eye to eye with what looked uncannily like a shaved monkey whose skin was covered with slate-coloured scales. Frozen with fear and shock and not knowing what to do for fear of upsetting the creature, Skye did nothing. She lay in her hammock and waited for somebody else to do something instead.

Eventually, Snowbroth broke the silence and introduced the group to the troll above Skye. It let out a loud click, and several more emerged from the trees around them.

A different troll, dressed in an ornate robe, stepped forwards and introduced himself as their leader Fen. He enquired as to where they were heading, and Snowbroth gave the agreed story of soldiers returning home.

The troll simply returned a small smirk and bid them to follow him into the trees. Not wanting to turn down the hospitality, they followed as quickly as they could.

The stars scrolled across the sky as they walked through the night until they finally arrived at the trunk of a long-dead tree that stood head and shoulders above everything else around them. As it towered above them, it looked more like a church tower than a once living thing.

Without stopping, Fen clambered up onto the trunk and pulled a branch hard. A clunking noise indicated that something was happening inside the tree. After a while, a piece of the bark started to peel back to form a bridge to the ground and to reveal a man-sized entrance into the trunk.

Without warning, the troll disappeared into the doorway. Skye and the rest were forced to follow him or turn back. They decided to follow and entered, single-file, into the darkness beyond. As she made her way to the door, Skye felt a dramatic chill, and the breath of the adventurers hung in the air.

As Skye's eyes adjusted to the utter blackness around her, she felt herself descending a spiral staircase. After a while, she started to pick out pinpricks of light in the walls, no bigger than a firefly. She walked for what felt like an age before she bumped up against Brabble in front of her as they reached the bottom and stopped. Brabble laughed and turned to her in the darkness.

"Be careful, little one. Brack cannot write a song about a hero undone by a flight of steps in the darkness!"

Skye giggled at the irony of dying in such a ridiculous way and held tight to Brabble's cloak for the rest of the descent.

Fen told them that he would have to go and inform the rest of the clan that they had arrived. Skye heard a heavy door close in front of them as they were left alone in the cold chamber.

Within a few minutes, Fen returned and told them that the trolls were ready to receive their guests and that a meal was currently being prepared in their honour. He opened the door in front of them and beckoned them to enter the room beyond.

If the size of the tree had stunned Skye, the vastness of the hall into which she now stepped caused her mind to freewheel. It was twice as large again as the biggest cathedral on Earth.

The lofted ceilings rose high into the shadows above and the whole seemed supported by only two giant wooden pillars in the middle of the floor. Each one appeared to have been carved from the roots of a giant tree above.

"Welcome to Landragog, our home since the first of our families walked this world. According to our legends, there once roamed a giant tree troll, bigger than any had seen before or since. His name was Landragog, and he roamed these lands looking for love.

"As time passed, Landragog grew lonelier and more desperate. He realised that he would never find love with another troll. To those that lived during those times, he was a freak of nature, far too big to ever live within the trees and something to be laughed at and driven away.

"Eventually, he moved so far away from the other trolls that he forgot who he was. The first creature that he saw was a fairy named Salverin. She was incredibly beautiful. Some say that she was Beauty itself, one of the lost Spirit Voices.

"Though she loved Landragog with all her heart, she knew that she would live forever and could not bear to watch her lover die. With a great sadness, she turned away and left him alone on this spot. In his grief, Landragog lay down and never rose again. Eventually, his body grew into a tree, our tree, and so grew our hall.

"Do not be afraid, little girl," Fen said, addressing

Skye's wonderment. "The tree that gave those roots still lives above us. Those are living supports for our roof. As they grow and twist, so does our great hall."

Skye stepped away from the group to take a better look around the great hall. Paintings and tapestries covered each of the walls. Skye was surprised to see one showing a series of pictures of trolls raising, playing with and educating a goblin. The inscription below was in a language that Skye couldn't begin to understand, but the meaning was clear enough.

"So, it is true then. He was raised by tree trolls," she said out loud, mainly to herself.

"Indeed, it is. We raised him well, if we say so ourselves."

Skye shot round in surprise at the voice behind her and found herself, once again, face to face with the troll who had startled her in her hammock earlier in the evening.

"Don't be so jumpy. Fen has asked that I escort you around our great hall and answer any questions that you might have. My name is Gonk and you are, I believe, Skye?" Gonk's voice flowed like the sap in the trees that surrounded them. It wasn't deep but had a deep quality that reminded Skye of the sound an underground river makes in a cave.

Skye nodded dimly and apologised for being so

jumpy. Gonk waved her apology away and started to tell Skye about how the tribe had raised Snudge from a child and were proud with what he was doing with the G'Oräk. They wandered for a while more until a loud bell rang.

"Dinner," offered Gonk, politely. "It will be served at the great table. Please, follow me."

Skye followed the troll to the wide table that ran half the length of the cavern.

During dinner, conversation turned once again to their reason for being in the woods.

Two Trees

"Now, my G'Oräk friends," began Fen in his crackling, gravelly voice, "why don't you be honest with me now that we are away from the prying ears of the rest of my council. What is it that brings you so very close to my great hall and so far away from yours?"

The rest of the council had made their excuses and left soon after the food had been finished. Skye and her friends now found themselves alone with Fen.

"As I told you before," answered Snowbroth patiently, "we are travelling warriors, and we are looking to find our way home."

"A merry excuse indeed and no doubt fit for the inns of Dune or Lörieas. But I know you, Snowbroth," the goblin winced at his name, "and I know that you are no simple warrior. I also know just what your friend Skye is." He pointed at Skye. "Why would a group of G'Oräk and Felmir be escorting a human down the Silver River? I think I know, and I hope that I am wrong."

"We have information—" began Snowbroth.

"We all have information," snapped Fen, "but we don't all go running off to act on it. Take a look at my walls, all of you." He gestured for them to look closely at the tapestries and pictures that hung beside them. "What do you notice about them? Or rather, what don't you see on them?"

Skye knew and had noticed it earlier.

"There are no wars or battles in any of them," she whispered.

"Good!" roared the troll. "Long may it continue! There is no blood on our walls because we do not seek blood and we make sure that blood doesn't seek us! If you go on your quest, Snowbroth, and chase your prophecy, you will surely bring war to our doorstep. Indeed, to every doorstep north of the Wandering Place."

"We are already at war, though little you know of it hidden away down here in the darkness," shouted Weard, standing in her place. "We were attacked two nights ago by a group of Nelapsi *inside our own walls*," she trailed off in a growl.

"She is right," agreed Corngaff. "Whether we seek it or not, the darkness is rising and the queen is growing ever stronger. She already commands an army that outnumbers ours and more are flocking to her every day. We cannot afford to sit and talk any longer. We have no choice but to try to stop her. Do not fear, though," he offered. "We do not seek all-out war any more than you do. Our plan is to defeat her without her even knowing it."

"Akeldama?" Fen whispered, daring not to say the word too loudly.

"We think that we can take it without her knowing and remove her source of power."

Fen fell silent. He stared hard at the walls around him, daring them to defy him.

After a while, he turned to Skye and said, "I have something to show you, something that I think you should see before you go any further." He stood up and left the table, waving his hand for them to follow him.

He unlocked a small, heavy door in the southern wall of the hall and led them down another long, winding staircase. At the bottom, Fen opened yet another door and led them in to a dimly lit cave.

Inside the room stood a tree that Skye recognised instantly. It was not the tallest or broadest of trees, but it was as familiar to Skye as the face of her mother or father. It was the cherry tree that had grown at the bottom of her garden back home on Earth.

The cherry tree that Skye and her mother had planted when she was only three years old and that they had looked after for years until, suddenly and without warning, it had died three summers ago.

Skye remembered how devastated she had been when the tree had died and how she and her mother had cried for days. It was one of the few normal things that she had with her mother; everything else was just so odd. Right now though, the tree was flowering with a pale pink blossom that glowed with a ghostly halo. Shocked, Skye felt tears rolling down her cheeks, and once again she felt her stomach being ripped from her as she gasped at the distance between her and everything she loved.

"I don't know if you know this, Skye, but you are not the first person in your family to visit Ithilmir."

This hit Skye even harder, and she struggled to stand as she reeled from the information.

"Your mother came to us when she was little older than you are now. She didn't have much of interest but stayed with us for a while. She never came across the G'Oräk, though she did take a huge interest in the woodland nymphs that float about here near the lakes."

Skye couldn't believe it. Her mother, her own mother, had actually been here before her. How had she made it back? Had she had to deal with what Skye was going through?

"There was no war when she arrived. The peace held stronger than it does now," offered Fen, apparently reading Skye's thoughts. "One day, she decided to leave and return to your planet. She had found a portal between the worlds, one that can sadly no longer be used," he added, noticing Skye's excitement. "As she left, she gave us a seed, a small token of her appreciation and something that she happened to have in her pocket at the time. We said our goodbyes. She went on her way and, as far as I can tell, lived a happy life on Earth.

"We had no idea what conditions the seed would need to survive, and so we planted it down here in the darkness. It is amazing, isn't it, how even the smallest seed will survive the most challenging of situations? A bit like you, Skye, don't you think?"

Skye didn't say anything. She didn't have anything to say. In her mind, she was back home questioning her mother about all of her adventures on Ithilmir and sharing her stories of her own adventures so far with her. Then the thought struck Skye that she might never get the chance to tell her mother what she knew. That she'd been a fool to doubt her beliefs and that she wanted more than anything to make up for it. Skye found herself rolling her mother's ring around her finger once more. She felt renewed vigour rising up inside her. She had to succeed, not just for the goblins whom she had grown close to but to get home. It was always about getting home. She had to keep that thought close to the front of her mind.

"Anyway," Fen continued, oblivious to Skye's internal dilemma, "the seed never grew. We tended it for generations and still nothing. And then, one day, when all hope was gone, it sprouted. It strikes me from your face, Skye, that this is not the first time that you have seen this tree."

After a long pause, Skye managed to compose herself enough to tell the story of her mother and their tree to the listening audience.

"Then it is clear to me, Skye, that this is a Spirit Tree, a direct link to the tree in your garden. I should imagine that as the tree you and your mother so tenderly cared for died, this one sprung from its soul. You will see that it glows. Is this normal?"

"No."

"I can only imagine, then, that it is the spirits of our ancestors that are locked within it that cause such an effect. We have long spoken to the tree in our prayers, and we often find them answered with advice from trolls that have long passed to the great beyond." The troll cleared his throat. "It is not the spirits that caused me to bring you down here. This tree is a symbol to us, Skye, that when all hope is lost, when all signs of a future have been snuffed out as with the little seed that your mother left behind, the brightest future may yet appear to us.

"When your mother left us, Skye, she didn't leave empty-handed. We gave her a small ring forged from silver mined beneath Landragog. As we cast it in our forges, we poured into it a small amount of our magic. Into the top, we set a pure crystal. There was nothing particularly special about the crystal other than the fact that your mother had taken quite the shine to it."

Skye shoved her hands into her pockets and felt for the ring on her finger. Surely it couldn't be the same thing? She daren't show them.

"The ring, however, held true power. The ring was one of the last pieces of magic that was cast in our hall and meant a huge amount to our people. Originally, it had been forged as an aid to our mages in the fight against the dark magic, but over time it came to represent our decision to remove ourselves from the curses that lay beyond our door. By surrendering the ring, we surrendered our power beyond our walls.

"As for how your mother left us? In the end, she left us in the same way as you joined us.

"Many years ago, my ancestors were gifted a small spyglass by a sailor from beyond the Selvern Sea who had sought refuge here within our halls. To begin with, the spyglass was nothing more than a trinket with which to spy on our enemies from afar, but soon our mages had taken to staring into the stars. It was there that they found their answers, their guiding voices.

"Over time that spyglass became synonymous with our beliefs. It was proof that there was something out there beyond our world that was controlling our destiny.

"It was a mage called Malagao who was first to grow restless with just looking at these worlds. He wanted to travel to them to gain their wisdom.

"At about this time, he disappeared from our halls. We later learnt that he had been training in darker magic at the Druidmotte. When he returned, it was with an evil glare in his eyes, and he soon declared that he had achieved that which he had set out to do. He would be able to visit the worlds that he sought simply by looking upon them through the spyglass. However, when our ancestors gathered around to watch display, it failed to work and Malagao fled in a vicious rage and was never seen again.

"After that, the spyglass remained an item of our belief but nothing more until your mother decided one night to stare into the night. She claimed to be able to see her own world through there, something that Malagao nor anyone since had been able to do. Upon viewing it again, she simply disappeared into the eyepiece.

"The spyglass and the cherry tree are the two cornerstones of our beliefs, Skye. One shows us what may yet arise whilst hope survives whilst the other guides us through our lives."

At this point, the troll lifted up his sleeve to show the group a faded mark burned into his arm. It showed a simple outline of a tree encircled with a thick line. He rolled his sleeve back down and continued.

"The ring that encircles the tree, that encircles our very existence, is the spyglass. Our view into heaven, for want of a better word. We wear this mark with pride, Skye. It is a reminder of our past and a warning as to where our future may lie if we make the wrong decisions. Every young troll within these halls is branded with this mark when they come of age as a reminder of their past. Beyond these halls, you will find others who have heard this tale and who follow our beliefs. You can be assured that those who wear this mark can be counted amongst your friends."

"Where is the spyglass now?" asked Skye desperately. For a moment, she considered abandoning everything on Ithilmir and returning home before reminding herself why she was doing this. She couldn't abandon her friends now, not after all she had seen and heard. She was in this until the end, however that may come.

"Alas it has long been lost. We believe it was stolen away by one of the many who sought refuge in these halls. That is one of the reasons we locked our doors to the outside.

"However, the tree still remains, and it seems to me that this tree is a link between what you have lost and what we have gained. Let it now be a shining light for you going forwards."

Fen broke a branch from the tree and offered it to Skye.

"The blossom will glow as long as the spirits live on, Skye. If the queen is as powerful as the G'Oräk believe, then all hope seems lost. It may be that you are a seed that is yet to grow."

Skye made a decision. She had to know. She closed her eyes and held out her upturned hand to the troll. In her palm rested her mother's ring. She heard the troll gasp but nothing more until she opened her eyes.

"This is very interesting indeed, Skye! Maybe

our cause it not yet so lost. That ring will give you power that you never knew you had. Very interesting, indeed!"

The troll turned to the whole group and said, "You go forth with our blessing and as our friends. Indeed, maybe the ring may once again come to symbolise power against the darkness. Do not let us down, my friends. The fate of our world depends on you all."

Skye sat under the tree for a long while after the rest of the group had left for their beds. She rolled the ring around in her hands, unsure of what to make of it.

"Do not worry unduly about the ring," Fen offered before he left to join the others. "You will find your own power within it. The magic that it holds will simply be an extension of your own. Each bearer will experience something different and will control it in different ways. You will find your own way. Goodnight, Skye."

After Fen made his excuses and left her alone, Skye prayed for the first time in her life.

"What should I do? How can I get home?"

She didn't know what to expect but was shocked when she felt a breeze rustle through the branches above her and a whispered voice filled the chamber.

"You know what you must do," it whispered. "Your course has been set for you."

Skye looked around her, stunned, "Will I ever seen my family again? Or Arthur?"

"We have no doubt that you will see them again in one life or another. You are braver than you believe, Skye Thistle. We know what you are."

"Who are you?"

"We are you, Skye. Your past, present and future. We are the remembered souls, your family who have passed away but also the souls of the friendships and dreams that have passed through your life. We are echoes of everything that you have ever been but also a glimpse of what you may become. You will be great, Skye Thistle, but only if you believe."

"Believe in what? What should I believe in?"

"Yourself."

She sat silently under the tree as she tried to regain her composure as tears rolled down her cheeks.

"Do you remember the prophecy, Skye?" whispered the souls.

"Yes, I think so," answered Skye as she wiped her eyes with her sleeve.

"Then remember the last line well. Those who came before! Not everything that your mother is or was left Ithilmir. Some of her remained, though she doesn't know it. Part of your mother lives on here on Ithilmir! Remember the prophecy, Skye, and do not be deterred from what you know you must do."

Skye jumped to her feet, but the moment had passed. She waited for a while longer before taking the branch that Fen had given her and trudging off to her bed on the floor of the great hall. She knew they had another long journey ahead of them the next day and could sense that there were not many hours left to sleep.

As soon as Skye lay her head on to her pillow, she fell into another sleep haunted by dreams, this time involving a tall cherry tree that shed its blossom to reveal that it was made entirely of bones, each branch pale and stained in the darkness. As hard as she tried, Skye couldn't gather up the blossom, and soon it turned into a river of blood flowing through her fingers. The spirits of the world howled about her screaming with an ethereal rage for bringing about their death with her war.

The queen rose above all of this carnage, laughing with a shrill cackle as she hacked the branches from the tree. As they fell around her, Skye noticed that each bone was engraved with a name that she recognised, family and friends from her past and present. On those that fell closest to her were the names of her parents and Arthur. Skye's eyes filled with tears as she realised that Arthur's branch split into two, the name of his future wife hidden in the dust. Scattered around this pairing were many smaller bones; their children. She tried desperately to see the name on the bone conjoined with his but whenever she had it in sight the branch would spin in the wind and she'd lose sight of it. No matter how loudly she cried out or reached out to the bones, she was never able to grab hold and pull them back towards her.

As the queen spun in the air, her face glowered over Skye, projected a mile high against the clouds. Skye looked into eyes more familiar than her own and screamed as she fell to the floor clutching the crumbling bones.

When she was jolted awake in the morning, Skye was covered in sweat and her face was wet with tears from sobbing in the night. Her finger was raw where she had been turning the ring over in her nightmares.

After Fen's speech the previous night, Skye found herself looking at the ring in a different light. It seemed to glow, somehow. No matter how hard she tried, she couldn't get it to produce any magic.

Despite never being interested in fairy stories as a child, Skye knew somewhere at the back of her mind that they sometimes contained magical items that were older than time and handed down from generation to generation. She had doubted very much that such things existed in the real world, but, she found herself reasoning, she now had no idea what the real world was or whether she was still part of it.

She found that she was doubting a lot of what she always knew to be true.

Around her, the air was crisp and cold, and Skye could see her breath forming as she exhaled. She pushed from her mind what she had seen in her dream and hoped that it was nothing more than an after effect of speaking to the tree of souls. The alternative was unthinkable.

"Winter is here, Skye," she heard Weard say above her head. "Make sure that you pack up warm and grab a blanket and a cloak before we leave. Curglaff wants to be back at the boat within the hour so don't be long."

Skye groaned inside but was shaken out of her mood as more important memories from the night before came flooding back. Her mother had been here with the tree trolls. She had given them the seed to the Spirit Tree in the cave below and had received her treasured ring in return.

Perhaps most importantly to Skye, she had then found a way to leave.

Most of her had left, anyway. Skye didn't know what it meant, but she would never forget the vision from her nightmare of the queen spinning in the air and her face filling Skye's entire world. A face that Skye recognised all too well. A face that she had spent years looking up into, each and every line and crease memorised and loved. It was *her* face that the Queen wore, the face of her mother.

Spy

Tentatively, Skye rose from her bed and packed up her belongings before grabbing the thickest fur blanket and cloak that she could find. Within ten minutes of being woken up, she was ready to face her future.

"I don't understand. What happened to the sun?" asked Skye as she left the tree trunk above the great hall.

As they had climbed back up the winding stairs, the air had grown colder with each step until, by the time she had reached the top, Skye was very glad of every layer that she was wearing. When she had stepped out the door, she had been greeted by an entirely new world. Where before there had been thick green trees and a well-worn but defined path, there now stood dark, wooden skeletons and little else. The whole of the forest had been covered in a thick white frost that crunched underfoot with each tentative step.

"The weather changes very quickly on Ithilmir," said Brabble, "particularly in the north. One day you are standing in a warm summer forest, and, as quick as thunder, winter is upon you. We knew this was a risk when we set out, though this is the earliest winter since before I was born and that's going back a long time."

"It is earlier because the darkness rides hand in hand with the cold." This was Snowbroth, speaking in his deep, slow voice. He had been the last to exit the tree trunk, having had late business with Fen down below, but now he strode ahead of the rest of the group and marched out into the whiteness beyond. "The last time we had a winter this cold this early was the last time that darkness ruled these trees. Within a year, beast and goblin starved and died when the rivers froze and the fires failed."

Skye and the others had started to jog to keep up with the elderly G'Oräk but now fell into a steady pace besides him.

"I spoke to Fen last night," Snowbroth continued, "and he seems to think we are out of our minds heading out in this weather. If nothing else, he agrees that something must be done, so our stay was not entirely without cause."

They reached the boat soon after and cast out into the river that was still mercifully unfrozen. They knew that their luck would not last long and that they needed to be safely at Hillmoss before it ran out. Marching overland in this weather would be slow and draining, but had the benefit of being under their own steam. If they were stranded north of Lörieas without access to the river then they would be easy picking for the bandits and poachers that roamed the hills and valleys in that area, not to mention any agents of the queen that had been sent to stop them.

"I've been thinking." Skye broke the silence after a long while on the river, during which they had made steady progress. "Will the queen be able to see us and what we are planning through Akeldama?"

"No, not unless she chooses to," said Longcraw who seemed to know a lot about the stone and often chipped in with information whenever the opportunity arose. "It is not all-seeing, and it cannot think for itself. She can only point it towards things and beings that she wishes to see. Until she knows of our existence and purpose, she will have no reason to aim it at us. Should she be made aware, however, then we are very much at risk and it is unlikely that we will be able to enter her domain unnoticed and without being challenged."

"Which is why," Yop added, "we must be very careful not to give away anything about our true purpose. The queen will have agents everywhere, listening out for any information. She cannot hope to rise to power without a contest, and so she will be expecting some of her enemies to make a move on her. It is to our benefit that she will expect a more ferocious attack with a full-on war, which is why I suspect that Snudge was happy to allow the League of War to continue their propaganda so openly. She will have received word of their preference and will assume that we will listen. Her arrogance will not allow her to believe that we would try anything else, and we hope to keep it that way."

They continued on in silence for the rest of the journey. To the annoyance of Skye and her stomach, they travelled right through lunch and on until dusk when they finally bumped against the shore just up river of the Wyvern's Wing Inn outside of Dune. Curglaff tied up the boat with the help of the two Felmir whilst Snowbroth repeated his warning from earlier and instructed the older warriors to drink nothing stronger than water. He didn't want them getting drunk and spilling their secrets.

Once inside the inn, Brack secured rooms for each of them and ordered food to be brought to their table in exchange for a song or two. He took up a position at the front of the room and didn't bother to wait for silence before starting to serenade his audience with songs of heroes that had died long before.

> *Down deep and dark and stormy roads,*
> *Her elegance and beauty told.*
> *Amidst a ravaged war-torn land*
> *A soldier ached to take her hand.*
>
> *Her golden hair like blossomed sun,*
> *His sword was dulled from battles won.*
> *A vision painted of lovers be,*
> *Alas their union could never be.*

Skye realised that this was a love song. It continued for many verses talking of the two characters and their love, separated by their warring families.

> *And as he saw her lying fast,*
> *Her soul expired and breathed her last.*
> *He took her sword and on it fell,*
> *But as he slipped, her chest did swell.*
>
> *Her heart and soul did join him soon,*
> *And danced amongst the Ever-Moon.*
> *Though lovers in the Shadowland,*
> *He always wept to hold her hand.*

With a sadness in her heart, Skye looked away so the others couldn't see her tears, though she soon realised that every goblin and Felmir were also drying their eyes.

Whilst they waited for the food and Brack kept everyone engaged, Skye noticed that Snowbroth was scanning the room looking intently at every other person, trying to work out who could be trusted and who should be avoided. Skye decided to do the same and so sat back and took in her surroundings for the first time.

The other customers seemed to be entirely goblin or near-human in one form or another. Here and there she spotted huddled families – refugees from the queen no doubt – but they kept themselves to themselves and were bothering no one. More ominous, however, were two huge men huddled in a dark corner some way away from but within sight of Skye's table. Their skin was thick and ebony and crossed with scars. Their eyes were sunken and appeared hollow like two black pits into their skull.

"Ash trolls," whispered Snowbroth, "A very old race of trolls that rose from the very first ash mounds that erupted during the battle between the Spirit Voices of the Before Time. You don't see many now. They left the north and headed into the deep south. Some say they even took to the sea and fled for the Marble Isles on the other side of the world. They are very strong and surprisingly quick but also very simple. They will do as they are told and nothing more."

"Perfect spies then," suggested Skye.

"Exactly. Keep your wits about you, Skye, and keep your sword close to your hand."

Skye felt her fingers tighten around the hilt of Burrower and realised that she had completely forgotten that she had it with her. She felt reassured to have it by her side even though the thought of having to use it terrified her to her core. Skye thought back to the lesson with Brabble. It had all seemed fun at the time, but now Skye really wished that she had tried harder and paid more attention.

Brack brought his last song to an end to great applause just in time to join the rest at their table for the food. All that the cook had been able to put together was a simple meal of stewed meat and vegetables with a loaf of hard bread to share between them, but it was better than nothing. They ate in silence, all afraid to say anything in case it was overheard, and soon they all stood up to head to their own bedrooms.

As they walked towards the stairs, Skye noticed that several Felmir and the ash trolls all stood up to follow them. She quietly pointed this out to Snowbroth though it hadn't gone unnoticed.

"Go to your room as normal, Skye, but once you

are in lock your door and climb out the window. Underneath the windowsill, you will find a sloping roof that will drop you quietly on to the ground below. We will all do the same and meet up behind the stables to the west of the inn. Move in silence. It is important that our unwanted guests believe that we are all in our rooms until they choose to break in and capture us. Hopefully, we will be far away by then."

By the time Snowbroth had outlined their plan, they had reached the doors to their rooms. They all bade each other a good night and entered their own quarters as though nothing was out of order. Once Skye had shut the door behind her, she quickly slid the double bolts across and quietly moved the dark wooden dresser in front of it just in case their would-be attackers tried to enter before she left.

When she finally managed to tease open the shuttered windows, she was met by a gust of frozen air. Sitting in the warm inn, Skye had forgotten how cold it was outside. It momentarily took her breath away. She recovered quickly and pulled the cloak out of her bag and threw it over her shoulders. Steadying herself, she swung one leg over the wooden window frame and on to the ledge outside. Every breath traced with steam in the air and seemed to crystallise in front of her. Bracing herself against the sides of the window, Skye swung her other leg over and had to take a second to get her bearings as her head spun with the height.

Behind her, Skye heard an order for her to open her door before the wood shook as somebody thumped it from the outside. Skye looked back down at the drop in front of her. It was a long way down, and she wasn't sure that she could push herself out. Again, behind her, the door shook in its hinges and dust floated down from the ceiling as the Felmir tried to batter down her door. Not wanting to face them any more than she did the drop, she slithered as far forward as she dared on the window ledge.

Sitting down on the very edge, Skye was able to slowly lower herself out on to the sloping roof but didn't take into account how slippery it would be with the fresh frost. Before she could stop herself, she lost her footing and slid on her back down the ice. She briefly had the sensation of flying before the air was knocked from her as she hit the hard, compacted ground below. Above her, she heard her door splinter open and saw two ugly heads silhouetted by the lamplight in the room.

The stars above Skye spun wildly as her head swam, but she forced herself to her feet and struggled off to the west, fighting with each step against the slippery packed earth underfoot and against her winded lungs. As she hobbled away, she heard footsteps behind her but didn't have time to check. She could only hope that those who had broken into her room had not been able to follow her that quickly.

After a hundred yards or so, Skye saw a white wooden building. It had the smell of stables, and she could hear the soft whinny of horses. She picked up the pace and scrabbled against the wall as she turned the corner and ducked into the darkness. Before she could catch her breath, a hand was clamped over her mouth and she was dragged to the ground and into a pile of cold straw.

Bogomils

"**B**e quiet," hissed a voice in the darkness. "We don't know who followed us." Skye felt the hand loosen its grip on her mouth. She turned to look into the face of Gondrag. He was surrounded by the rest of the group except for Longcraw and Yop.

"We cannot afford to wait for them for long," Skye heard Weard whisper. "We must be back at the boat within the next few minutes otherwise we are all at risk."

They didn't have to wait long before Yop came skidding around the corner and fell, sobbing to his knees.

"Longcraw," he stammered, "he didn't make it. They burst into our room as he was climbing out and shot him in the back with a crossbow." He burst into a fit of sobs until Geldrig clapped a hand over his mouth and hissed at him to be quiet.

"We cannot mourn now. We must go, especially if they have already seen us leave," said Snowbroth as he headed towards the back of the stables.

"Where are you going? Our boat is the other way," shouted Brabble.

"Our boat will be well-guarded, you fool," hissed Snowbroth. "They know how we arrived and will guess how we will leave. We must leave the river behind us now. There are good fellhorses in this stable. We should take one each and leave now."

Snowbroth didn't leave them any option and hastily handed each of them the reins to a large beast. The fellhorses were taller than any Skye had seen before and broader with far thicker legs and shoulders. Their hair was long and shaggy and hung to their knees. They were all darkest black with bright white manes that glowed even in the darkness of the stable.

It took three goblins to help Skye up on to her fellhorse, but soon they were all mounted and galloping out of the stables and into the darkness. Yop had managed to compose himself well enough to lead the way. Skye soon looked back to see the inn as a dot on the horizon. She couldn't see anybody following them, but that didn't reassure her much. If people were looking for them this close to home, there would be more along the way.

They rode east across cold, open tundra dotted here and there with low purple scrub brushes. They rode as fast as they dared in the darkness, slowing down occasionally when the ground underfoot became too frozen or uneven. Despite no sign of anyone in pursuit, they pushed their fellhorses hard until dawn when they finally slowed and stopped beside a small brook to take on water and eat a small breakfast of hard biscuits and fish caught fresh from the icy stream.

Afterwards, Skye helped the group collect large stones from the riverbed, and they built a cairn in honour of Longcraw. Weard lit some of her incense sticks, and the G'Oräk prayed and chanted in their own language. They never told Skye what was said.

It was decided that they would take it in turns to keep watch whilst the rest of the group tried to catch up on some sleep. However, even though her legs and back were sore and aching from a night in the saddle, Skye found that she was unable to get to sleep. She spent the next few hours sat up with whoever was on duty. She offered each one to sit up on her own, but she got the impression that they didn't trust her to remain watchful. Skye didn't blame them. She didn't feel very brave and certainly didn't want to have to fend off a group of trolls or Felmir without their support.

When she finally took to her bed, Skye was able to get a good idea of who was on watch and who was just returning, so much so that she was able to count the hours away by the changing of the watch. It was whilst doing this that Skye was surprised to see one of the goblins making his way through the sleeping group barely halfway through his shift. Judging by the way the goblin moved, Skye knew that it was Yop. Instead of heading to the watch post, he made his way out of the campsite and off into the night. Skye swore to herself that she would ask Yop about it in the morning, but the whole incident made her uneasy.

As she rolled over to try to finally get some sleep, Skye felt the weight of Burrower against her leg and was shocked to realise that she was starting to draw comfort from having a weapon so close to hand. Before it had made her scared, nervous of what it represented. Now she found herself hardened and determined to do whatever it took to get home to see her family again.

The next morning, they rested longer than usual, allowing the weak sun to rise almost directly above them before Snowbroth decided that it was time for them to make a move. Even so, Skye had found it too uncomfortable to bring up the situation with Yop. She decided instead to keep a closer eye on him to see if he acted oddly again.

"Lörieas is five leagues to the south as the Silver River flows, but we must steer clear of the water for a while and head inland. We can be sure to find friends there. Lörieas has always been an ally of the G'Oräk. For now, we head south-west and through the Wizened Peaks. This will bring us out to the north of Lörieas and should give us an easy ride towards the postern gate."

"Will that not be obvious to whoever is searching for us?" asked Weard. "Won't they be expecting us to head for Lörieas and wait there to ambush us?"

"Quite possibly, but we don't have a choice," answered Snowbroth. Nobody dared to argue.

At first, they rode with pace, still nervous of being followed. Soon, however, they settled into a slow rhythm and enjoyed the weak heat from the sun on their backs. The wind was still bitterly cold, but the frost was thinner on the ground the farther south they headed. The fellhorses made easy work of the soft grasslands but started to struggle as they approached a deep range of rocky hills.

"The Wizened Peaks. We must be careful of ambush in here," Corngaff whispered. "These hills are hunted by the Bogomils."

"Bogomils?" questioned Skye, "More evil

creatures?"

"Not evil. They don't fight for good or evil, just for themselves. They do what they must to survive. The Bogomils are a tribe of gnomes that have bred through the generations a species of dragon that can be ridden safely. Their dragons are much smaller than the dragons of old, barely as big as you. But for a gnome, they are magnificent beasts. They swoop down into the valleys and attack travellers such as ourselves. They don't normally kill them, just rob them. That way, they argue, they can rob you again on your way back!"

"They sound lovely!" said Skye sarcastically, "Is anywhere safe?"

"Not this far south, I'm afraid."

Skye pulled her hood up over her head and settled down into the saddle, her eyes scanning the cliff tops for any sign of movement. For a few hours, they continued unmolested and were able to reach the crest of a mountain before lunch. From the top, Skye could see straight down into the valley below and a towering city on the horizon.

"Lörieas," grumbled Geldrig, "a place me and my brother once called home."

"It looks quiet. Where are all the wagons in and out? Where is the trade?" whispered Curglaff. "We should proceed with caution."

Skye shivered at the thought of more trouble and was more than happy when Weard suggested that they settle down in the shelter of the rocks to eat. Lunch was sparse, but Weard had managed to pick up some mushrooms on the journey through the mountains and had made a fine soup. Each member sat in silence as they ate. It was rapidly turning too cold to talk.

Skye was breaking into a chunk of hard, stale bread when the silence was broken by a piercing scream echoing down from the clouds above. Within seconds, others took up the cry, and Skye and her companions fell to the floor clutching at their ears.

"Bogomils!" cried Curglaff from behind a large rock. "Take cover!"

Skye managed to drag herself to her feet and ran to the rock just as a hot flame shot from the sky and scorched the ground where she had been lying. She looked up as she ran and saw a herd of blue dragons whipping through the sky, twisting and turning over each other as they fought to attack their prey.

Riding on top of each was a small creature that looked for all the world the same as the gnomes that Skye's mum worshipped in the garden. Each of these gnomes, however, was entirely yellow except for where their bodies were tattooed with a dark blue ink. There were a lot of tattoos, each one a different pattern. As

Skye watched, the swirls moved and flowed across its owner's skin, never staying still for more than a second in much the same way as the fabric on Weard's bag.

Skye noticed all of this in the seconds it took her to make it across the open ground and to the overhanging rock that Curglaff had ducked behind. Just as she was about to throw herself behind it, she felt a hard crack against her shoulder that sent her tumbling forwards. The last thing she saw was the rock racing towards her face as, with a sharp pain in her temple, she was knocked unconscious.

When Skye opened her eyes, the sun had started to fall below the mountains.

"You've been out for a long while, little human. Do not get up too quickly. You will still be dizzy. That was quite a knock you took to your head."

Skye was pleased to hear the calming voice of Weard, but when she tried to move she felt a dull ache throb through her shoulder.

"It isn't broken," Weard reassured her, "You took a hit from a dragon, but luckily it didn't bite you. Dragon bites are not pleasant and do not heal well."

"Did everyone make it?" Skye asked, visions of the dragon attack still swirling through her mind. She swore she could still hear the shrieking echoing in her ears.

"We are all alive, though many are injured. Gondrag has twisted his ankle and Yop has a nasty burn across his face, but they'll all live. Snowbroth is gone, though," Weard finished with a sadness in her voice.

"Gone? Where? How?" Skye stuttered, her stomach dropping even more.

"One of the dragons picked him up. He was alive, but we don't know why they took him. Bogomils don't often take prisoners, just treasure."

"What do we do?"

"All we can do is wait until tomorrow. If he isn't returned, we must continue without him. Our task remains the same."

Skye felt like she could cry. How could they continue without Snowbroth? He was their leader and their guide. Skye felt surer than ever that their quest was doomed to fail.

That night they built as big a fire as they could, though it was more a pile of smouldering logs than anything that would warm them through. On it, Weard and Brabble managed to cook up a paste of root vegetables which they eagerly spread onto the last of their stale bread. It was neither tasty nor filling, but it took some of the edge from their hunger.

Expecting another attack at any point, they took

it in turns to keep watch throughout the night. Skye was surprised when Yop woke her up with a nudge not long after the moons had risen.

"'Your turn, Skye. It's all been quiet so far, but keep your eyes about you."

"Thanks, Yop," Skye yawned. "Can I talk to you for a minute about something?"

"I can't right now, Skye, sorry. I have important things to do for Snudge. You understand?"

Skye wasn't happy with the way that Yop looked on edge. He was shifting his gaze from side to side and wouldn't look her square in the eye. Skye tried to press him to talk, but he insisted that he needed to leave and that he couldn't waste any more time. As he argued, he turned away from Skye and, once again, headed away from the camp. Before she could call him back, Yop had turned and disappeared behind a rock.

Skye took Burrower out of its sheath and climbed up onto the rocky peak that they had been using to keep watch. For an hour or so, Skye stared into the blackness of the night seeing nothing other than the occasional firefly darting through the cold night.

As she stared, she felt her eyelids start to weigh heavy and to close despite her best intentions. Just as she felt sure that she couldn't keep awake for a minute longer, she was jolted back to attention by a soft whisper overhead and a thud and rustle from a tree not a hundred yards south of where she sat.

Sinking back into the rock, Skye increased her grip on her sword and pulled her hood up over her head, better to disguise herself in the darkness. Her eyes were wide awake now, and she was able to make out a shadow silently making its way through the rocks towards their camp. Skye knew that she should alert the rest, but she was frozen to the spot with fear. All she could do was watch and hope that whoever or whatever it was would pass by their camp undetected.

After a while, she realised that the shadow that she had been focussing on was that of a large tree stump and that she now had no idea where the creature had moved to. With panic rising inside her, Skye forced herself to her feet and turned to raise the alarm. As she stood, she came face to face with the intruder.

"Snowbroth?" she cried aloud, more with relief than surprise.

"Do not disturb their sleep now, Skye. They will need every minute of it, as will you. We can let them know tomorrow that I am returned."

"Where have you been? What happened?"

"All in good time. For now, know that I am well and that we are safe here. The Bogomils have agreed to keep watch over us. Even so, I will take the watch from here. You must go and sleep. I will explain all tomorrow. We have a long ride ahead of us."

"But Lörieas is only half a day away," croaked Skye. "Why such a long ride?"

"I'm afraid we aren't going to Lörieas," whispered Snowbroth, lowering his stare. "Lörieas has fallen."

Lörieas

"Fallen?" shouted Geldrig, "When?" It was early the next morning, and any elation at Snowbroth's safe return had disappeared with his news about Lörieas.

"A week past, at least. The Bogomils fly over a very large area and do not often visit this site. When they last flew over Lörieas a month ago, it was as lively and busy as ever. Now, however, it lies empty and the dead rot in the street."

At the demise of their former hometown, the Felmir had been inconsolable. It had taken all of Snowbroth's persuasion to prevent them from riding off immediately to take revenge on any enemies that might still be hunting amongst the debris.

"Nothing living remains," Snowbroth had assured them. "Any who stayed to loot the dead have long been driven out by the phoenix that have moved in to feast on the carrion.

"The Bogomils were good enough to take me on a scout of the area yesterday. There is nothing there for you now, my friends. Nothing there for any of us. Instead, we must loop past Lörieas and head across the Wandering Place to seek out the Druidmotte. There I hope we will find support, information and rest. It is a week's trek from here if all goes well, and so we must set out now whilst the sun is still rising."

Most of their horses had bolted during the dragon attack the day before, but Brabble and Brack had managed to retrieve nearly all of them and they were now tethered and grazing on a balding patch of grass. After all of the excitement, it was decided to not overburden them, and so the beginning of the journey saw the horses used only to carry bags and tents. Skye was not happy with this arrangement. Her shoulder was still extremely painful, and her ankle was still sore from the glibberig attack. Her arm felt a lot better, but she knew that leading a horse for any length of time would make it sore again.

For most of the morning, they slowly walked down a steep incline that led them inch by painful inch closer to the foot of the mountain pass. Every now and again, they would see a shadow move across the land as a Bogomil scout flew overhead.

Every so often, the group would stop in their tracks and duck behind boulders or bushes at the sound of footsteps approaching. Invariably, it turned out to be yet more families fleeing their villages in the south. Snowbroth engaged the first few in conversation, but their stories soon became repetitive, tales of villages razed to the ground, farmland scrubbed bare and of women and children murdered in front of their husbands and sons. After a while, they just gave a polite nod and went on their way.

Occasionally, they would stumble upon families or lone men who hadn't been so lucky and who lay dead and rotting by the side of the road. They gave these a wide berth, and Skye noticed that the goblins said a small prayer each time they passed.

Around about midday, they stopped for a quick lunch at the foot of the pass before pushing on south towards Lörieas. Snowbroth had told them that they would have to skirt around the very edges of the city wall in order to get back onto the main road through the Wandering Place, but there was something very ominous about the dead city of Lörieas. All morning they had heard wailing screams from within the walls but could make out no movement.

With every step towards the city, Skye felt an ever-growing presence of death. The smell was overwhelming. The closer they got, the thicker the swarms of flies buzzing around their heads grew. A short distance north of the main city gate, Yop called everyone to a halt and placed his finger to his lips to silence them. This close the screams seemed to come from the very walls themselves and surrounded the travellers on all sides. With each scream, the branches in the trees would whip around as though in a strong wind and cast their dry leaves to the ground.

"The city is weeping for its dead," muttered Gondrag as he ran his fingers across his chest to ward off evil spirits. "There is much sadness here, but no evil. You were right, Snowbroth."

"I am truly sorry for your loss, both of you," offered Snowbroth. "We should continue on, though. The air here is foul and will bring upon a sickness if we stay too long."

"You go on if you must," grumbled Geldrig. "Me and Gondrag are staying behind. We owe it to our people to see what we can save."

"We will join you then. You leave us no choice. We all go on or none at all," asserted Curglaff. "We have travelled too far to go it alone. What harm will it cost us?" This question was to Snowbroth who Skye noticed was shifting uneasily beside his horse.

"Very well, if that is the choice of the group, we shall stop and help salvage what we can, but we must not linger long. As I said, there is a foul air here, rich with the stench of death and despair. It is infectious. I can feel it seeping into my veins as we stand and chat idly." Snowbroth shuddered. "If we must go, then we go now and be out by first moon. I will not spend a night in that place so long as I can move my legs."

Gondrag and Geldrig grunted their appreciation to the group and led them with confident strides around the outer wall until they came to a small gate well-hidden behind a climbing bramble covered in dark, foul-smelling flowers. Brack made short work of it with his small hand axe though it took the Felmir awhile longer to break through the rusted lock that barred the gate against intruders.

"Whoever laid waste to the town certainly didn't enter here," grumbled Yop under his breath, shivering as Geldrig grunted with a final blow against the aged metal. "The main gate was obviously breached."

"Or the skies," whispered Gondrag as the gate finally swung open. "Everybody move quickly but quietly into the gate. *Now!*" Gondrag finished with a shout as a dark shadow eclipsed the weak sun and a screaming beast twice as big as a horse landed on the city wall high above them. The creature towered over the wall and spread its wings wider than a house. Skye looked up as it opened its mouth and fine pointed teeth shone as it screamed with rage. Large, ivory horns curved away from the top of its scaly head, and fin-like ears turned this way and that. Sickly yellow eyes burned bright like fire pits constantly scanning the floor for food. Stumbling on the narrow walkway atop the wall, it scrabbled with clawed toes to get a purchase, stones crumbled from their mortar and rained down onto the ground below, threatening to crush them all.

"Wyvern!" screamed Brabble as he grabbed Skye by her hood and dragged her into the tunnel behind him.

Skye never worked out how they all managed to dodge the hailstorm of rocks from above, whether through nimble feet or sheer luck, but they all made it safely into the damp, unlit corridor beyond the gate. From their bags, Weard, Brack and Brabble all removed cloth torches and set them alight with thick, yellow-headed matches.

With the torches lit and her eyes adjusting to the darkness, Skye started to relax a bit. For her part, she withdrew the glowing cherry tree branch that she had been given by the tree trolls. Though it glowed with a pale luminescence, it filled the shadows more effectively that the oily torches up ahead. Every now and again one of the group would wander too far from the spluttering light and with a curse would trip or stub a toe against one of the many loose rocks and roots that covered the uneven ground.

Even during the uneasy peace that had, until

recently, lasted in this city, this corridor would not have been often used. Against the wall old weapons were stacked, largely rusted and bent or blunted. Here and there were more rural items that belied a history of use as general storage, not just for arms. The floor was littered with rakes and scythes mixed in amongst the swords and armour.

Skye was fascinated to find a broken jewellery box cast into one of the corners. The contents had been scattered across the floor, but rings and necklaces were visible in the sand here and there. Before Skye had time to look at them in more detail, the rest of the group urged her further into the passageway.

When they were sure that they were out of reach of the wyvern, they settled down for a drink of water. In their haste to escape, they had left their horses tethered outside the gate along with all of their food in their packs. Whilst they sat and drank, Yop and Curglaff volunteered to retrace their steps and retrieve what food they could. As they set off with the torches, the shadows around Skye and the group grew and soon they were plunged into a moody half-light lit only by the branch placed on the floor in the middle of the group.

"We have retrieved most of the packs and much of the food," started Curglaff upon his return, "but, alas, our horses are gone. No doubt picked off by the wyvern."

"Is it still out there?" asked Snowbroth, eager for more information.

"*They* are still out there," answered Yop, sitting down with his back against the wall and fishing through a pack for some bread, "At least six I'd say, though they fly fast and high. I'll be honest, we didn't stick around to count."

Wyvern. They all knew what bad news this was. There was no going back now, but none of them knew how much or how little cover would be offered once they made it into the city. Geldrig and Gondrag offered to scout ahead, but Snowbroth insisted that they all push forward together, lest they end up spending more time than they needed in the foetid tunnel.

"Is your shoulder still troubling you, my friend?" asked Weard when she saw Skye falling to the back of the pack as they meandered further under the wall.

"I can't shake the pain inside it. It doesn't feel like a bruise. It feels much deeper. More like something in the very bone."

Weard pulled Skye to one side and offered her the torch to hold.

"Let me take a closer look. I didn't get chance to tend it properly after we were attacked."

Weard pulled the shoulder of Skye's cloak down and held the torch close.

"There appears to be a small but deep cut below the shoulder blade. If that was caused by the dragon, then there may still be dragon scale in the wound. This is bad, I fear. It will not kill you, but it will not heal fully until it is removed and there is no way that I can do it in this light. As soon as we are away from here, you must let me try my best to fix it. For now, I am afraid that you must endure the pain as best you can."

Skye nodded solemnly as she pulled her cloak back over her shoulder.

"Thank you, Weard. It seems I am forever owing my life to you. I hope one day I can repay you."

"You will, my little friend, you will."

The two of them raised the torch high above their heads and jogged carefully over the rough floor. They came up so quickly on the rear of the pack that they almost fell head first into Yop. When she regained her balance, Skye looked up and saw why they had all stopped in their tracks. Ahead of them and beyond another open gate stood the most beautiful city that Skye had ever seen. As soon as they'd left the Wizened Peaks that morning, Geldrig had given them all a short history of his home. The news of its destruction had hit him and his brother hard and they'd spoken with pride as well as anguish as they'd told of the once great city.

Built almost entirely out of a pink, iridescent

marble, the city of Lörieas had once been home to over ten thousand souls, a mix of goblin, men and even some of the more well-behaved Nelapsi. Together they had built a city to rival any on the Silver River.

Specialising in the trade of fine fabrics, Lörieas had rapidly grown to be one of the wealthiest cities in the north and its influence reached out across the land. It controlled politics as far south as the exotic Rumm Islands.

Lörieas was not an ancient city compared to those built by the first Shrunken. Alastor was more venerable by a scale unimaginable. Lörieas was merely a few thousand years old. Despite this, it rose higher and packed its city walls with more culture and boasted more history than many of the older cities and towns. As trade had boomed and money filled the town's chests, the early governors had spent heavily on resplendent churches and houses for the rich. After a time, the less wealthy began to resent the luxuries that the rich were afforded and dissent started to grow amongst the workers.

For many years, the tension simmered under the surface, and the governors used this to their advantage. They spread vicious rumours that the lower species were to blame, that the Nelapsi and goblins were the cause of the difference in wealth. They started to push these creatures into poverty with higher and higher taxes until they snapped and tried to fight the system. This was then used as evidence that they couldn't be trusted, that they needed to be gone. Over the years, the governors systematically turned men against the other races and the other races against each other until eventually they were forced beyond the walls and out into slum cities in the surrounding lands.

The Nelapsi were the first to go, leaving swiftly and in the darkness. They fled south and soon found the welcoming arms of the first evil. The goblins and orcs followed soon after, many headed north but yet more joined the Nelapsi in the south. In this way, Lörieas found itself without any of its toughest fighters and in return armed what would soon become a feared enemy.

The men that were left were not slow in realising that they had been duped and that rather than increased wealth, their hatred had instead meant that they now needed to fill twice as many jobs as before for little extra money. Meanwhile, the purses of the elite grew ever heavier.

In the uprising that was to follow, many men lost their lives but by the end, the city was rid of most of its corrupt governors. One, Golconda, was allowed to stay to set an example to anyone else who tried to grow fat on the ill fortune of his people. He was forced to live a life of penance in a small wooden hut in the darkest corner of the city and had to beg for money in the streets.

With their corrupt leaders gone, the city was placed into the hands of a warrior chosen for his valour in battle. His name was Alberich. He was instructed to only do what was right for the people of Lörieas and would not take a salary. Despite his pleading though, those species that had been driven out could not be persuaded to return.

For many years, this system served the people of Lörieas well, and once again the city had begun to prosper. Even now, looking around at the empty houses and crumbling towers in front of her, Skye could imagine the beauty that had been and how the city might once have buzzed as in the tales that Gondrag had told as they ventured from the gate and explored the ruins.

Surrounding them all, the signs of war marked the buildings like scars on a soldier's body. Small fires burned everywhere, and the once fine stone houses looked scorched. Every now and then, a loud crack would echo around the eerily silent streets as a stone fell from a church wall or a now blind watchtower.

For over an hour they picked through the rubble and debris, moving dead and rotting bodies into a large pyre in the city square. All the while they sought for anything that might give them a clue as to what had caused this devastation. Gondrag and Geldrig sobbed quietly, occasionally letting out a whimper as they saw somebody they knew or recognised a landmark that had once meant something to them.

"Whoever did this has cleared the place out. There's not even an arrow left behind," cursed Curglaff as he lifted a stone twice his size away from a doorway.

"Not quite," offered Brabble, holding out a bow and quiver as tall as he was. He slung the bow over his shoulder and attached the quiver to his belt.

As Brabble stood boasting of his find, a pile of rubble avalanched down from a rooftop behind the group. They spun around, swords drawn, as the rocks fell to the ground narrowly missing a cowering Felmir. In the shadow of the building, he looked twisted and evil, naked except for a dirty loincloth. When he stood, however, he was nothing more than a weakened old man.

"I have gold!" he barked to nobody in particular. "I can pay for whatever you have!"

"Be off with you, foul old hermit. Who knows what danger your wretched shouting is bringing towards us!" shouted Brack as he tried desperately to scare the man away.

"That is no hermit," spoke Geldrig, pushing his way to the front of the group. "That is Golconda, the last remaining vagabond of the Lörieas government." As he spoke, he drew his sword and placed it to Golconda's neck. "Your greed killed my family, my friends. Your *thirst* for gold killed Lörieas. Tell me, why shouldn't I strike you down?"

"I have gold!" babbled the old man again without even seeming to recognise the sword pricking at his neck.

"Leave him be." Snowbroth eased Geldrig's sword away from the former governor's neck. "He is beyond knowing what he has done. His death would serve no purpose other than to be another mark on your soul."

Reluctantly, Geldrig holstered his sword and grunted at Golconda "Leave this city now. If I see you here again, you will not have my more well-mannered friend here to save you."

However insane Golconda was, something registered in his head as he shot to his feet and ran, giggling to himself in a high-pitched squeal, out into the main road and out of sight.

It soon became obvious that there was nothing to be gained from searching the city further, and even the Felmir agreed that it was best to leave. They turned and made their way back towards the gate.

When they were halfway back, Brack stopped dead and motioned them all to squat down low. Peering over a pile of marble bricks, Skye could see a tall, thin creature working its way through the dead bodies a hundred yards ahead. Its skin was pallid, and she could see thin blue veins tracing a map under the surface. A hood covered its head, but the rest of the body was naked. Whatever it was moved with a lightness and agility that was almost catlike.

As the creature moved between the bodies, Skye could see it picking through the pockets and grabbing anything of any value and even occasionally taking a bite out of the flesh. Skye retched and turned her head away from her friends. She didn't want them to see any weakness in her.

Absently, Skye started to play with her ring. Once again, it reminded her of home, of the only chance to go back to what she whole-heartedly yearned for. It reminded her of everything that she was fighting to get back to.

Fight

"Nelapsi," hissed Brabble as he returned from the top of the pile of stone. He drew his sword silently and tapped Skye on her shoulder snapping her back out of her thoughts of home. "Don't worry, Skye," he said softly to her, nodding towards her mother's ring. "I've seen you play with it before when you're nervous or worried. I know you miss your home, Skye. You'll get back, I promise. We'll sort this queen out, no problem, and then I'll personally make sure that we find a way to get you home again." He smiled at her with his crooked, goblin smile, and Skye found herself relaxing and pulled Burrower free of its scabbard.

"Thank you, Brabble, you've been more a friend to me since I arrived here than you ever had to be. I know you were unsure about a human joining your adventure and I'm sure that I'm more a hindrance than a help, but thank you." She smiled back at him and steadied her feet against the pile of rubble. Skye glanced around and saw the rest of the group do the same, silently drawing their weapons ready to attack.

"Everybody, in a circle around me!" Snowbroth broke the silence with a loud yell, and Skye was dragged roughly into position. Each solider faced out, and Skye could see why Snowbroth had seemed so eager. Like a scurrying swarm of ants, scores of Nelapsi were circling in on the group, crawling down the high city walls or scurrying from underneath heavy rocks or piles of discarded wood. Wherever there was somewhere to hide, it seemed, Nelapsi were pouring out. All of them were dripping blood from their mouths where they had been feeding on the fallen soldiers that still littered the pavement.

In the skies above, phoenix circled and called to one another, ready to descend to celebrate their gory feast.

Without thinking, Skye reached to her belt and unsheathed Burrower. Its weight felt reassuring in her hand. All around her, she saw the goblins hefting their swords from one hand to the other, tensing at the shoulders ready to attack.

"Do not attack them," screamed Yop into her ears. "Let them come to you. Do not break the circle. Trust those around you to protect your back, and you damn well make sure that you protect them if they need it!

"Remember, they are vicious things that will rip the skin from your body if you let them get you on the ground or if you get cornered by a group. But if you stay on your feet and keep them on their own, they are weak and easily killed. Just don't fall over!"

Nervously, Skye nodded that she understood and took up the stance that she had been taught by Brabble in the shadows of Snudge's house.

Skye broke into a rhythmic cry. "Fight! Fight! Fight!" she repeated over and over to herself, remembering all the times that it had been chanted on the school field. She doubted it had ever been chanted before a battle, though.

As the first wave of Nelapsi broke over the pile of rubble in front of her, Skye noticed the strange way that they ran. They couldn't fly, but they leapt and bounded as though gravity had less of a hold on them. The covered ten paces for each of Skye's and were soon on top of the group.

Skye felt time move slowly until every movement felt as though she was moving through treacle. She caught sight of the first creature as it leapt from the top of the pile and saw into its dark, bloodshot eyes as it fixed its gaze on her face. Somewhere deep inside her, Skye saw her future. It was, above all else, short.

Her arm took control and rose in slow motion towards the demon in front of her.

With a strong swing of her arm, she parted the head from the neck, and the Nelapsi fell to the ground twitching as its dark blue blood flowed down the cracks in the pavement. Skye watched it flow like a river following the contours of the well-worn slabs. Her arms screamed at her as they recoiled from the force of cutting through bone and sinew. She felt herself throwing up, horrified at what she had done.

She didn't have time to dwell on it, though. As quickly as it had slowed, time came rushing back. Skye redoubled her grip on her sword and looked for her next victim. A mist clouded her mind as she remembered all of the times that she had been too cowardly to fight back against Keith Boggart, of all the hanging loogies and knuckle rubs that she had ever endured, and she channelled all of that anger into her arm.

With a swift punch, she drove the handle of her sword into the head of an oncoming Nelapsi, crushing its skull. With flick after flick of her wrist, she sent heads and limbs flying as hordes of creatures fell upon her screaming their curses. Many of those screaming defiance as they attacked her managed to slice into Skye's skin with their claws, but the adrenaline coursing through her veins stopped any pain from registering.

Underneath her feet, the ground became slippery with the blood and limbs of the fallen, and she had to fight with each step to keep her feet. The smell was unholy. Every breath reeked of death, and Skye took to breathing only through her mouth, but even then she could taste the decay.

Her heart raced in her chest. She knew that one false move would be fatal. Though most of the Nelapsi had no weapons, their claws and teeth were sharper and filthier than any weapon Skye could care to imagine. Already some of the wounds on her forearm were starting to burn and itch.

Suddenly, as she thrust forward skewering one of the creatures on her sword, her left leg slipped and she dropped to her knee.

Issuing a scream from hell, one of the demons leapt from behind a pile of his fallen comrades and aimed straight for Skye's face. She felt her eye throb as its bony ribcage smashed into her and knocked her back to the ground. Her head swam as it cracked against the hard cobbles, and she felt sick with fear. Reacting instinctively, Skye ducked and twisted, and grabbed the loose skin that hung from its emaciated back. She pulled hard and dragged it away from her own face, its sharp claws digging into her cheeks as it fought to hold on. Eventually, it came free and she threw it as hard as she could over her head, wincing as it flung out a claw in one last-ditch attempt to grab hold but succeeding only in grazing her neck with its claws. As the creature came to a rest next to her, she stood quickly and stamped down on its head feeling it pop like an insect.

Skye's face throbbed with pain and she could feel it start to swell into what would be a dark black eye. Her arms ran with blood from the many scratches but reassuringly, none of them looked to be too deep.

Despite the odds, Skye could see that they were winning. Bloodied bodies lay around them, but they were all Nelapsi. None of her friends seemed to even have a scratch.

As she looked around, Skye momentarily took her eye off the enemy and with a thud, felt herself knocked over and flattened to the ground with a group of Nelapsi on top of her. They were incredibly light, and she was able to claw them away from her face. As quickly as she flung them away, more landed on top of her. She felt their piercing claws ripping at her clothes and into her skin, but still she fought them off.

Just as her arms screamed in agony and her legs collapsed like lead and she felt that she was about to succumb to their sheer numbers, she felt them all thrown off with one fell swoop of a heavy sword. She looked up into the bloodied face of Brabble who helped her quickly to her feet.

Behind them Skye saw Curglaff and Snowbroth fighting back to back, circling as enemies flew at them from every direction. Each one was dispatched with an effortless swipe of their sword or fist, and Skye realised that it was very much like a ballet. Each warrior moved in sequence with his partner, making sure that neither was ever exposed or overwhelmed. Skye realised that she was proud to be fighting alongside such heroes. She knew no songs would be written of this day – it might not even be remembered at all – but to her, it was a turning point in her life. She was no longer solely concerned with what she had left behind on Earth. She now cared about her legacy here on Ithilmir.

The tide of Nelapsi was now slowing and fewer were sticking around to fight. Most were fleeing in the face of the unending wrath of the defenders. With a final thrust, Skye skewered the last creature and fell to her knees exhausted. Around her, the goblins and Felmir were hugging and congratulating each other for a battle well won.

Suddenly, out of the corner of her eye, Skye saw a wounded creature rear its head above the roof of a building behind them. Before she could cry out, it pulled a broken crossbow from behind its back and took aim. The string snapped with a loud crack, and Skye heard the thud before she'd even taken a breath. Turning around, she saw Brabble take a step forward and look down at the feathered shaft that thrust out from his chest. Silently, he fell to his knees, blood trickling from his lips.

Without thinking, Skye raced over to her friend oblivious to the arrows still being loosed from overhead. She grabbed Brabble around his waist and lowered him into her lap. She was surprised at how light he felt. She stared into his eyes begging for him to return her gaze, but his eyes were fixed somewhere that no mortal could see. His breath was weak and rattled in his chest. Skye shook him hard and screamed at him to listen to her, but even as she did so he stopped breathing and relaxed into her arms. Right then, Skye wanted to scream and rage and fight the entire world. She would have drawn her sword and ran at a thousand orcs her anger was so intense. But she had nothing left to give. Almost as quickly, she felt the bile rise in her throat and her head swim with grief. She collapsed into a sobbing heap as she was overcome with the emotion of the battle.

Through half-closed eyes Skye saw Brack remove his bow and loose an arrow at the murderer high above. The arrow flew true and smashed through its chest, sending it tumbling over the wall and onto the ground below. It brought no joy to those left behind who ran over to Brabble and hugged him close, begging him to come back to them, desperate to see any trace of life in a body beyond saving.

Through tear-stained eyes, Skye forced herself to her feet and dragged her aching body over to join the rest in their mourning. Yop and Brack were sent out to scout for any remaining Nelapsi, and they took no pleasure in sending the last few souls to their death. When they returned, they lit a fire and built a shallow grave for their fallen comrade.

As the evening wore on, Snowbroth made as poor a supper as they'd had so far though few of them felt like eating. Those who did sat in silence as they ate. Each member of the subdued troupe took the time to rest and reflect on his or her own personal feelings and not one of them was without tears in their eyes. Even the more battle-hardened goblins who had lost friends and family in past battles were deeply affected by their loss. After a while, Brack quietly broke into song.

A braver soldier never fought,
He died in Lörieas.
He stood beside us valiantly,
And gave his life for us.

His soul forever wanders far,
His memory we keep.
Sailing high through Shadowlands,
We'll keep his shadow deep.

Though his body lies below,
His spirit carries on.
We'll charge with him to battle more,
Remembering him with song.

The song did little to lift their moods, but when Brack started again they all raised their voices in Brabble's memory and sang until they were hoarse. The rest of the night was filled with song and stories of Brabble.

That night, Skye got very little sleep and her dreams were haunted by scrambling creatures that crept from every nook and cranny and attacked her with diseased teeth and rotten claws. When she woke, she felt as though her arms and legs had been replaced with wooden stumps during the night, and every movement reminded her of how much energy her actions the day before had cost her. The air felt truly poisoned as they broke up their tents and picked at a light breakfast. At Snowbroth's beckoning, they made their way back to the gate before morning light broke over the city wall.

Torment

Skye was sure that what they saw when they emerged from the dark winding tunnel was a mirage. An illusion sent to test them. When the group stepped blinking in the cold winter sun, they found their fellhorses grazing happily on the long grass that grew at the base of the city wall.

"They must have run and hidden at the first signs of the wyvern," cried Skye as she ran and hugged the smaller horse that she had grown accustomed to riding.

The appearance of the horses and the knowledge that they wouldn't need to walk did a lot to lift their spirits. Before long, they were laughing and joking as though the troubles from the previous day had vanished. As they breathed in the cleaner air, they felt the decay and pestilence of Lörieas leave their bodies. They felt refreshed.

They spent the day in the saddle, taking a slow pace to spare the horses. This meant that the icy wind cut through them like a knife. It wasn't long before, Skye had wrapped herself in every layer that she had in her pack and was bent low in the saddle to keep her body heat in and to deflect the worst of the wind. Through the tiniest of gaps in her hood, she could make out the riders in front of her, but as they approached the Wandering Place the weather took a turn and they started to feel the cold damp of a snowstorm approaching.

Skye had spent many happy days on Earth sledding and playing in the snow in her garden or in the local park and had always waited excitedly each winter's evening to see if she could see the tell-tale fluffy flakes that might mean a day off from school. Never before had she experienced snow like the storm they found themselves lost in. Snow fell in a thick white sheet and was forced by the wind through the fabric of their cloaks.

Before long, each rider found themselves soaked to the skin with no way to get warm or dry. As it worsened, Skye found that her field of vision narrowed until she could only make out her companions as silhouettes against the whiteness of the sky.

Every now and again, Skye found that she needed

to shout out to work out where she was and found on more than one occasion that she was farther away from the rest than she liked and was in very real danger of wandering off completely.

"This is why they call it the Wandering Place," howled Brack above the screaming wind. "When it snows, you easily lose your track and end up wandering in circles until you freeze solid. When it is hot, the temperatures become unbearable and throw up mysterious mirages that lead travellers away from their chosen path. Many a warrior has come to his end in this place. We must stick together or else die apart."

Time after time, Skye found herself heading towards a silhouette that she assumed to be Weard or Brack or one of the others only to stumble over the carcass of a tree when she finally reached it. Each time she would shout out and follow her friends' replies until she was back with the group.

Eventually, though, there came a time when they didn't reply. Skye shouted and screamed until her throat was sore, but still she heard no answer. Knowing that she would freeze to death if she stayed where she was, she had no option but to head out in the direction that she thought her friends would be heading.

In the swirling snowstorm, it was hard to determine which way to steer her horse, but Skye knew that they had been heading into the wind for most of the journey, and so she decided to head off that way. She ignored the fact that the wind was constantly changing direction like a weathervane in a tornado. She couldn't afford to sit around and think. She had to take action.

For what felt like hours, Skye trudged through the blizzard, fighting endlessly to keep her cloak wrapped around her. After a while, the wind wasn't so biting cold anymore. In fact, she realised, she couldn't feel it at all.

She eased her fellhorse to a standstill and dismounted. She stood up straight for the first time since they had entered the Wandering Place. Lowering her hood, Skye realised that whilst the wind was still blowing strongly enough to shake the branches in the trees it seemed to swirl around her and leave her untouched.

Unsure what to make of this, Skye left her mount tethered to a tree stump and proceeded with more caution. Soon, the swirling snow changed to form a thick, oily mist. As it rose, it curled itself around Skye's ankles.

Behind her, Skye heard a scratching sound moving through the scrub. She spun on her heels and shouted out to it.

"Who's there? Brack, is that you? Weard? This isn't

funny, guys!"

When nobody replied and the scratching drew closer, Skye took off in the opposite direction, all thoughts of finding her friends abandoned. She knew she had to get away from whatever it was that was hunting her in the snow. She hadn't run for long before she tripped over a large stone that rose from the ground. As she leant against it to help herself to her feet, she realised that it was a gravestone. It was simple and carved from a dull grey granite, but it was unmistakable. Screaming, Skye backed away and spun around. As she turned, the mist retreated and Skye was able to see where she was for the first time.

She wasn't in the Wandering Place anymore.

She was stood in the middle of a grey field covered in dead grass, as though all colour had been drained from the landscape. Here and there were dotted odd trees, each one grey and leafless and still. There was not so much as a breeze, but the air was still cold enough to sting.

What concerned Skye the most were the graves. Stretching all the way to the horizon in front of her were thousands, maybe even millions, of gravestones. Each one looked identical to the next.

Moving slowly between them, Skye noticed that they were all marked with the same date, as though the owners had all died as part of a mass extinction. She knelt down next to the stone closest to her and brushed away the snow. Immediately, she recoiled and fell back onto the cold ground.

"No," Skye screamed. "It can't be. She isn't dead. I just saw her!" she sobbed.

She moved closer to check again. The name on the grave was there as solid as the rock into which it was engraved.

WEARD

Skye scrambled to the next stone and scrubbed away the snow.

BRACK

Crying at each one, Skye moved from stone to stone. At each one she read a familiar name. Eventually, she reached the last stone in the row and stopped dead. She couldn't understand what she was reading.

SKYE THISTLE

"But I'm here. I'm not dead yet!" she screamed to the sky.

"Not yet, child, but you will be soon. All of you will be."

The voice was cold and shrill and came from all around her. Skye spun around looking for anyone or anything. She was alone.

"Who are you? Who said that?" she wailed.

"I think you know who I am, little girl. I am your destiny!" echoed the voice.

"You are Queen Camarina," Skye stated. "But why can't I see you?"

The wind picked up again and stirred the leaves at Skye's feet into a small cyclone. When they settled back down, the field was filled with a rhythmic whisper. As it grew louder, Skye realised that it was the echoing sound of scraping dirt.

As she stood rooted to the ground, Skye watched with horror as the soil started to sink into each of the thousands of graves in front of her. Distorted, rotten hands broke through the surface and clawed the dirt away. Skye screamed silently and tried to turn around. No matter which way she turned, the graves were in front of her.

With the corpses came a horrible, soulful groaning that bounced around the cemetery and filled Skye's head.

"Why did you kill us all, Skye?" cried a thousand dead goblins. "Why did you doom us all to die?"

"What is this?" Skye screamed above the noise, "This can't be real. I didn't kill you. Why are you lying? I just want to go home! I never wanted this!"

"Murderer!" they chanted. "Traitor! Destroyer!"

Skye fell to her knees and pulled her hood back

over her head to drown out the noise, but it filtered through the thin material and echoed in her ears as they chanted their accusations over and over again.

Suddenly, Skye felt her hood ripped from her head and a cold, bony hand grab her chin roughly. Her head was forcefully twisted around, and she looked up into the rotting face of Snudge.

"I trusted you, *human*!" spat the goblin leader, bits of dirt and skin falling from his bones even as he spoke. "This is what we get for trusting in a filthy, dirty human!"

Another head formed in the mist, its eye sockets black and empty, blinded by a wound across its face.

"You said I was your *friend*!" hissed the ghost of Brabble, "Why did you lead me to die? Why did you betray me?" he howled into the wind.

"What have I done?" Skye sobbed. "I didn't do any of this! Why are they dead?" Skye screamed and closed her eyes shut.

She felt a shift in the air and dared to open her eyes. The graveyard was gone, and she found herself kneeling on the frozen wasteland of the frozen Wandering Place, a sharp biting wind whipping through her hair and chilling her to the bone.

"I haven't killed them," she spoke to the wind. "That wasn't real."

"No," replied the voice of the queen, louder than the rattling gale. "You haven't killed them *yet*. But you will."

"Never!" shouted Skye. "They are my friends!"

"You will kill them, Skye, when you lead them to *war*!"

The Wandering Place was suddenly filled with the sounds of battle. Skye stumbled and fell as she tried to run from the dark army attacking from all directions. As she pulled her head into her arms, she expected to be cut down at any minute, but instead the army passed right through her with a ghostly silence.

Skye looked up and saw the tide of evil wash over an army of her friends. The soldiers floated and drifted as they fought each other, each one nothing more than a shape in the mist. Skye watched in horror as the queen's legion worked their way through the goblins killing them as they stood.

"I know you are coming, little girl," shouted the queen over the crash of sword on shield. "You will die before you reach my tower, and I will unleash an army bigger than any this world has ever seen. Your friends will die, Skye, and it will be your fault!"

Skye sobbed as the queen paused and the ghosts floated away.

"Unless…"

Skye lifted her head to listen.

"Join me, Skye. You would be a powerful ally! Together we could lead my army to victory and rule the whole of Ithilmir! We would be unstoppable!"

"And you would spare my friends?" Skye asked.

"They would live lives of relative safety, yes. As our slaves, of course. Goblins, Nelapsi, gnomes…they are all nothing but lesser animals. The armies of humans are built to lead! We will take our rightful place above all else and lead Ithilmir into a new era of peace! Think about it, Skye! You will be a hero!"

The last word jolted Skye back to reality. She couldn't consider it. She wouldn't allow herself to be drawn in. She knew that anything the queen offered her would be tainted and a trap.

"No," Skye whispered. "I will not join you. I will destroy you, and I will destroy everything that you are. You will not be remembered, Queen. You will be forgotten and left to rot in the Shadowlands! I will go home, and I will leave Ithilmir a place of peace!"

Inside her, Skye felt her anger rise and boil and grow until she felt it rear up behind her eyes. On her finger, she felt the ring start to grow hot and to spin. She closed her eyes tight and felt the white-hot pain inside her skull wash over her. Clenching her hands together, Skye felt the power contained within them.

She slowly pulled them apart. Held inside them was a small ball of white light, burning brighter than anything that she had ever seen.

Something snapped inside her, and Skye screamed a horrifying bellow and launched the ball of light into the air. As it left her hands it grew and exploded until the whole world was bright white. Skye recoiled and shielded her eyes.

Skye felt the queen's rage race across the landscape like a terrible hurricane and felt it rip through her soul. Her howl of anger echoed around the landscape and froze the snow in the air. Skye felt the air freeze in her lungs and her blood seize in her veins. Her eyes grew wide as the face of the queen appeared in front of her, shaped from the mist and snow. As Skye collapsed to the cold ground, she knew now that there could be no doubting what she had seen. The queen's face.

Skye could no longer hide away from who she knew the queen to be. It made no sense, and she still couldn't bring herself to believe what she had seen. The queen had tucked her into bed a thousand time. It was her mother.

Druid

"Skye? Is that you?" Skye lifted her head towards the voice drifting through the snow. "Brack? It's me. I'm over here!" she cried, looking around desperately.

Slowly, a growing silhouette made its way through the falling sheet of whiteness, and Skye was overjoyed to see the rest of the group following on behind. She leapt to her feet and ran to give them hugs.

"What's wrong, Skye?" asked Snowbroth as Skye's cheeks streamed with tears. "You've barely been lost more than a minute."

"A minute! It felt like longer," stammered Skye, not wanting to seem even more like a small child.

"We heard you talking to somebody?" asked Weard as she put her arm around Skye and led her back the way they had come.

Skye panicked. She didn't know if she dared tell them what had happened, what she had seen. She didn't even know if it had really happened or if she had just hallucinated in the cold.

"Oh, I was just praying. Praying for you to find me." She smiled at the goblin. "It worked."

Skye shivered, though it had nothing to do with the freezing temperatures.

For a while they trudged on through the snow until their horses started to slow to a halt and they were forced to take shelter behind a rocky outcrop that shielded them from the worst of the weather. Try as they might, they couldn't light a fire and so resigned themselves to a night shivering in their wet clothes. To preserve what heat they could, they huddled together and tried to push whatever dry garments they had left underneath their wet clothes.

The horses were left to fend for themselves.

Around dusk, the light faded quickly from the sky, taking the snow and wind with it. Even though the temperature still wasn't above freezing, Skye felt a small relief from the bitter, biting wind.

As if to celebrate the change in weather, one of the group started to sing another mournful melody. This time, it wasn't the sweet, almost childlike voice of Brack but rather the gruff and soulful Gondrag. He sang from the heart. Skye couldn't decide if the song was about him or just somebody that he had known well.

> *In Lörieas city, a girl waited for me*
> *at the top of a tower all happy and free*
> *with hair that was golden as midsummer sun*
> *and a head full of poems of battles to be won.*

> *I remember our meeting as though yesterday*
> *as lost as I was my poor heart found the way,*
> *through valleys and mountains and rivers so cold*
> *I presented myself full of valour so bold.*

> *Soon the war started raging, and soldiers were called*
> *and I found myself outside our fair wall.*
> *As each arrow flew, the further we roamed.*
> *The sound of her songs would carry me home.*

> *I ended my tale with a whimpering sound*
> *as my body was left here to rot in the ground.*
> *But as I lay dying I saw her sweet face;*
> *it was the last thing I took from this Wandering Place.*

For a while everyone sat stunned, except for Geldrig who had obviously heard this tale before and sat silently weeping. Without warning, Gondrag stood up and shrugged off his blanket. With a grunt, he walked away and set up his tent on the outskirts of their camp. The rest of the group left him with his thoughts and retired to their own damp beds to spend a fitful night fighting to stay warm.

In the morning, they arose to a weak sunlight. Far in the distance, Skye could just make out a towering hill that was dotted from top to bottom with black specks.

"The Druidmotte," muttered Snowbroth as he saddled his horse and caught Skye staring open-mouthed. "We'll be there within a week if the weather favours us."

As it was, the weather was on their side. It took less than five days before they left the worst of the cold behind them and the Druidmotte stood much taller against the horizon.

By the time they were ready for lunch on the third day, they had left the snow behind entirely and were making their way across the dead salt plains that bordered the Wandering Place on the western side. There were no signs of life in any direction. No plants grew, and Skye doubted whether fresh water ever fell. The land underfoot was parched and cracked. In some places, the ground had split so viciously that they were forced to take long detours around canyons too wide for a horse to jump.

It was whilst they were rounding yet another

ravine that they stumbled upon it. Erected by the side of the track were four wooden pyres. Each one had been burnt almost to the ground, but there was so mistaking what had happened. The four skeletons still hung where they had been tied to the posts. Two of the skeletons were no larger than Skye. This had been a family simply trying to escape the ravages of the war that they wanted no part in.

What shocked Skye the most was that she wasn't shocked by what she saw. By now, she was so hardened to the death and despair of those fleeing the south that she expected nothing else. The only difference this time was how savage it was.

"What do the symbols mean?" asked Skye, referring to the shapes that had been scrawled into the sand.

"*Rahul*," read Brack. "It means traitor in the old tongue."

Once again, the goblins said their prayers as they passed and then they moved on. It was all they could do.

Eventually, they made their way around the last of the obstacles and found themselves alongside a green pasture in the shadow of the Druidmotte itself.

"Our horses can take us no further, I fear. They are weak and hungry and have been ridden harder than they were ever bred to," Snowbroth declared.

"They've served us well enough," offered Curglaff, "I'd always prefer a boat, myself, but there are worse ways to travel than horse. Let them be free if free they so choose. We can always find horses once this is over. There is many a creature down on his luck enough to sell us a nag or mare for a cut price."

They walked their horses to a nearby field on the border of the salt plains where the grass appeared more lush and set them racing away and into the distance. As she watched hers trail behind, Skye felt a pang of sadness. She'd never had a pet at home, certainly not one that she could grow attached to. She felt that her horse had served her better than she deserved. She hadn't even named it she realised. She hadn't dared in case she lost it or it was killed.

"I shall name you Arthur," she whispered, "after the only other person who put up with me as well as you did."

Once they had released the horses, they made their way to the bottom of the hill that was home to the Druidmotte. Skye hadn't been sure what to expect, after all Weard was a druid of sorts but seemed perfectly normal. Normal for a creature that, until recently, Skye was convinced didn't even exist. What Skye hadn't expected was a campsite. All around the hillside and on every patch of flat space, small tents were pitched, many with a bubbling pot outside that smelled delicious after days with little food.

"Whatever you do, little human," Weard whispered out of the side of her mouth as they approached the first tent, "do not eat anything that you are offered. These are interesting goblins, and they make interesting food. Unfortunately, interesting is not something that you little humans can handle."

"It'll poison me?"

"Or worse. Many of their potions are designed to show you another world or another time. Only druids can handle this potion, not even our goblin friends could cope with focussing on two worlds at once. If a human tried it?" Weard let out a long whistle. "Just trust me, little human. Stay clear of the food!"

They had reached the first tent by now, and Snowbroth and the rest had wandered inside to talk to the druid who owned it, leaving Skye alone with Weard.

"Why are there so many tents here? Are they the Druidmotte?" Skye asked her friend.

"The Druidmotte is a group of goblins, of druids, that sit atop this hill and distill the wisdom of the ages. They say that they can still speak to the Spirit Voices of the Before Time. They say that they can understand all that has been and all that is to be. They say a lot of things."

"Don't you believe them?"

"I do not know. However, Snudge does and, for now, they are the only chance we have to find out what is happening in the south. I do not think that any of us expected it to be as bad as it appears, but those that are fleeing do not tell of much hope."

Skye nodded. "So, are the tents where the Druidmotte live?"

"No, the Druidmotte live where they work, on the top of the hill. These are the druids who have come to seek the advice and wisdom of the Druidmotte. They will wait on this hill until they are seen, however long it takes. Some are seeking the wisdom to guide their villages. Some are seeking knowledge that will bestow upon them great treasure or fortune. Some are here on errands of great importance, and some are here to serve only themselves. Whatever their cause, they must all wait the same."

"How long must we wait?"

Weard motioned to one of the druids who was walking back up the hill to a tent much closer to the peak. She spoke to him in a tongue that Skye didn't understand, and it was a while before their conversation had concluded.

"This druid, he has been waiting for seven seasons

he says."

"Seven years?" gasped Skye, "We can't afford to wait seven years!"

"Indeed, I understand that this is what Snowbroth and the others are currently in discussion with the other druids about. He will be trying to speed up our passage up the hill."

Weard sat down on the grassy hill and offered Skye a chunk of bread from her pack. "For now, though, we must wait. As we wait, we should eat and keep our strength up. Even if Snowbroth is successful, I doubt we will be seen until the morning and so, after this, we will find tents for us all and a fire to warm our clothes."

Whilst they ate, Skye had a chance to look properly at the druids that scurried around them. It struck her that scurried was the most appropriate word. Even though they were all goblins and of a venerable age, there was none of the pride or strength that Skye had grown accustomed to with the G'Oräk. Instead, they stooped low as they walked and pulled their heads into their dark cloaks. None of them bore the silver handprint of the G'Oräk, but each cloak was embroidered with its own sigils that gave an air of mystery to them all.

Here and there, amongst the stars and moons, Skye noticed an all too familiar symbol, the cherry tree inside a ring.

Weard caught her noticing one such sign and offered, "It is not just the trolls who worship the cherry tree in the darkness, Skye. Word spread, and many of our cultures are familiar with the story even if most consider it just that, a story. Also, do not forget that Fen and his kin are deep believers in the magic of our world. They will have mages here seeking advice as we speak. Especially now that they have once again accepted the outside world into their tunnels!"

"Why are they all so hidden away?" Skye asked as another druid grabbed his pot of boiling broth and ducked into his tent.

"They spend too long stuck between one world and the other. They don't know who, what or even when is real and so they fear everything. To them, we may appear as ourselves or as an unimaginable horror. That is why I say don't eat the food."

"Are they saveable?"

"They don't want to be saved. They don't even think there is anything to be saved from. To them, their world is whichever world they currently inhabit. They know nothing different." Weard paused and surveyed the scene in front of them. "They are the lost goblins, indeed. They are also our only hope. For now, though, we should make a camp."

Weard never had chance to find a tent as at that moment Snowbroth and the rest emerged from a tent towards the top of the hill and called Weard and Skye to them.

"We are truly honoured, indeed," the old goblin said. "The Druidmotte have agreed to see us at once. They understand the importance of our quest and are eager to help wherever they can. This is a better outcome than we could have hoped for. We must leave now."

Druidmotte

Once they had passed through the great stone gates that had served as an entrance through the tall wooden wall that crowned the top of the hill, Skye and her friends were led into a well-manicured stone courtyard dotted here and there with ornate statues and fountains. The gentle trickle of falling water was the only sound that punctuated the otherwise silent atmosphere. None of the noise and activity that had been outside transferred into this inner sanctum. Skye found the overall effect to be very peaceful.

Leading off the courtyard were several doors. The druid that had met them at the gate led them towards one that was no different from the others. He was hunched in a dark blue robe dotted with silver stars and hadn't uttered a word to the group since they had entered, instead guiding them simply by dragging Snowbroth by the hem of his robe. Skye noticed that his eyes were bloodshot and dim from consuming too many of his own potions.

Once they had been ushered through the door, Skye found herself inside a large, well-lit room, not particularly long or wide but of a truly enormous height. Looking up, she couldn't make out the ceiling, but an occasional flutter and a falling feather told her that there was life up there somewhere. Sitting in a large circle in the middle of the room, surrounded by tall molten candles and foul smelling incense were the Druidmotte. Skye counted twenty different druids sat around the circle, though she couldn't identify any of their faces as they were all bent double with hooded heads. They didn't look up when the group entered but instead carried on with their ritual.

"We must sit and wait," urged Snowbroth, taking a seat on the flagstone floor.

Skye folded her legs and made herself as comfortable as she possibly could. The floor was uneven, and she found that no matter how she arranged herself there was always a sharp corner sticking into her legs or ankle. Her limbs still complained terribly with battle fatigue, and Weard still had not had time to remove the dragon scale from her shoulder. Skye wondered if she would ever feel fully healed again.

"I don't like this at all. I've never had any messing with magic," whispered Curglaff during a lull in the chanting.

"Be quiet!" growled Gondrag, "Believe what you will, but do not anger our hosts."

"I wasn't angering them," Curglaff snapped back, "I was just saying that it makes me uneasy, is all."

"Gondrag is right," scolded Snowbroth. "We would do well to remember that these are our only hope at the moment. This is their closing ritual. They will see us soon."

In the end, the druids finished their chanting soon after and their guide reappeared from a dark corner and summoned Skye and the group forwards to stand inside the circle of goblins.

As they walked forwards, Snowbroth muttered under his breath, "Let me speak for the group. Keep your counsel all of you."

"When you left," began one of the voices as soon as they were all inside the circle, "there were ten plus *that*," he nodded at Skye, "in your midst. Where are the rest?"

Skye noticed the hatred in the voice at the mere thought of a human. She suddenly felt very alone again.

"We lost two along the way," explained Snowbroth, "to agents of our enemy."

"And which enemy is that, do you presume?" asked another voice, this time from behind Skye.

"You know as well as I do," snapped Snowbroth. "She who calls herself Queen Camarina. She is rising again in the south, and her reach is ever-widening. We have come here before you seeking counsel."

"We know all about these *ideas*," hissed yet another voice. "We received a message not three nights ago from a goblin you know well. He told us that you had set out under the cloak of a coward to avoid a just war?"

"Elflock?" stammered Curglaff

"Hold your tongue," hissed Snowbroth. "We do not need to give them more information than they already have."

"We know all! We see all! We *are* all!" chanted the circle together.

"You cannot tell us anything that we do not already know, little goblin, but you are lucky." Skye recognised the first voice to speak. "We have looked into the future, and we do not believe that your little friend's war is the correct path to follow."

Skye felt herself relax a little at the thought that Elflock's attempt at sabotage hadn't worked. The thought of all-out war still filled her with fear.

The first voice continued, "We have already considered your case. We saw you flee from Lörieas. Your approach towards Liorath's Peak has not gone unnoticed and there are eyes everywhere.

"All is not lost, though. We foresee that you will still complete your quest. There is much danger ahead and a heavy cost to pay. We fear that your journey will not end with you all reaching your destination."

"What of the prophecy?" asked Snowbroth, ignoring the last comment.

"You know that many years ago we foretold a prophecy."

"A dark shadow will fall in the south. Those who seek to fight shadows shall be delivered a warrior from the skies to combine the forces of old and chase into the Shadowland those who came before." As with the G'Oräk, the circle of druids spoke as one. Skye felt the hairs on her neck stand on end.

"The prophecy is correct," spoke a deeper voice from the circle, "but unhelpful on its own. Skye."

Hearing her name startled Skye to attention.

"Yes?"

"We cannot know if you are the child spoken of in the prophecy, but you are here and you will help us." This was a statement, a fact. Skye knew she had no choice. "But we must tell you now, we see death, the death of a human. The visions are not clear anymore. Ever since Queen Camarina started looking into Akeldama, our ability to see the future has diminished. Skye, are you prepared to do anything you can to help us?"

"Of course, I want to get home most of all, but I will do whatever I can to help my friends."

One of the hooded figures rose from the circle and walked over to Skye. He moved his face close enough to Skye that her own face disappeared inside his hood. Up close, Skye saw that his skin was more weathered and his face more twisted than any goblin she had seen before. It was cracked and seeping around the mouth, and his eyes were weeping in the corners. When he spoke, it was with a hoarse whisper that only Skye could hear and his breath smelt foul as it wafted over her face.

"Follow me, and I will show you all that you can ever be."

He took Skye by an unresisting shoulder and started to lead her away into a dark antechamber. She looked back towards Weard for reassurance, but the healer just nodded gently and bowed her head.

The chamber was small and damp and was lit by a single spluttering candle that burned with a smoky flame. In the middle of the floor was a stone plinth sat in the middle of a complex system of runes scrawled into the sandy floor. On top of the plinth stood an ornately carved mask that showed a face in complete agony. It had a dull shine in the candlelight, almost like gold but not quite. The eyes were picked out with dark green emeralds and the lips with polished rubies.

"My name is Orthos, I am the most senior druid here. You can trust me, or rather you can trust me more than you can trust some of my fellow druids.

"This mask was created by the first wood pixies thousands of years ago. It is cast from pinchbeck, an extremely rare metal that is no longer found anywhere on Ithilmir. Anybody who wears it will be able see all that the druids see. Skye, it will open your mind to the pasts, presents and futures of our world. You must be sure that you can handle that if you are to look."

"Pasts? Are there more than one past?" Skye asked, curiously.

"But of course. Are you familiar with the idea that every action you take diverts you onto a different path in the course of your life?"

"Of course."

"Then surely it follows that if there are an unlimited number of futures that may or may not happen, there must be an unlimited number of pasts in which they did or did not happen?" He looked at Skye's face. "Do not look so confused. I am telling you nothing that you didn't already know. You just may not know it in this life. Unfortunately, it does mean that what you will see may be completely useless to us. It may represent a future that could never happen or may never happen or has even already happened. There are things that even us druids cannot control, but I am interested to find out what you see. Are you ready?"

"Wait."

"Yes?"

Skye decided to open up and told the druid everything about what she had seen in the Wandering Place and what the queen had told her. She didn't tell him about her mother's face, though. She still wasn't sure what that could mean.

"Interesting," murmured the druid. "It could mean everything to your quest or nothing at all." He paused. "Thank you for telling me, Skye. For now, will you indulge me and wear the mask?"

"Will it harm me?"

"Physically? No. Other than that, I cannot say."

"I will wear it. Will you stay here with me?"

"I will be here until you return. Please, relax your mind."

The druid lifted the mask from the plinth and

offered it to Skye. It was encased in solid gold and reflected what little candlelight there was with an oily sheen. The eyes were inset with piercing green stones and the cheek was carved with strange markings. The lips were picked out in brilliant ivory and etched to look like sharp teeth. When Skye took it, she felt heat radiating through the metal and staggered under its weight. She wasn't sure how she would hold it up for long enough to see anything.

Nervously, Skye raised the golden face to her own. Looking out through the emeralds, the world took on an eerie green hue. As soon as it touched her skin the heat left the metal, and Skye felt it flow through her body in much the same way as warm porridge on a cold winter morning.

At first, nothing happened. Skye looked across to the druid who just smiled and nodded. Suddenly, Skye felt like her brain was on fire, and she felt the mask soften and move in her hands. She felt it flow and wrap around her face until she was sure that it had covered her whole head. Out of nowhere, Skye's vision was filled with flashing images that moved far too quickly to make out any details. She had the vaguest sense of war and death, of armies crashing into a rocky tower like the sea upon a cliff. All the time, a giant glass orb swirled in and out of focus catching her unawares and threatening to crash straight into her face. With a loud scream her entire focus was filled with a hideous snarling mouth, filled with sharp teeth and bloodied gums.

She felt herself flying over the barren landscape of the Wandering Place, now scorched with burning earth, and on towards a dark and forbidden forest that felt still and dead. Onwards she flew towards the ever-growing tower of rock that she knew to be Liorath's Peak. As she drew closer, Skye saw a massive army amassed in its shadow. She could make out regiments of orcs, goblins and Nelapsi but in even greater numbers were those descended from the first human arrivals, evil and twisted but all too familiar. They numbered in their thousands.

Suddenly, Skye felt a tug and she was thrown high into the air and onto the top of the tower of rock. A fire reached into the night sky and around it danced a band of druids similar to those in the Druidmotte, only these weren't just goblins. There were druids of all species and they were all dancing in a frenzy as they threw strange herbs and coloured powders into the fire. Over them all floated the Dark Queen.

As the dancing reached its climax, the queen spun around suddenly and Skye's vision was filled with a sharp pair of slate grey eyes. But for the colour, they were all too familiar. The queen floated away, and Skye saw her in her full, evil glory. Before she could react, she felt a sharp snap and everything went black.

Skye opened her eyes and found she was laying on the sandy floor in the chamber. The mask was lying next to her in the sand, it no longer had the shine or magic that it had before. Looking down into Skye's eyes was Orthos and behind him stood Snowbroth and the others.

"Quick, before your memory fades, human," the druid urged her. "What did you see? What is to come?"

What should she tell them? Skye was still reeling from her vision and the last thing she wanted was to upset or anger their hosts or worse still invite further questions that she didn't know the answers to. She had come this far though, and she owed them at least something of what she had witnessed in the mask.

Skye took a deep breath and told them most of what she had seen. She still didn't tell them it all, it was all too much to deal with.

Plan

Before the group left the Druidmotte, they wanted to make sure that they took full advantage of any information that the druids had that could help them with their journey. Snowbroth had been in long discussion with Orthos whilst Skye and the rest sat on stone benches in the courtyard and listened to the play of water in the fountains.

When Snowbroth returned from the darkness some hours later, it wasn't with information but rather to summon Skye back in to the inner sanctum.

"You are needed, Skye," whispered Snowbroth as he led her gently by the hand. "We are discussing our journey from here, and there is information that it is only fair that you hear."

Skye didn't like the ominous tone in Snowbroth's voice but was powerless to resist as he led her gently across the yard towards a small wooden door. Skye had to stoop to fit through the low entrance and was led down a dark flight of stairs.

At the bottom, they came to a dead end against a stone wall. Snowbroth tapped out a complicated sequence on otherwise identical stones, and Skye heard a click within the wall. As she watched, the whole wall swung open to reveal a small, sparsely furnished room lit by many candles.

A low wooden table was placed centrally in the room. Around it sat three druids. Their hoods were pulled back. Skye was surprised to notice that one of the druids was female.

"Come and sit with us, Skye." She spoke in a soft and slow voice. "My name is Roke the Foreseen. Would you like a drink?"

Remembering what Weard had told her, Skye declined politely.

"A wise choice, indeed. Skye, we have looked into the future, and we have information that we think that you need to know."

Orthos interrupted to speak to Skye directly, "You must remember, above all else, Skye, that whatever we have seen represents only one of many possible futures. It may also represent a past that hasn't or will never happen. You would be wise to heed what we tell you, but do not trust it entirely. Trust to your instincts to guide you, and you will not go far wrong. Do you understand?"

"I understand," Skye said, though she was more nervous than she let on.

"We have seen your journey to Liorath's Peak. It is fraught with danger and confusion," said the third druid. "We have word from our spies that Queen Camarina is expecting you to make a move towards the tower but that she is expecting a more forceful attack from the north. We do not know how she has this information. It is possible that you have been betrayed, but it is equally possible that she has simply learnt how to use the full power of Akeldama. To remove as much risk of detection as possible, it is our vision that you will move around the Peak and infiltrate it from the south. A longer journey for sure, but much less likely to attract her attention as you approach.

"The concerning thing is that to reach the south entrance, you must skirt alongside the eastern edge of the Gloom. This journey should take you five days at a steady pace, and yet we see you entering Liorath's Peak within three nights. We fear that something must happen that requires you to move quicker than we would like. You must keep your guard about you at all times. Am I clear?"

"Yes, sir," Skye answered. "Will we travel by foot?"

"No," the druid continued. "We will provide you with fast nightwolves to ride." The druid noticed the look of fear pass across Skye's face and continued before she had chance to interrupt. "Goblin druids have ridden these beasts into battle for many generations. They are fierce but gentle beasts that will defend you should the need arise and deliver you with speed. You need not fear them, Skye. If they want you to live, then you will. If they don't? Then being afraid won't make the smallest difference!" He started to smile at her obvious discomfort before continuing in a far more sombre tone. "There is one more thing, Skye." Skye looked the druid in the eye as he continued. "We see you arrive at Liorath's Peak well enough, but we fear your company will not be at your side. We do not see more than this, but be prepared to face whatever you must with fewer allies than you would like or none at all."

This news chilled Skye to her core, but this time she held strong. She knew that, now more than ever, she needed to show the strength that she was beginning to find within herself.

"Remember," reassured Snowbroth, "none if this is carved in stone. What is yet to come may be similar or dissimilar to what has been seen or even both at once. We can only use this as a guide. As it happens, the information to travel south first and to try to enter the tower undetected is a much welcome piece of information. It has saved us much wasted time and heartache. This is the path we must take. Are you agreed, Skye?"

Skye was shocked. None of the group had ever looked to Skye for advice before, instead relying on their own superior knowledge and instincts to guide them.

"If that is what you think best, I will follow wherever you lead."

"Skye, you heard what our hosts said. You may end this journey alone. The path we take must be of your choosing, I will not lead you somewhere that I may not be able to follow. We will leave now and sleep. Our hosts have provided us with dormitories within these walls, and we need not make a move until the morning. Make no mistake, Skye, when we move tomorrow, you must lead us with strength and conviction. The G'Oräk amongst us respect you and are grateful for your presence as to a lesser degree are Gondrag and Geldrig. None of them will follow you into battle though if they think that you will lead them into a needless death.

"Think hard tonight, Skye. Is it to be all out war

on the queen's front doorstep along with the songs and valour that so recently you assumed were the sign of a hero, or will it be a sneaky and otherwise less heroic attempt via the south?"

Snowbroth stood and bowed towards the hosts. He helped Skye to her feet and she followed suit, bowing to each druid in turn. Snowbroth took Skye by the hand and slowly led her to the door.

"One more thing," offered Roke, "I see treason and treachery in your quest, Skye. Be more careful than ever of who you trust as you approach the tower."

With their final warning heeded, Skye and Snowbroth headed back up the stairs and out into the Druidmotte hall. The G'Oräk led Skye across the floor and through yet another anonymous door in the eastern wall and into a room full of pallet beds. Most were occupied with the other members of the group who were already in a deep sleep. Snowbroth offered Skye one of the beds and told her to sleep and think.

Although she tried her hardest, Skye couldn't decide what to do. Her mind was filled with the images from her vision earlier in the day and the message that the Dark Queen had delivered in the Wandering Place. Skye was still trying to figure out what her mother had to do with all this and what it meant.

Her? It doesn't make sense.

Eventually, Skye succumbed to a deep sleep, happy for the release from the agonising decisions that swirled around her mind like a thin fog, desperately close but impossible to grab at as they floated by.

When Skye awoke, it was still early and the rest of the group were still asleep. She rose quietly and went for a walk around the grounds. She tiptoed across the main hall and left via the door to the courtyard. Outside, the sun was crawling above the horizon, but the air was already feeling colder than the day before. Skye knew that winter was on its way south as well, and they couldn't afford to delay their departure any longer.

She took a walk around the tall wall that marked the outline of the inner courtyard and found her way to a set of wooden ladders propped up against the stones. At the top was a square, wooden tower into which Skye climbed. As her head emerged above the parapet, her breath was taken away. All around her she had an uninterrupted view all the way to the horizon. Away to the north she could almost imagine she could see the North Wood and even see Snudge stood outside his house in the forest. In the west, she could just about make out the snowy expanse of the Wandering Place that so recently she had thought would be her grave.

Skye turned and looked to the south. She saw

the towering monstrosity of Liorath's Peak looking imposing even from this great distance. She had expected to see a vast army amassed in the surrounding grasslands, but it seemed eerily empty.

Looking out over the land before her, Skye knew what she had to do. All of this land, every square inch in front of her, depended on her defeating the person who she was now starting to think of more and more as the Dark Queen.

If Skye failed, all would be lost. She could not afford to risk all of these lives for her own vanity. She knew in her heart that an attack from the north would be both expected and doomed. She felt that this was the future that she had seen in her vision and, more so, the vision that the Dark Queen had shown her in the Wandering Place. Her only hope, the only hope of all around her, was to sneak in through the south and steal Akeldama away undetected.

Skye tried to avoid thinking too much about what the druids had said just before she left. She couldn't afford to doubt those around her. She would rely on them to keep her safe as they approached the tower, and she wouldn't allow herself to suspect any of them of treachery.

Just as she was coming to this conclusion, Skye came to a rather more upsetting one. There was no way the nine of them would be able to sneak around the Peak and in through the southern entrance undetected. There were too many of them. Her only hope – indeed their only hope – was for Skye to enter the tower alone.

With her plan in mind, Skye climbed back down the ladder and set off to wake the group. She knew they would fight her on it, but she also knew that if she were to gain their respect she would have to hold firm. On the way back, she stopped off at Orthos's room and talked through her plan with him in some detail.

"I've made up my mind," she told her friends once they were all woken. "We will head south this morning and skirt past the Gloom. We must keep as close as is safely possible to the treeline to avoid detection from Liorath's Peak."

This was met with nods from the rest of the group who barely looked up from their breakfasts. Skye caught Snowbroth's eye as she continued.

"The plan will be to ride south of the Peak and to approach under cover of night. That way there is less chance of being spotted by her spies."

"South?" asked Yop. "What is wrong with a northern approach?"

"The druids have seen a future in which the

Dark Queen already knows of our presence and our intentions," explained Snowbroth. "They think she may be expecting a much bolder attack from the north, and so we must aim to catch her by surprise." He looked across at Skye, "It is a bold and wise decision from Skye. We would do well to follow her."

"Then follow her we will, right up the queen's throne and back out with Akeldama," replied Gondrag bluntly.

"No," whispered Skye, "you won't."

Even Snowbroth looked shocked at this.

"What do you mean, Skye? Surely you are not questioning our commitment to this cause?"

"Of course not, Snowbroth," she answered calmly. "If I am to have any chance of remaining undetected, even at night, I must enter the tower alone. Instead, you will continue on the Scirion Mountains that run to the south of the tower and proceed to the west.

"You will make as much noise as you can and draw as many of the queen's soldiers away from the tower as possible. That way, I hope, I will be easily able to slip in amongst the chaos."

Skye had expected the group to be annoyed at her decision, at her denying them the chance to join her in the key element of the quest. What she hadn't expected was the shouting and angry fist banging that followed.

"This is ridiculous, Snowbroth!" shouted Geldrig above the din, "She is too young to send in alone! I won't allow it!"

"Indeed," cried Weard. "Skye, this is too much you ask. We cannot send you to your death. You will not win in a battle against the Dark Queen's guards!"

Calmly, Skye stood up and motioned the rest to sit and be quiet. Surprisingly, they did as she asked. She sensed that, despite their outrage, they somewhat respected her intentions however foolhardy they considered them.

"I do not intend to fight anyone. Alone, I will be able to work my way towards and into the tower without much risk of detection. I spoke to our host last night, and he has shown me a brief outline of how the tower was laid out last time it was taken. I am confident that I can find my way in and out. Also, I have reason to believe that the Dark Queen will not harm me if she can possibly help it."

"Don't be so *childish*!" snapped Brack, "Whatever makes you think that?"

"I am not prepared to go into detail yet. My vision gave me some confidence, and I believe I should follow it to its conclusion. As for the rest of you, our host has assured me that the nightwolves we will be riding will outpace anything that is likely to chase us from the tower, wyvern's excepted. When you have lost your pursuers, you will make your way to the copse that lies to the south of the Scirion Mountains and make camp to await my return.

"This is possibly going to be a mission that I will not return from. I can't, and I won't, allow you to follow me on it. This is my decision. I will not be swayed."

Snowbroth asked Skye to leave the room for a moment whilst he discussed it with the rest of the group.

"We trust in your courage, Skye," he said, "but it is the future of our world, not just you, that is at stake. Allow us this courtesy, please?"

Reluctantly, Skye rose and left the room. She wandered twice around the courtyard before heading back to see where her fate lay.

"We admire your bravery, Skye," Snowbroth said quietly, "and we believe that your plan is foolhardy and reckless but nonetheless is the most likely to work. It is somewhat pleasing to see how much you have grown during the short time that we have known you, Skye. The 'Dark Queen,' as you call her, should be very fearful. Of course, we will ride with you, Skye." Snowbroth paused and looked around the group before continuing, "And then we will leave you."

Link

Skye left the group to finish its breakfast and made her way to their dormitory to pack her belongings. Once done, she wandered back out into the courtyard and towards the ladder that she had climbed the night before. At the top of the ladder, she was surprised to find Roke staring out towards the south.

"There is true evil on top of that peak, Skye," the druid said without turning around to face her. "I wonder why someone so young as you would set forth with such confidence."

"I have seen a future that I cannot ignore," Skye said. "Whilst this adventure could have many different endings, what I have seen cannot be undone or changed in any of them. What I have seen will happen and has already happened."

"What did you see that has stirred so much fire in your belly, timid human?"

How could Skye persuade them to believe what she had seen. She didn't even believe it herself. She chose to stay quiet and join the druid in looking south.

"You may, of course, keep your counsel as is your business, but, remember, we may yet help you before you leave our home."

Skye took a deep breath. "My mother," she said, flatly. "I saw my mother."

The druid didn't say anything.

"Yes," she finally said after a long pause. "That may be correct."

"I beg your pardon?" exclaimed Skye, exasperated. "You knew this?"

"No. How could we? We may have seen the same vision of the same queen, but I have never seen your mother before. We have heard stories of her, of course. She was one of the earliest humans to travel to Ithilmir. But most living druids have never seen her face. But I think it makes sense."

"How?" Skye asked, not able to draw her gaze away from the druid who still refused to look her in the eye.

"Snowbroth told me of the cherry tree that grows within the halls of Landragog, tended by Fen and his tree trolls. I am correct in thinking that it is linked to one in your mother's garden back home?"

"Yes, though it has died."

"Of course. I believe that when your mother left the seed for that tree behind, she left part of herself behind as well. A link to herself in your world. Though I'm not sure your language is able to accurately describe it."

"Her soul or her memory?" asked Skye, knowing full well that a few weeks ago she would have dismissed any of this as complete nonsense.

"Yes and no. I am sorry, Skye. I am not sure how to explain. I think that a living link to your mother remained in our world within the seed. There it lay dormant, ready to fly free but biding its time. Something triggered that tree to grow and the one in your garden to die at the same time. I believe it was your mother's link breaking free that did so. It brought your mother's energy back to our world."

"Then why the queen?"

The druid looked thoughtful for a while before answering. "I think the best explanation would be to think of the link to your mother as a living thing. Once it was free, it sought shelter and a willing host to support it. From what I understand, after speaking with Snowbroth, the sprouting of the cherry tree coincided with the first rumours of evil spreading in the south. It is my belief, as horrid as it seems, that the rise of Queen Camarina, of the Dark Queen, provided an open mind in which the link to your mother could take refuge."

"So," Skye began tentatively, "my mother is Queen Camarina?"

"Again, Skye, the answer is both yes and no. Queen Camarina was and is an evil creature spawned from an evil line of half-humans descended from the first arrivals on Ithilmir. Over time their spite and greed was distilled to an almost pure evil. She is the result. The very fact that she was nearly human possibly made it easier for her to accept your mother's spirit. Left alone, she would still have risen to power though who knows if she would have been as powerful."

"Is that why my mother was always trying to speak to the goblin prince or whoever she always talked about?"

"No. That is just one of your mother's quirks. Your mother would be well aware that goblins and the like exist on our planet. She may have been seeking them out in your own world. We don't exist there, of course. Equally, she may have been plagued with visions from Ithilmir, visions of her host mind. Imagine your mind being tuned to two different realities, one sharp and clear and the other fuzzy and on the edge of recognition." The druid's voice took on a darker, more severe edge. "Imagine how that would feel Skye. That is how your mother and the queen view the world, always interfered with by the other.

"You will be familiar to the Dark Queen on some level, Skye. That you can count on. I doubt that she will know who you are, though. She will only have faded memories, and I do not think that she is aware of the link with your mother. Who she is at heart is still the evil half-breed that crept from the shadows many years ago. Do not look to her for mercy. You will find her wanting."

Skye took a minute to let this all sink in before thanking the druid for her help. Taking her leave, Skye climbed down the ladder and found the rest of the group ready to depart.

At the entrance to the Druidmotte, nine nightwolves had been tethered and were sat on their haunches waiting. Each wolf was half as tall as Skye as they sat there. As she placed her hand against their warm bodies, she felt solid muscle rippling under their pitch-black fur as they moved slowly in position. There were no saddles on their backs nor reins around their neck. A mixture of emotions fought for Skye's attention, fear at the sheer size and power of the beasts but also a growing desire to appear brave and trustworthy to those around her. She was relying on them trusting her plan to take them into the queen's territory. To show weakness now would undermine that. She straightened up and forced her hand to stop shaking long enough to reach out and hold onto the shorter fur on one of the wolf's haunches.

"Here!" instructed the goblin who guarded the gate as he grabbed a longer patch of fur on a wolf's neck. "Grab them by the neck and don't let go. They are fast and strong and will attack with you on their backs. They are more lethal than any weapon you possess, so I suggest you let them do your fighting where possible."

Skye was led to a handsome wolf with piercing blue eyes. As she approached, it leant forward to allow her to climb easily onto its back. When it rose, Skye found that her feet dangled freely above the ground and her legs struggled to wrap around the thickness of the wolf's chest. Under her hands the fur felt soft and smooth, more like a cat's than the rough bristles that she had expected.

"From here, it is half a day's ride to the boundary of the Gloom." Roke had appeared behind them and stood firm in the gateway. "If you take my advice, you will make camp just short of there before continuing in the morning. Anything that you face as you pass that soulless forest will be better faced in daylight, and you will not make it past before nightfall tonight no matter how hard you ride.

"After that, it is a three-day slow ride around to the south of the Peak. Do not make too much haste if you can avoid it. It will attract more attention. Travel slowly and in the shadows of the forest where possible.

"Beyond the forest lies a series of shaded hills called Kalmir's Range. It is little known and unexplored. It used to be the home of a small band of Shrunken, but they have long left it to the wild. You will not be spotted travelling through there and is worth the extra effort."

Snowbroth thanked the druids for their help and hospitality. With a click of his tongue, he led the wolves and their riders back down the hill, weaving between the druids' tents. Skye felt sorry for them all waiting so long just to hear vague words from their elders, but she also knew that she had gained some comfort from her vision and her visit with Roke.

When they reached the bottom of the hill, Snowbroth led them south and away from the tents and into an area of thick meadows. Even though there were still flowers amongst the grasses, Skye could feel the chill rising in the air and felt moved to take her cloak from her pack and rest it on her shoulders.

"The queen will have ears everywhere we tread

now," Snowbroth told them as they left the hillside. "We must travel in silence as much as possible and keep ourselves low and hidden."

For many hours, they travelled in this way, each hunched down against their nightwolf's back, making every effort not to make a sound. As the air started to cool even more and the sun sank lower in the sky, they started to look for somewhere to camp. On the horizon, Skye could make out the black shadow of the Gloom and knew that tomorrow she would have to face that and more.

Gondrag warned against lighting a fire so close to Liorath's Peak, and so they spent the night in darkness, eating cold vegetables and strips of cured meat that the druids had sent with them and listening to the sounds of the insects in the grass. As they lay down to sleep, Brack started to sing a gentle lullaby in a half-whisper.

Over hill and under skies,
I go to sleep and rest my eyes,
A sweeter song she sang to me,
A peaceful, tender melody.

Over hill and under skies,
I go to sleep and rest my eyes,
Though tomorrow soon will come,
Take heed, my child, today is done.

Over hill and under skies
I go to sleep and rest my eyes,
Things are sent to challenge you,
But if you're brave you'll see them through.

Skye fell asleep with tears in her eyes thinking about the lullabies that her mother used to sing to her. She hoped more than ever to hear them again.

The Gloom

The next morning, Skye awoke to a hard frost on the ground and her blanket set stiff around her body. She stood up and broke the crust enough to pack her blanket away in her bag. The rest of the group were starting to wake up, as the sun was rising weakly over the horizon. Curglaff and Geldrig had set out before dawn to scout the way, and Snowbroth insisted that they breakfasted whilst they waited for them to return.

The morning passed quickly as they sat around the camp waiting for their friends. The sun was edging above the trees when the scouts finally returned with optimistic news.

"It is about an hour's ride from here," Geldrig told them as Curglaff wolfed down a quick meal of cold meat and recovered his breath. "Though that is mainly due to the fearful speed that these creatures can reach!" He nodded towards the nightwolf that he had ridden. "Truly amazing beasts."

"And of the enemy?" asked Snowbroth, eager for their full report.

"Nothing. A few remaining men who have fled the queen's reach and a few more who didn't make it that far but nothing more sinister than that," answered Curglaff between mouthfuls. "We skirted along the edge of the forest for a league or two and saw nothing through the trees. Either they aren't awake yet, or even the evils of the forest are too scared to roam near to the queen's realm."

"We must hope it is the latter," muttered Gondrag as he rose and climbed aboard his nightwolf. "It's almost noon already. We must ride now, or else we may not clear that sickened place by nightfall."

They resumed their positions from the day before and rode single file, pressed into the backs of their charges with their hoods pulled over their heads, partly for secrecy but mainly for protection against the falling temperatures. At this slower pace, it took nearly twice as long again to reach the outskirts of the foreboding forest, but none of them dared suggest stopping for food. Instead, they picked up the pace slightly and headed out across the open scrubland that bordered the thick, tangled treeline of the Gloom.

Circling in the sky high above them were several phoenix. Skye pointed them out to Brack.

"That is not good news. There will be death today if the phoenix are circling. Stay close, Skye, and keep your wits about you."

Skye could feel the evil in the air and could hear the whooping and hissing of dark creatures lurking in the trees just beyond sight. She knew that they couldn't risk going any faster but wished that they were able to leave this place far behind.

Suddenly, a deep trumpet echoed from the trees and rebounded across the arid landscape around them. It seemed to creep inside Skye's skull and threatened to shake her thoughts loose. Unable to let go of her wolf to cover her ears, Skye ducked her head even lower into its body.

As she leant forwards, she felt something whistle past her face nicking the skin of her cheek just below her eye. She raised her hand to her face and saw it covered in blood.

Looking around her, Skye saw volley after volley of thick-stemmed arrows flying from beyond the trees to their left. Each sheet of arrows threatened to rip into her body and send her flying. Ahead, Gondrag howled as a shaft punched into his side and dented his body armour. Skye knew that her leather cloak wouldn't offer as much protection.

Eventually, Skye's brain kicked into gear, and she heeled her wolf to full speed overtaking the rest of the group.

"To me!" she cried. "*Away!* Follow me!"

She had no idea where she was going, but she knew that they had to escape the range of the deadly bolts flying through the air. She pulled on the hair on the wolf's neck and veered it sharply away from the forest. Looking over her shoulder, she saw the others following. As she watched, she saw their attackers leave the forest canopy and begin their pursuit.

"Orcs!" Gondrag screamed and pointed towards the hideous creatures emerging from the trees. Each was taller than a man and wide across as a bull. Their faces were twisted with rage and criss-crossed with scars. Sharp, yellowed fangs hung over their lower lips and thick ropes of saliva hung from them whenever they screamed their piercing war cries. A thick blade hung from the belt strung around each waist, and every orc carried a fearsome crossbow in its hands. Bolts flew from these weapons of death like rain, and it was only the distance that still stood between the orcs and their quarry that provided any protection.

Skye still didn't dare release her grip enough to

draw Burrower, but Skye made sure that she could feel its welcome weight against her hip. As she looked back, she saw that the orcs were riding small flying creatures similar to the wyverns they had encountered outside of Lörieas only smaller and much more bat-like. Worse still, they were slowly catching up with them.

Skye turned in her seat and heeled her wolf to go faster even as she knew that it had no more to offer. Every time she glanced back, she saw the orcs creeping closer. She knew that her and her friends were outnumbered by more than ten to one. To her horror, Skye saw Brack pull his wolf to a halt and turn and draw his bow. Though he shot fast and true, he was only able to fell a handful of orcs before they surrounded him and he was crushed under their onslaught. Skye heard a scream of sorrow pierce the air before realising that it was her own voice, wrenched at the thought of losing yet another friend. She tried to turn her wolf to return to help Brack, but she was no match for the wolf's strength and so she surrendered to his will and continued to flee. She knew that she would have to wait to mourn her friend properly until all of this was over.

The nightwolves didn't manage to stay ahead of the orcs for long before they were finally overcome. The first attack came from the west as a group of three flyers attacked Gondrag. Skye watched over her shoulder as his wolf leapt into the air and ripped the head from the orc's mount as though it were catching a ball. The orc crashed to the ground and was trampled under the heavy feet of the wolf. The second orc approached more slowly and felt the steel of Gondrag's sword for its trouble. The third tried a full-out attack, and Skye was horrified to see it leap from its winged beast and land astride the wolf with its blade raised ready to hack into the Felmir's head. The orc punched hard between Gondrag's eyes, and Skye saw her friend collapse into the back of his wolf. The sunlight gleamed on the blade as it started to trace an arc through the air, but before the orc could strike his blow, the wolf had snapped its head back and dragged the orc to the ground without breaking its stride.

The first assault on Gondrag appeared to spur the other orcs on. They attacked freely, swooping in from all directions. Skye held on for dear life as her own wolf leapt and felled one orc after the other.

"Good boy," she muttered each time. "Keep going!"

Whenever his bite missed, Skye was there with Burrower to hack and flail at anything she could reach. Her technique was messy and rarely struck home, but it kept the orcs at bay long enough for the wolf to do his job. Around her, she heard screams and grunts and realised that Yop had disappeared in the melee.

She couldn't see his wolf anywhere and felt a stab of sadness. She had quite liked the goblin even if he had been quiet most of the time and moody when not. Most annoyingly of all, she'd never find out where he had disappeared to during the night. Where he had sneaked off to that was such a secret?

She didn't have time to dwell on it though. The phoenix were circling overhead and screeching their loud cries to remind the warriors that they were there to pick up the pieces after the fighting was over.

For what felt like hours, they raced across hard land that jarred the bones and brought them ever closer to the dark shadow of Liorath's Peak. It was too late to divert towards Kalmir's Range.

Without warning, Skye felt a sharp thud against her wounded shoulder and looked behind her in time to see an orc land on her wolf's back. Time slowed, and all Skye could see was the mist as it breathed its foul stench and the dark yellow puss that oozed from its teeth. She saw the blade swing round towards her neck. She waited. Ever closer, the blade crept along its arc, its chipped and blood-encrusted edge dull in the low sunlight. But it never connected. Skye ducked her head the only way she could and felt herself roll from the side of her wolf and land heavily on the compact earth below. She pulled herself into a ball and rolled hard and fast across the ground until she came to rest in the grass.

Skye rolled onto her back and stared up into the sun. She thought back to the day in the school field when she had lay looking up into the silhouette of Keith Boggart and considered just how different she felt now. Keith Boggart would never scare her again. After an orc, she could handle a fat, bald bully. She wondered if the orcs would just give her a knuckle rub and leave her be. The mere thought of that and the true impact of her situation were suddenly too much for Skye to contain. She burst into a sobbing laughter.

Propping herself up into her elbows, every joint in her body screaming in pain, Skye surveyed the carnage around her. Her friends had circled ahead and were heading back towards her but were still being pursued by the orcs and their mounts. They were heavily diminished though. Through fuzzy eyes, Skye could still count six mounted friends with wolves leaping and attacking.

Looking down at herself, Skye realised that she had come to a rest against the body of a dead orc. Its head had been mostly removed from its body, and its stomach lay open, the result of a nightwolf attack. It was clothed in a thin armour and the chest was painted with a crude outline of a dead cherry tree. One of its legs lay heavily across Skye's, and she leaned forwards to lift it free. As she lowered her head, a shadow cast over her, and she heard a hissing laugh from above.

"What's this then? Pretty little thing!"

Skye looked up into the dark red eyes of her attacker. Behind them, she saw her nightwolf lying dead on the ground, an orc blade jutting out from the back of its neck. She held back a sob.

"It's my lucky day." As the orc spoke, it licked its blistered lips slowly and dribbled through its sharpened teeth.

Skye saw her foe raise its blade high above its head and step forwards. She closed her eyes and braced herself for the impact. She waited. Instead, she heard a deep thud and a sigh.

She dared to open her eyes and saw the orc still stood above her but with a confused look on its face. Green blood trickled from the corners of its mouth, and it had dropped its blade. Instead, it was holding on to a thick arrow shaft that stuck through its chest.

With a final grunt, the orc toppled to the ground, narrowly missing Skye. A nightwolf pulled up in front her with a familiar goblin astride it.

"Brack!" she shouted, far too overwhelmed with

relief to consider her noise. "I thought—"

"They'll not kill me yet," he answered as he helped Skye to her feet and onto his wolf behind him. "They were flying. It was all too easy to roll underneath them and head the other way. They were too eager to catch you lot up."

Skye hugged the goblin tight from behind and smiled as they rode to help the rest of the group. By now there were fewer than a dozen orcs left. As soon as Brack started firing arrows at their backs, they soon withdrew back to the forest.

Once the orcs had fled and Brack had filled everyone in on his amazing escape, thoughts turned to Yop. Nobody had seen him fall and they couldn't find his mount, but there was no doubt that he was dead. As they had with each of their fallen friends, they built a simple cairn out of whatever stones they could fine and bowed their heads in prayer.

Their numbers even more diminished, their conversation returned to their current situation. Their battle had taken them far away from the Gloom but much closer to Liorath's Peak than they had hoped and too far away from Kalmir's Range for it to be of any use.

"She will know we are on our way," Skye argued. "Those orcs may have been a wild tribe, but they were all wearing armour bearing the queen's symbol of a dead white tree. I cannot go into detail now, but the rise of the Dark Queen is linked with the rise of the cherry tree within the halls of the tree trolls. I believe that she has taken it as her symbol. If so, these orcs were sent by her to ambush us. She is expecting us."

"What would you have us do?" asked Geldrig. "Should we find a place to rest until nightfall?"

"There will be no safe places here," Skye answered. "We must ride now and ride hard. We must follow the plan as before. We ride south and loop around. You will carry on and draw out as many of her soldiers as you can. I will find a way into the tower."

"Are you sure this will work?" asked Weard. Skye noticed that the healer was pressing her hand to a bleeding wound on her left arm.

"No," Skye answered flatly. "But I must do it anyway."

Brack leapt from his wolf and surrendered the mane to Skye. He climbed up behind Curglaff and held on to his hood.

Skye sat high in her seat and looked ahead towards the growing shadow of the Peak. She took a deep breath and bellowed as loud as she could. "We ride!"

Beneath Liorath's Peak

The ride to the base of the tower was fast and hard. Skye could feel her tired leg muscles screaming their annoyance with every bound. Brack's nightwolf was strong and powerful, and Skye could feel it doing its best to make the ride smooth. Even so, Skye was grateful when they finally came into sight of the southern side of Liorath's Peak.

What they saw when they arrived made a mockery of anything that Skye had planned.

Thousands of armed soldiers, representatives of all imaginable creatures but mostly of half-men, goblins and orcs, were scattered across the plains in front of them. Some were tending to dwindling campfires or setting down thick canvas tents, but most were racing around responding to an order to come to attention. Those garrisons that were more organised or well drilled were already forming into neat squares that were beginning to give the grasslands a patchwork effect. The ground was littered with debris and it was clear that the soldiers had been here for some time.

"She knew we were heading this way!" whispered Skye loudly enough for the rest to implore her to be quieter.

"Indeed she did," grunted Gondrag, "She must have messengers in the skies to know so quickly that we were arriving tonight. These soldiers have been ordered to attention. They are expecting something to happen soon. There is no way through now. We must change our plans and travel to the north entrance."

"There is no time," urged Skye defiantly. "I will make my way through to the south entrance as planned. If I wait until dusk, I will be able to make my way past the soldiers unseen." She tried her hardest to seem brave. Skye still believed that she stood the best possible chance on her own but on the inside her walls of bravery and defiance were crashing down. She'd known as soon as she'd set eyes on the amassed army that her chances of leaving this place alive had dwindled to almost nothing.

Nervously, Skye rubbed her thumb across her ring and immediately her vision was filled with the familiar dragon's tooth mountains of the Shadowlands. There was no wind blowing through the trees now, but the thick mist coiled snake-like around the protruding rocks. In the distance, a small figure was picking its way through the strewn boulders. Skye found a small rock and sat down to wait. Time had no place here in the Shadowlands. She felt like she waited for no more than a second yet the second took longer than a day. Slowly, the figure came into focus, and Skye couldn't help but leap to her feet and she ran and embraced the familiar figure.

"Brabble!" she cried as she flung her arms around her old friend. There was no substance to him though. He was simply formed from the white mist, and Skye found herself falling forwards to the ground. She pulled herself to her feet and turned to face the goblin who now looked old and frail and yet more full of vitality than Skye had ever seen him.

The figure wavered in front of her, flickering in and out of focus and always obscured by the thick fog, but there was no mistaking the gentle warmth that Brabble's friendly green eyes radiated. As she watched, she heard the goblin's voice inside her head.

You must continue, Skye! I know what you saw in the mask. You can still achieve what you set out to do. The queen can be defeated! You can still go home!

"How?" Skye asked. "The queen's army is too big.

There is no way past!" She was getting angry and frustrated. She wanted her friend to be alive, not here in the Shadowlands.

She knows you are here, Skye. She has known for a long time. I cannot tell you how. You must discover that for yourself, but proceed with caution. She is curious about you. She cannot figure out where your allegiance lies, and she sees that as something that she can use. It is you and you alone that she seeks. Be careful! Look for another way past her army. There is always a back way if you know where to look.

As the mist coiled away leaving no trace of Brabble, it suddenly reared up in front of Skye. Her whole vision was filled with the shape of her mother's face, only there was no warmth or love there. Her face had darkened, and her skin was mottled and hung loosely from her bones.

You will never defeat me! the queen's voice wailed inside Skye's head so loudly that she was convinced that the queen's soldiers would hear it. *You are mine, Skye Thistle, and I will destroy you!*

"You are a foolish little girl!" snapped Geldrig as he dragged Skye to her feet. The ring burned on her finger, but she didn't dare to remove it. Her friends seemed oblivious to her vision and seemed more concerned with her plan to proceed alone. "How do you plan on travelling past them all?" the Felmir continued as Skye stood opened-mouthed trying to calm her nerves.

Skye thought about what Brabble had said and about something that she had noticed when they first edged past the queen's army.

"They are stationed a good distance away from the base of the tower. I can sneak back the way we came and make my way behind the rearmost regiments, through the gap and to the base of the tower. It will work. I am certain." Skye felt her confidence growing the longer she argued her cause. If the queen had really been there in the Shadowlands and knew that she was here, then she would want to claim Skye for herself. Skye didn't know whether the vision was real any more than the one she had dreamt at home or had suffered through in the Wandering Place. It irritated Skye that she couldn't shake the feeling that they had been able to reach the tower so easily. Other than the orcs who Skye suspected were little to do with the queen and more bad luck, they had been able to approach the tower unmolested.

It may just be good fortune, she told herself, but she doubted it even as she thought it. *This is my battle*, Skye thought, *and I will fight it on my terms if I'm able!*

"She is right," offered Snowbroth thoughtfully. "We must do as she asks. Would you still have us draw out the army, Skye, now that there are so many?"

"I would ask that you draw attention away from the tower. The queen will not engage her entire army for a few rascals like you, I am sure. But with their attention drawn towards you I will be better able to sneak behind them." Again, Skye spoke with a calm and steady voice, but it belied her thumping heart and churning stomach. Expected or not, she knew that the queen hadn't invited her to a tea party. There was only one way that the queen sought to end this.

"From here, the base of the tower is close, close enough for them to hear any loud noises," whispered Snowbroth. "You must be careful and quiet in your approach, Skye."

"I will. Don't worry," she reassured him. "Hopefully you will be making enough noise and distraction to take the attention away from me anyway. Remember, don't make any noise until you are far enough away. The last thing I need is them snooping around here."

Brack took Skye to one side and showed her how to wrap her sword and other metallic items in cloth to make sure they didn't clink against one another as she rode. She thanked him with a hug and returned to the group as they were settling back into their saddles ready to ride.

"If I don't make it back…," Skye started.

"You will," interrupted Weard. "Our future depends on it, as does the future of everybody you hold dear."

"I will do everything I can. At the very least, I will steal Akeldama. If I need to, I will throw myself off the edge of the peak with it to make sure it is destroyed."

"The orb can only be destroyed by magic, Skye," explained Corngaff who Skye noticed had picked up a lot of knowledge about the orb whilst they were with the druids. "I fear that all you will be doing would be throwing away your own life. Be safe, Skye, but, above all else, be smart."

Skye nodded and climbed aboard her wolf.

"Remember, wait until you are west of the tower before you start your distraction."

With that, she retraced their steps and made her way towards the rear of the army.

After using a couple of dead vines to tether her nightwolf to a tree in the shadows, Skye moved silently behind the meagre cover of the bushes and trees that lined the hillsides, she made her way past the gathered forces of the queen's army. Regiment upon regiment upon regiment disappeared into the distance, all standing to attention and all heavily armed and ready to fight. Each wore upon their faces a decorated war mask carved from wood or forged from metal.

Except that they weren't.

As Skye moved unseen past the soldiers, she started to notice tell-tale signs. The shaking hand here, the badly held sword there. Underneath their war masks these soldiers were scared. As she looked closer, Skye realised that half of the men were no older than herself. These were the men and boys who had been dragged from their villages to fight for the queen. The men and boys whose only experience of a fight was outside of an inn or jostling with their friends where the stakes were low. Out here they were terrified. To Skye's horror, one of the boys in front of her broke rank, sobbing to his commander.

"Let me go home, you monster!" he screamed as he threw his mask and long spear to the ground. He fell to his knees and sobbed. Skye saw the man who had been stood next to the boy falter as he made to drag him back to his feet. Skye saw the same face echoed through the filter of time etched upon the older man's face. It was the boy's father. Skye saw the agony pass across his face as he realised what his son had done and the futility of trying to help. At that point, Skye saw just how beaten the villagers were. She knew that no parent would allow their child to come to harm if they could help it, but out here in the middle of a war, when these men and their families were harassed and beaten to within an inch of their miserable lives, their resolve became nothing. Instead, he stood to attention and stared into the distance.

The orc in charge of the soldiers saw the disturbance that the boy had created and bustled over, seething with rage. He leant down and dragged the child up by his neck.

"You want to leave the queen's army, boy? You want to go home to Mummy and your darling little sister?"

The boy sobbed quietly and nodded his head.

"Then off you go!" smirked the sergeant, releasing the boy from his grip and pointing away from the unit.

He risked a fleeting look towards his father who simply closed his eyes. The boy took off at a sprint, tripping over his feet as he tried to put as much distance between him and this hell as he could.

As Skye watched, the sergeant nodded his head and the archers loosed a hail of arrows.

The boy fell dead.

His father simply stood and watched. As Skye fought back the urge to grab the man around his shoulders and implore him to do something, anything, more to protect his dead son, she noticed tears running down his cheeks. The man was clearly not yet so broken down as to not mourn his son's passing, instead the callous mathematics of the evil war ahead took precedent. There was nothing he could do that would save his son, and so he had done nothing.

Crying silently to herself, Skye continued towards the darkest shadows at the foot of Liorath's Peak. Behind her, she hoped that her companions had set off in the opposite direction. She prayed that her plan would work and that they would go undetected for long enough for her to find an entrance to the Dark Queen's domain.

Far off in the distance, Skye heard the sound of her friends blowing war horns and screaming and shouting. Immediately, she heard a retaliating cry from the screaming hordes of the enemy. Skye cowered into the shadows as the hard sound of weapons being mustered and troops marching out filled the sky. Somewhere, a war drum starting beating a slow rhythm.

This might just work, she thought, not even daring to whisper it out loud.

Skye wandered back and forth looking for an entrance to the tower, retracing her steps time and time again, scouring every face of the rock for what felt like hours. It wasn't until she took a few steps out of the shadows that she noticed a roughly hewn set of steps carved into the stone.

She made her way forward and tried to locate the bottom step. She found that they were cut deeper into the rock than their shadows suggested, but it was still hard work climbing them.

There was no doubt that her adventures so far had made Skye fitter and stronger than she had ever been before in her life, but she still found herself regretting wasted PE lessons at school. Her legs felt like dead weights hanging from her body, and her arms protested with each grab. Her hands were chaffed and blistered, but still she climbed on.

Halfway up the rock face lay a ledge that hung out from the wall, counterbalanced by a large stone at the other end. Behind the stone and carved into the wall was a dark crevice. Skye crawled forward into the crack, turning sideways in order to fit.

The gap narrowed against Skye's waist as she edged further and further inside. She worried that soon she would become wedged. Just as she began to despair, she gave a final push and popped out into an airy corridor.

Even though the walls, floor and ceiling were still carved from the same rock as the narrow crevice, they had been polished and finished with fine engravings. This was obviously a passageway that saw use. The floor was worn with the tracks of people passing back and forth for generations.

Skye found herself dabbing tears from her wet

cheeks as she thought about her friends outside, giving their lives so that she could succeed. She had no way of knowing how many still lived.

Spurred on by their sacrifice Skye pushed herself forwards. Her hand never far from Burrower and the ring resting reassuringly on her finger. She hadn't dared to touch it since her vision, but it still brought her comfort to know that it was close by.

Silently, with her back to the wall, Skye made her way along the passage as it wound slowly upwards. Eventually, it exited into a wide, circular room lined with heavy wooden doors. Skye tested them all and found nearly all of them locked. Through the grates hammered into each, Skye could see more endless corridors.

Seeing the single open door as her only option, she pushed against it, cursing as it grated loudly against the stone floor and its hinges screamed in defiance.

Ducking back into the shadows, Skye waited for a few minutes to make sure that she hadn't been heard. When she felt sure, she headed along the new corridor with renewed urgency.

All along the wall, torches were hammered into the rock. As much as she would have loved more light to see by, Skye knew better than to light them. Instead, she withdrew the cherry branch from her pack and held it above her head, the soft glow removing some of the darker shadows.

All at once the wall started to crumble under Skye's fingertips, and she staggered forwards into a solid wooden door. Skye felt around the door for a latch and found a strong metal hoop that had rusted almost through. It took all of her strength to twist it loose and unbolt the door. Learning from her previous mistake, Skye made sure that she pulled the door slowly, though this time it swung open silently. As the door pulled back, a dim light crept through the crack and flooded the corridor. Though it was no brighter than a single candle against the deep darkness that Skye was used to it seemed brighter than the sun.

Not wanting to open the door fully, Skye slid through the crack and into the room beyond, shutting the door slowly behind her with a heavy thud. In fact, the room into which she stepped was lit by four thick candles which had been positioned around the outside of a circle about as wide as Skye's arms. However, it was what was inside the circle that took Skye's breath away.

In the centre sat a perfect stone sphere that rippled with a black inky quality like the surface of a pond. It shimmered with a beauty that Skye found difficult to resist. As she approached, Skye saw that the surface wasn't exactly smooth, here and there were pits where slivers of stone had been chipped away. Skye was transfixed.

She knew immediately what is was. It was Akeldama.

Betrayal

Nervously, Skye made her way towards the orb. As she got closer, the stone changed colour again and started to glow an intense aquamarine. Out of nowhere, it started to scream with an ear-piercing sound that made Skye recoil in pain. As soon as she backed away, the noise disappeared. She edged closer, more slowly this time, and again the room was filled with the horrendous noise. Unsure what to do, Skye ran back to the door through which she had entered but found that it had latched shut and there was no way to open it from her side. Stuck, Skye backed away into a corner. She cursed herself for being led into such an obvious trap. It had all been so easy that she'd allowed herself to become complacent.

From high up in the rafters came a slow thrumming sound. The noise grew louder and louder as it got closer and closer. It reminded Skye of the rhythmic chuffing sound of a steam engine slowly working its way through the English countryside. Silently, appearing suddenly out of the darkness, dropped a giant creature twice as tall as Skye and with twice as many heads. As it landed, it folded a pair of thick wings behind its back, the leather creaking against the strain.

As it circled the room, Skye could hear the animal sniffing the air. The beast's two dog-like heads moved independently of each other, sniffing in separate directions. They talked to each other with a series of high pitched squeaks that Skye strained to understand.

"Where are you, little *thief?*" one head hissed loudly.

Skye ignored the question and slid around the wall. She didn't notice the rock on the floor and stumbled over it sending it flying across the room. Immediately, the creature snapped round, and Skye found herself looking into two sets of dark red eyes. Each head had a long snout, similar to a fox, and a set of hideously disfigured teeth. As twisted as they were, they were lethally sharp. Skye gave up any idea of hiding. She rose to her feet, drawing Burrower.

The blade of her sword caught the candlelight as she danced across the floor, sending rainbow reflections dancing across the walls. Skye tried desperately to remember the techniques that she had been taught before they set off on this adventure, but her aching limbs made it hard to get any rhythm with Burrower. She circled the room quickly, keeping her sword in front of her face at all times, expecting an attack that never came. All the while, the orb was glowing brightly in the middle of the circle, screaming whenever she approached too closely.

Every now and again the creature would half-heartedly lunge forwards and attack with one of its snouts, but Skye was able to easily parry them. It soon became clear that the creature was being cautious, even scared. Skye knew that she didn't have time to wait for it to attack properly. For all she knew, Akeldama had alerted more soldiers who were on their way to the room at that very moment. Worse still, every minute she spent inside the tower was another minute that her friends and companions were fighting for their lives.

Taking matters into her own hands, Skye feigned a dodge to the left before leaping over the glowing stone and lunging at where she hoped the heart of the beast would be. Unfortunately, the creature didn't fall for the feint and rolled its shoulders, throwing Skye back across the room and into the stone wall. She felt the air rush from her lungs, and she doubled over, gasping for breath.

"Silly thief!" the creature hissed loudly, "You are weak and stupid, and we are not. You cannot beat us. The queen will rule the land. Whoever you are, thief, you will be destroyed and you will be forgotten."

Skye stood up straight and gulped in mouthfuls of air, trying hard to calm herself. In an instant, the creature leapt across the room with open wings and pinned Skye to the wall with its sharp claws. She could smell the animal's breath as it moved its heads closer to hers and a cold, wet tongue licked at her face, tasting her.

Shuddering at the sensation, Skye tried to move her hand into position so that she could strike out with Burrower, but it was hard going. Her attacker had her pinned tightly.

"Stop wriggling, thief! Why resist? It only prolongs the inevitable!"

Skye sagged with acceptance, and her shoulders dropped. In that moment, the creature loosened its grip and Skye was finally able to move her hand. She twisted Burrower and thrust it upwards. She felt it slice through the thick leather of the wings and saw with satisfaction the shredded mess that it left behind. The creature howled in pain and staggered back clutching at its bleeding wound.

Seizing her opportunity, Skye leapt forwards with

all her strength and hacked Burrower down over its head. She felt her shoulder jar as it sliced into one of the necks, stopped only by the thick spine. As she tore her blade away, the head fell limp and hung horrifically from the half-severed stump. The other head still lived and screamed with rage. The beast staggered to its feet and lunged at Skye, but it was moving with anger now without thought. Skye dodged the first attack, but the sharp claws ripped into her shoulder and opened a fresh wound. As she turned and howled, the creature snapped at her side, and she felt its teeth pierce her midriff. Acting on instinct and adrenaline, she hacked her sword down into the animal's back. It slashed across the flesh and opened a deep cut from wing to wing.

Again, the creature screamed, and this time it tried to flap its wings to escape. The damage done by Skye meant that it couldn't leave the ground. Skye rushed across the floor, thrusting her bloodied blade upwards under its ribcage. She felt the cold blood gush from the wound and over her hand, but still she stood, twisting the blade slightly inside the creature. She watched the last signs of life flicker from its eyes. Only when she was sure that it was dead did she push her foot against the creature's chest and pull Burrower free. She looked down and saw that her hand was covered in thick purple gore and her arms and hands were criss-crossed with scratches, some of them very deep. She staggered over to the corner of the room and threw up, the intensity of the situation overwhelming her.

No matter how she turned it over in her head, Skye had taken the life of another creature. When she had killed that first Nelapsi in the streets of Lörieas it had been hard, the final strike had come from within her and it had scared her. She'd felt momentarily sad for the creature, even though it had been trying to kill her. Even during that battle, it had grown easier with each monster that she slew. This time, she hadn't even thought about killing this beast. She had struck out and attacked and did what needed to be done. It helped that they were trying to kill her, but Skye was worried about what she was becoming. She was only fourteen years old. This is not what a normal fourteen-year-old should be doing.

She reassured herself that this was just a means to an end, that once the task was over she would never have to hold a sword again. It didn't make her feel much better.

When she had calmed down, Skye made her way to the centre of the room towards Akeldama. Not wanting to waste any time, Skye picked the stone up and placed it into her bag. It was a lot lighter than she had imagined. It felt hollow, almost like it was made of glass. It was ice cold to the touch, as though it removed all warmth from anything in its presence. Despite it only being a stone, Skye couldn't help but get the feeling that it was somehow alive, maybe even sentient. She felt uncomfortable referring to it as an *it*.

"I'd put that down if I were you."

The voice came from a ledge above Skye in the shadows halfway up the stone wall.

"You were very impressive against the orcs, Skye. Brabble taught you well."

The voice made Skye wretch. She was overcome with a rising tide of fury and despair. She felt the anger boiling up inside her again. She felt the ring burning on her finger and the power flowing. She fought the burning power. She was scared by what she might do.

"Yop?" she stammered, "What are you doing in here? I…we…thought you were dead."

"Dead?" he chuckled, "No, not dead. You see, I could never make it here on my own, but you were all so very eager to sneak in and take what I wanted that I couldn't pass up the chance."

"You want Akeldama? Why?"

"Elflock is right, Skye. We cannot defeat the queen by sneaking in through the back door and stealing away in the night. Akeldama will give us the power for all-out war against her and any other evil that rises ever again. We will be safe forever. Can't you understand that?"

Skye drew Burrower and approached Yop, who dropped down silently from the ledge. He didn't draw his sword but circled around the wall away from Skye.

"You are in league with Elflock? You traitor!" she hissed.

"In a hundred years, Skye, I won't be a traitor. I'll be a hero." He was moving more quickly, edging further and further away. "Elflock is right. We do need a war. It will defeat the queen, sure, but it will cleanse our people, Skye. Imagine, all of those who are not worthy to call themselves G'Oräk, all of those who aren't *pure* goblin. We can send them off to fight for us. 'For the honour of the tribe' we will tell them. And then they will die, and we will be left with a pure race. A stronger race."

"That's horrible," Skye spat. "That's genocide."

"Oh, call it what you will, you *naive* little girl, but we cannot have our race watered down."

Yop brought his hand from behind his back holding a short dagger. He lunged forward and slashed at Skye's chest. The blade sliced through her cloak. She felt it cut into her flesh, not deeply, but it was still very painful. She staggered back and managed to recover her footing in time to dodge the goblin's next thrust. She dropped to the floor and rolled away. When she stood, she found that Yop hadn't followed her. He was stood on the opposite side of the circle chuckling quietly to himself as he wiped her blood from his blade.

"Look what happens when species are allowed to mix." He nodded towards the door. "Queen Camarina? Snudge told us that she was descended from the first race of men. The first human to help *Snudge*. He let her loose on our world. He has never been a very good judge of character, has he?"

Skye dropped her head and thought. Slowly, she raised her head high.

"No," she whispered, "he hasn't been. But not with me." She lunged across the circle and thrust Burrower over Yop's defensive arm and towards his face. "With you," she screamed.

Yop parried the blow just in time, but not before Burrower's tip scraped along his cheek and cut across his eyelid, blinding him in one eye. Howling in pain, he dropped his dagger and scrambled up the wall and back onto the ledge above.

"Snudge cannot win, Skye," he wailed. "His time is short. Elflock *will* command the G'Oräk."

With that he disappeared into a crack in the wall and was gone.

Skye sat back against the wall, her head spinning. She had to let the others know. She had to get a message back to Snudge to let him know that he was in danger. She didn't know how she could do that, but she knew that Yop would be heading straight back to Elflock to tell him that she had Akeldama.

Skye fought back the urge to throw up again. They knew that she had the stone. They would stop at nothing to get it from her. She wasn't safe whilst Elflock was free to do as he pleased.

You're doing it again, she thought. *This is too easy, too neat. How did Yop manage to get into the tower so easily? Surely you don't believe that he's done all of this for Elflock?*

Skye knew that she didn't have time to think about the whys and wherefores right now. She had a mission to complete. Fortunately, it seemed that her former ally would lead her straight to the queen, and so she made her mind up to follow Yop wherever he was headed.

Making sure that Akeldama was safely secured in her bag, Skye turned to follow Yop up on to the ledge. She couldn't climb as well as the goblin, and it took her a good while before she was sat, out of breath, on a thin stone that stuck out from the bricks. Feeling around, she found the crack and breathed in so that she could edge through before dropping out into another corridor on the other side.

This time Skye found the corridor well-lit and with nowhere to hide. Expecting an ambush from Yop at any time, she quickly made her way to the end of the passageway and soon emerged through a brick-lined doorway onto a large open platform on which burned a towering bonfire.

Skye stopped dead, choked into silence by the scene playing out in front of her. The large fire raged in the middle of the barren summit. Thrusting upwards erupting from the centre of the flames was a large wooden spike onto which was strapped a writhing wretch of a boy shrouded in smoke. Skye felt the sickness rising in her throat and fought back the urge to vomit.

It was Arthur.

The Dark Queen

Skye stopped breathing. Arthur was screaming in agony as the flames licked across his body. As he twisted on the spike, his arms and legs bound behind him, Arthur looked directly into Skye's eyes.

"Help me!" he screamed. His words reached Skye's ears, but she couldn't process them. This was too much. It wasn't fair! Arthur wasn't part of the deal! She had never wanted him to be part of all of this. Her main reason for wanted to go home so badly was to see him again.

Skye watched on from the shadows too afraid to move. She'd raced headlong into the cavern and had almost paid the price. Her arms were still bleeding in places where the foul two-headed ghoul had savaged her. Arthur was crying now, his tears running dry in the intense heat of the flames. Smoke rose around him, and Skye had to strain to see him clearly. She wanted to race out onto the tower so badly to save him, to pull him down from his mount and tend to his injuries, to be the supportive one for once rather than the one needing support in their friendship. She had to physically hold onto the doorway lest she run out to her doom. Her fingernails were digging into the bricks and mortar, and her fingers bled as she clenched the wall with all her might.

Arthur's screams changed now from begging for help to the soft unholy wails of a body whose soul has given up. Skye couldn't fight back her tears any longer and sobbed uncontrollably as his body stopped moving in the flames, and he relaxed almost as though he were asleep. Skye dragged herself back further into the shadows and buried her head in her hands in an effort to silence her cries. As she wiped away the tears, she forced herself to look once more into the fire.

Something wasn't right.

Skye watched the forlorn figure closely. She realised that Arthur wasn't surrounded by smoke as she had originally thought, the smoke was drifting and forming into the shapes themselves. The Arthur in the flames was merely an image, an illusion created by the drifting vapours of the very real fire. It was a trap.

Skye wanted to scream a mixture of happiness and

feral anger. At that moment, she hated the queen more than she had ever thought possible. How dare she try to take the most precious thing in Skye's life? How dare she think that Skye would be so weak as to throw herself at the queen's mercy so easily? After all that she had been through?

It did mean one thing, though. The queen knew that Skye had arrived and was trying to entice her out onto the tower. Skye knew that to run out now would be folly. The queen would be waiting and would destroy her in an instant. She had to think.

No matter how much Skye knew that what she was seeing wasn't real, the obvious anguish that Arthur – that the creation, she reminded herself – had shown was far too realistic. She'd had to turn her eyes away from the gory illusion as it unfolded for her benefit. What if Arthur really was in pain or worse, and this was just a reflection of that created by the queen's dark magic? The thought of anything happening to Arthur was too much for Skye to bear.

In her bag, Skye felt Akeldama rattling against her hip as though it were trying to escape. She brushed her fingers over it, trying to calm it, but still the orb continued to move, agitated at its imprisonment. She could sense the darkness reaching out and clawing at her thoughts. Then it struck her. The orb was reading

Skye's mind and was feeding her innermost fears into whatever magic the queen was using. The queen knew nothing of Arthur or what he represented. All she saw was what Skye feared the most. The queen obviously felt that would be enough to destroy her spirit. Skye was determined to prove her wrong.

She glanced back towards the fire. Arthur was no longer burning in the flames. Now the vision had changed, morphing into a vision of Skye's father strapped to the wooden spike as unseen hands flogged him with thin whips. Skye flinched as they cut into his flesh and his ethereal screams rang around the tower. His blood flowed freely charting a course like rivers down his back. Skye breathed deeply as she watched her kind-hearted father suffer the most brutal torment.

This isn't real, she reminded herself over and over. *Your father is fine and safe back on Earth, just like you will be as soon as this is over.*

Only it wasn't her father anymore, now it was her mother twisting in agony as she hung from gallows, a thick rope noose tied around her neck. Her veins were bulging and her eyes large in her distorted face as she clawed at her throat in a desperate bid for air.

Enough!

Skye pulled herself together and stepped forwards onto the tower. Immediately, the visions disappeared leaving only imprints in her eyes and the flames roaring into the night sky. She shivered despite the intense heat of the fire and made her way slowly to the edge of the cliff expecting at any moment to feel the sharp sting of magic as it ripped her apart or the excruciating warmth of a blade thrust into her back. Nothing came, though. Skye looked down over the edge and immediately reeled at the dizzying drop.

Off to the west, a tall column of dust rose into the dawn sky. She hoped that it was the goblins riding away. She could see scores of tiny ants in pursuit and was relieved to see that they were not catching up.

"They will tire, my dear, and then they will kill them."

Skye didn't want to look around. She knew that voice. It was as familiar as the breakfast she had every morning or the feel of her own mattress under her back. Alone in the Wandering Place, the voice had sounded cold and distant, nothing like her mother's. Here though, it was uncanny. The queen was taking on more and more of her mother as she grew stronger.

"I know who you are, Carmine," Skye said without turning around.

"It doesn't matter who I *was*, Skye. It matters who I have become!"

Skye was forced to turn around and face the queen.

She was shocked by just how much like her mother the queen looked. Even down to her dress. It was far more glamorous than anything her mother would ever wear, but it was definitely cut from the same cloth. It was as though the queen had taken one of Skye's mother's dresses and improved it tenfold. On her head she wore a small, silver tiara that reflected the light of the fire brightly. Her feet were bare but perfectly porcelain in their appearance, untouched by the dirt beneath them.

Her face, as well, was more similar than before. Her skin was pallid and grey but still managed to glow with an inner beauty that had long left Skye's own mother. Her eyes glimmered with a green shine that seemed to pierce Skye's soul. She could feel it grating across her brain like a rake and had to close her eyes and look away to make it stop.

As Camarina looked into Skye's eyes, she stopped, taken aback. For a moment, something seemed to confuse her, and Skye hoped that she wouldn't recognise her. Could the queen access Skye's mother's memories? Would she know about the link at all? Shaking her head, the queen let it pass and returned her attention to Skye.

"How can you hope to defeat me, Skye?" she asked, quietly.

Skye looked away.

"*Look at me!*" screamed the queen as a flash of light erupted around Skye.

Skye found herself picked up by an invisible force and brought face to face with the Dark Queen. As she looked deep into her eyes, Skye saw nothing but pure, dark power. She could convince herself that she could see the whole universe in those eyes, stretching away to infinity and all controlled by the powerful witch in front of her.

"You can see it, Skye, can't you? You can see how insignificant you are compared to me. You are *nothing*."

It was all true, Skye knew. The queen was only confirming what Skye had always feared. She was too powerful, too beautiful to look away from. Skye was angry and upset. Tears streamed down her face as she realised the pointlessness of it all.

"Be careful, my queen. She is a tricky one."

Skye snapped her head around and saw Yop walking out on to the platform.

"*You!*" she cried, though it was nothing that she hadn't already suspected whilst back in the cavern under the tower.

"Oh, be quiet, you fool," he spat. "Did you really think I'd be fighting for Elflock? That warmonger?"

He knelt at the feet of the queen and bowed his

head.

"You are the only one that I serve," he snivelled. "She has the stone in her bag," he offered, standing up.

The queen's eye flicked back to Skye and down to her bag. Skye saw a glint of metal as the queen flicked a knife across her stomach. For a moment, Skye expected to feel the sharp pain of the blade, but when she looked down she saw that the queen had simply cut her bag straps. Skye watched in horror as Carmine removed the orb from the satchel and placed it carefully on a flat stone to her side.

"Thank you, goblin." She spoke to Yop without taking her eyes away from Skye. "You have served me well. Without your information each night, I might not have been as prepared for our little guest as I am."

Realisation dawned on Skye.

"So that's where you were sneaking off to you traitor...you...*rahul*!" she spat, struggling to find words to do the goblin's betrayal justice. She'd known that Yop had betrayed them since she'd found Akeldama and had even suspected that he might be helping the queen, but the sheer and utter horror of what that meant struck her all at once. Brabble had died, as had Longcraw, to try to defeat the queen. They had been doomed from the start by one of their own. They had died for nothing. Worst of all, Skye found herself realising, she had never had a chance of making it home once Yop had decided on his course of action.

"My queen, it is an honour," he bowed again, ignoring Skye's outburst.

"It *was* an honour," the queen began. The goblin looked up confused. "Now that I have the girl, I don't really need you, do I?"

Yop opened his mouth to protest, but his words were stolen from his mouth. The queen waved her wrist through the air, and Skye watched in horror as a deep cut opened up across Yop's throat. There was no blade needed. This was dark magic. This was the power of Akeldama.

Skye almost felt sorry for her treacherous friend as he gasped for air and clutched at his wound. It took him a long time to die, but the queen never took her eyes away from Skye.

Once again Skye looked deep into the queen's eyes. Something had changed since she had first stepped foot on the top of the tower. It was as though the queen had been wearing a mask of innocence, something to draw Skye into her power. Now the mask had been lowered. Taking the life of her former servant had drained something from the queen, part of her soul. Skye remembered being told that the queen would forfeit part of herself each time she drew power from

Akeldama, and Skye was witnessing that very fact.

The closer Skye looked, the less of her mother she saw in the queen. Her features were certainly similar and she had no doubt that there was a link, but below the hard features of the face there was no similarity. There was no warmth behind the eyes. There was no love. Roke had told Skye that the queen's appearance was just a vessel that her mother's spirit needed to live. Skye couldn't help think it was the other way round.

Her mother hadn't left part of her spirit behind. If she had, then the queen would be more like her mother's personality. Instead, her mother had left behind an imprint of her image, a reflection in time. The evil that had risen in the south had found this reflection floating around without a soul and had taken over like a parasite. There was nothing of her mother inside this monster, just darkness.

When Yop had finally breathed his last, the queen flicked her wrist again and Skye found herself floating through the air, still held in place by an invisible force field. She struggled desperately against her bonds as she floated beyond the edge of tower and stopped, suspended thousands of metres above the ground that waited far below.

"I could let you go, Skye. It would be the simplest thing."

Skye couldn't get any words out. All she could focus on was the gaping void.

"This is power, girl. You think that your goblin leader has power as he sits on his throne and tells those vermin what to do? That's not power. That's *weakness*. He allows his subjects a *choice*, as though they matter!" She laughed maniacally, and Skye felt herself thrown through the air.

Skye felt herself released as she fell and rolled to a standstill at the queen's feet. She stood up and clumsily drew Burrower in front of her.

"You silly girl!" The queen laughed cynically. "Your metal is no good against me! You have seen my power. I could destroy you with a flick of my hand."

Carmine slowly circled Skye. As she passed, she brushed her fingers through Skye's hair.

"Such a pretty prize," she whispered. "Killing you would be such a waste. Maybe you need to be mounted on my wall like a stag?" She twitched her head, and Skye flew across the tower and crashed into an old brick wall where she was held in place.

"Or perhaps you'd be better as a figurine?" she cackled.

This time Skye was thrown towards a crumbling marble plinth, and she found her limbs moving into unnatural positions, posed like a statue in a stately garden.

Time after time, the Dark Queen threw Skye around like a marionette, amusing herself each time with a different pose. Eventually, Skye collapsed to the floor, sobbing and exhausted. Her joints screamed their defiance, and every one of her wounds ached.

The queen approached Skye and leant down to stroke her damp cheeks.

"You poor thing," she mocked. "You thought that you could just walk into my home and leave with my power? You wouldn't even have made it here if I hadn't let you. The goblin was useful, certainly, and you've shown more tenacity than I thought you would. Do you know how valuable you are, Skye?"

"The prophecy," Skye choked.

"Yes! You don't have to fulfil it, though. You could still join me!"

"Never!" Skye screamed and lashed out with Burrower. She was too far away to do any real damage, but she sliced across the top of the queen's bare feet and watched with satisfaction as they opened up and blood flooded from the wounds. The queen howled with rage and backed away towards the doorway. Akeldama glowed brightly as she drew on all of its power, ready to destroy everything that Skye was and had ever been.

Seeing her chance, Skye leapt through the air

and knocked the stone plinth over, sending the orb crashing to the floor. As it landed on a sharp rock, it splintered and the light inside it dimmed. A shard of glass shot away and fell beside Skye's hand. She grabbed it up before the queen noticed. The orb rolled away from Skye towards the edge of the tower. She heard the queen squeal in her rage as it disappeared over the edge and fell from sight.

Screaming in defiance and pain, Skye shook her head clear and jumped to her feet. Bellowing, she raced across the platform towards the queen ready to attack. The queen cackled loudly and waved her hands in front of herself. Skye felt a force pick her up and throw her to the floor, but it was not as strong as she had expected. As she looked over at the queen, Skye knew that something was wrong. Camarina was staring at her hands with disbelief.

"My powers," she whispered. "What have you done?" she screamed at Skye, spit frothing at the corner of her mouth as her rage grew.

"Akeldama is gone. Without that you are nothing. You forget that your power is not your own. It was borrowed. Your power is weak, *Carmine*." Skye spat the words with venom. "Those creatures," she pointed towards the battle in the distance, "they follow you through fear, not through respect."

Skye pulled herself upright and lowered her voice so that the queen could only just hear her. As she spoke, she approached and circled her weakened enemy who sat shivering on the cold ground. In her hand, Skye felt the ring heat up as her anger grew. Without looking down, she knew that it was glowing. Skye could feel power coursing through her arms and into her soul. It felt as though somebody had poured sherbet into her brain.

Not yet, she thought, *the time will come.*

"There was a time when I thought that I wanted all-out war, you know," Skye whispered as she continued to walk around the stricken queen. "There was a time when what I thought I wanted was to be the hero. I wanted a fight at your gates, and the chance to watch you die in battle. I thought that I wanted songs sung about me."

"You can still have that!" cried the queen.

"I was *stupid*," hissed Skye. "You don't deserve that. You are a weak little creature who feeds off the fear of those around you. I followed a group of goblins and men that I barely even knew. I didn't follow them because I was afraid of them or afraid of you, though I must admit I *was* afraid of them. I followed them because I knew deep down that they were honourable, and I kept following them when it got tough because

I learnt to respect and trust them. You know what? Because of that, they trust and respect me. That is why they are out there now fighting for their lives so that I can come in here and defeat you. If you died now, would your monsters still fight for you? Would they lay down their own lives to avenge you? I doubt it."

She continued to circle the queen, growing ever more confident.

"I am here to kill you," said Skye, matter-of-factly. "If this were a story, I would let you live and send you away weaker to learn your lesson. This isn't a story though, and I can't take that chance. I have to kill you, Carmine, so that I can rest easily at night knowing that my friends are safe."

Skye drew her sword above her head and lowered it to the queen's neck.

"Consider this a blessing, Carmine. I am releasing you from the evil that you have created."

The queen's eyes flickered away from Skye for a split second. In the moment that Skye followed her gaze, the queen ducked and rolled away drawing her arms up in front of her chest.

Skye felt the magic drawn from the tower before she saw it materialise in a glowing ball of red fire between the witch's hands. Without thinking, she closed her eyes and felt the anger rising inside her once again. On her finger, her mother's ring glowed white-hot though there was no heat on her finger. This time Skye let the power grow. She let it course through the soles of her feet and travel through her veins and tingle at her fingertips. She opened her eyes and saw the growing orb of light that she held in her own hands. This time, she knew she had to more to come. She could feel a darkness coming from somewhere deep inside.

Inside Skye's pocket, the sliver of Akeldama started to glow and vibrate. Inside her head, the voices started to whisper to her.

"Use us!"

"End this now. You have the power!"

Skye found herself embracing the power. She had never felt so strong in her life! Her fingertips shook as she accepted everything that her ring and the stone had to offer her. All at once, the light exploded outwards from her core like ripples on a pond.

The queen screamed as the blinding light ripped through her and her body was torn apart. As she faded away into dust, a ghost of a shadow flew out of the light and into the sky.

As it fled, it whispered, "I'll rise again, Skye. You shall not destroy me!"

Escape

Skye blinked her eyes open struggling to believe that she was still alive. The clouds overhead continued to be bleak and grey and the temperature remained icy cold, but Skye was certain that she felt a shift in the air as the queen's power wavered as her soul had fled. Out on the plains the queen's forces had all stopped and were staring into the sky as their mistress disappeared into the ether. Whatever spell she had cast over them with her fear and destruction appeared to melt away with her. Skye soon heard horns calling a retreat to the remaining evil forces. She breathed a sigh of relief that those goblins who still stood were no longer in immediate danger.

At the southern edge of the tower, behind a derelict throne, a crumbling gateway was set into a wall. The wooden gate had long since rotted from its hinges, and it hung limply across the path, standing only because it rested against the stones of the gateway itself. Scratched into the dark wood was a handprint, not dissimilar to the one that the G'Oräk wore on their clothes. Skye made a point of trying to ask more about the history of her new friends when her mind was less fuzzy. For now, she would settle for sleep.

A loud crack echoed around the tower as Skye pushed the gate from its resting place and sent it crashing onto the stone floor.

The queen had fled. Skye had been so close! She kept reminding herself that she had only succeeded in part of her task. She wasn't sure where Akeldama was or whether it would or could be found, and she hadn't managed to destroy the queen. That had always seemed the harder of the two tasks, especially since she had learned of the link between the Dark Queen and her own mother. She wasn't sure that she could ever look into those familiar eyes and strike a killing blow, no matter how evil the shadow was.

She felt reassured that the queen wasn't aware of the link. That would be more dangerous than Skye dared to think about. For now, she had to console herself with the fact that the queen's power had been severely weakened.

Skye sighed and edged through the debris, using the

wooden gate as a platform over the crumbling ground. Hanging over the edge of the tower were a series of wooden rungs bolted into the rock face. Looking down, Skye was again overcome with sickness and fear. She was higher than she had ever been before, and she knew that the only way home lay at the bottom of the makeshift ladder. Each rung was only as thick as Skye's wrist, and there was no space behind them to wrap her fingers into. She would have to make do with gripping tightly with her fingertips and wedging her toes in below.

There was little wind once she lowered herself below the top of the tower, only a refreshing breeze broke the calm dawn air. Below, smaller carrion birds joined the phoenix on the battlefield. She hoped that they wouldn't be feasting on any of her friends. It helped to think of her companions waiting below to congratulate her. She dreaded telling them that she had failed.

Breathing slowly, Skye lay down onto her stomach and lowered her legs over the edge. The rough stone floor scratched at her stomach through her ripped T-shirt as she twisted round. The wound that Yop had inflicted across her chest opened again and started to bleed. She felt her elbows scraping against the sharp rocks. Slowly, she lowered her legs down and shuffled her body backwards.

Rung by rung, Skye settled into a rhythm of moving one foot and one hand at a time. It took her well over an hour to climb halfway down the slippery ladder and soon the sun was casting a weak light onto her back.

Before long, she found herself back on the ground and praying to whoever happened to be listening that she would do everything she could to never be that high again.

Full of shame at her failure, Skye made her way around the base of the tower until she found the tree to which she had tethered her nightwolf the night before. To her horror, it wasn't there.

Behind her, Skye heard a crack in the woodland. She spun round on her heels, drawing Burrower. Any remaining confidence evaporated instantly, and she cowered back into the shadows trying to spot whatever was out there hunting her and ready to attack.

Slowly, Skye worked her way backwards until she felt the reassuring sensation of cold rock against her back. Something didn't feel right, though. Skye felt the hairs on the back of her neck stand on end.

"Just because you got rid of the queen, do you think you're some kind of hero? Want me to sing a song about you *Skye Thistle*?" The laugh was familiar and very welcome and Skye relaxed as the voice washed over her. She turned around and gave her would-be-attacker a long hug.

"Brack!" she shouted, "You had me scared for my life!" She started to playfully hit the goblin around the arms as he feigned injury.

"Where are the others?" she asked after they had finished their roughhousing.

"Hidden in the woods. They have your nightwolf with them. They are ready to hear of your brave deeds, but, more importantly, they are ready to go home."

"I couldn't agree more," said Skye, dreading what she would have to tell them.

She allowed Brack to lead her away into the trees. It wasn't long before they arrived at a clearing made warm and bright by a small but healthy fire. A small deer hung on a spit, roasting slowly. Every now and again the fire would leap higher as a drop of fat spilt onto the embers.

A quick count of heads left Skye dismayed. There were three less than they had set out with the previous night.

"Where is Corngaff?" she asked, "And Geldrig and Gondrag?" Her eyes were filling up with tears.

"Corngaff and Geldrig have gone to find food for the wolves and wood for the fire," Snowbroth started.

"Gondrag is no longer with us." Their leader lowered his head to the ground.

"What happened?" wailed Skye.

"He fought well and went to his death with honour." Geldrig had entered the clearing without Skye noticing.

"I am so sorry." Skye fell to her knees at the Felmir's feet. "It is my fault," she sobbed.

"Get to your feet, little hero." Geldrig's reply was soft and forgiving. "My brother fought last night because he knew you were a cause worth fighting for. He died doing what he loved best. He was a fighter, and he has died with a fighter's honour." Geldrig looked directly into Skye's eyes. "You wanted songs of heroes and villains, of battles won in glorious style? Yet you weep for my brother as a huge loss. How would you command ten thousand men to die the same?"

"I was foolish," Skye stuttered, lost for words.

"We were all foolish when we were young. It is how we move on from our foolishness that defines us. You will learn from this and be a better leader because of it. One day you will lead armies into battles worthy of song, and I shall be there at your side." With these words, Geldrig lowered himself in front of Skye and knelt on one knee, head bowed before her.

"I would be honoured to fight alongside you,

Geldrig," she whispered, "but I have failed in my quest." She lowered her head and sat softly on the grass.

"How is this?" asked Corngaff, sitting beside her and putting his bony arm around her shoulder. "Did you not retrieve Akeldama?"

Skye told them of her battle on top of the tower and of how she had lost Akeldama. For now, she left out Yop's involvement.

"That is indeed less than ideal," Corngaff continued in his soft tone, "but we always knew that slaying the Dark Queen in her own stronghold was not going to be easy. The stone was always our main aim. Without it, her powers are severely weakened. Whilst we may not have it, she doesn't, either."

"Geldrig and Brack, you will scour the base of the tower near where it fell as soon as we leave here. If you can find it and bring it back to us, all the better," instructed Snowbroth as they nodded their agreement.

"She is or was powerful," Skye warned. "She can control Akeldama's magic. She was able to throw me around like a ragdoll without lifting a finger." Skye yawned. "As soon as the orb fell over the edge, she seemed weaker, more vulnerable."

"It is quite possible that Akeldama was destroyed in the fall, though I doubt it," spoke Snowbroth from across the fire. "For now, I think we have had enough excitement. We should eat before the meat is spoilt, and then we will take a slow ride home."

They ate heartily and well into the afternoon. Skye had never felt as hungry as she suddenly did when she smelt the cooking meat. Part of her was relieved that her companions were not far angrier at her for not killing the Dark Queen, but another part of her was considering the consequences. She would be back. Skye knew it instinctively. She wouldn't go away and just disappear. She was too stubborn. Skye didn't mention her fears. She was too interested in hearing how the battle had gone during the night.

Brack told the story with a mix of excitement and awe. From the moment they had left Skye, they had been under attack from small groups that had broken from their regiments.

They dispatched most of them with ease and were able to break out into the plains beyond. There they had sounded their horns. When they were out of range of the archers, they had stopped to give the queen's soldiers time to form ranks and attack. As soon as they had left the tower and the group knew that Skye was as safe as she could be, they had turned on their heels and pushed their wolves to ride as hard as they could.

For most of the night the goblins had led their

foe a merry dance across the plains, heading into the woodlands if ever they came too close. All told, Brack argued, their enemies were in the thousands. Some were happy to disagree with him, and soon they numbered in the millions or even more, depending on who took up the story.

It wasn't until dawn started to break, around the time that Skye was finally making her way onto the top of the tower that they had to stop and fight. Their wolves would run no more, and Snowbroth was afraid that they might turn on their riders if they didn't rest.

At the edge of a thick woodland they had dismounted and formed a line, ready to embrace the army as it attacked. Most of their pursuers had long since quit and headed back to the tower, unbeknownst to Skye. In the dark shadows of the trees, they had met less than a hundred enemies, well-trained but tired from the chase.

At this point, Corngaff took up the story. He said that their enemies had fought hard but were falling nonetheless. Eventually, they heard the sound of a war trumpet and through the ranks pushed a huge, lumbering dark troll. Three times as tall as any man, it had crushed its own allies under its feet as it sped towards the group.

It was here that Gondrag had met his end. He had

raced ahead to tackle the beast on his own and had been swatted aside with one swing of the troll's mace. The rest had circled around, moving constantly to confuse it. Every now and again one of the enemy would try to circle round but they were dealt with easily.

One by one they had lunged to attack the troll, slowly cutting into its flesh whilst those on the front kept its attention. Eventually, the beast had succumbed and fell to the ground. At that point, what remained of the enemy had fled even before hearing the call of the queen's retreat.

For her part, Skye told her friends how she had channelled the magic of her mother's ring. She didn't talk about the darkness that she had felt from the stone. She had scared herself with how comfortable she had felt drawing on the darker magic.

Finally, all of the food had been eaten and the nightwolves well rested. With aching bodies, each member mounted their own ride, Skye rode on Gondrag's nightwolf, and they set off towards the north. Towards home.

Promise

The journey home was as uneventful as the journey to Liorath's Peak had been dangerous. They stopped off at the Druidmotte to rest and talk of their success to the druids. They nodded appreciatively, but, on some level, Skye suspected that this was all according to their plan.

Not wanting to battle with the snow again, they took a longer route across the southern tip of the Wandering Place, though it was still bitterly cold and Skye was forced to unpack all of her clothes that had since been packed away.

At Lörieas, Skye was dismayed to see that it was still in ruins, though some people were returning to claim their belongings or just anything that they could find. Geldrig had left them at this point to help his fellow countrymen with a promise to return to Skye's side should she ever need him. She had given him a hug and thanked him for everything that he had done for her. He left them with his face blushing red.

Before long they were spending the night in Dune, though this time they chose a different inn, not trusting the Wyvern's Wing anymore. The night passed without incident, and they all managed to eat a good meal and rest well.

It wasn't until they were back on the river on a borrowed boat that Skye felt the company really start to relax and accept that they were out of danger for the moment. As they rowed slowly upstream, Skye closed her eyes and listened as Brack broke into song:

'Twasn't long ago you were d'livered to us
You came through the woods all bluster and fuss
But ho! Skye listen t'me
I'll sing you a song of our sweet victory,

Hey ho, listen to me,
Hey ho, sing it with me!

They'll come a time not far from now
You'll think of our names, and you'll bend in a bow

We've fought side by side in this battle, have we
I'll sing you a song of our sweet victory!

Hey ho, listen to me,
Hey ho, sing it with me!

The queen, she is vanquished, she's left our fair land,
No thanks to us, we just lent a hand.
'Twas you who sent her away with a squawk,
We were just here to slaughter the orcs!

Hey ho, listen to me,
Hey ho, sing it with me!

At the last verse, they all fell into laughter, and Skye knew that somehow she would help them win their war. She didn't have a clue how, but she made a promise to herself that she wouldn't just leave like her mother had. She owed them more than that. She owed them her life.

Before nightfall, they had made their way to the dock from which they had begun their adventure and with eagerness in their step they pushed through the forest and on towards Snudge's mansion. Snowbroth knocked heavily on the door whilst the others stood back. When Snudge finally shuffled to the door and pulled it open, muttering under his breath about the ungodly hour, they all sprang forwards and bundled him into his own hallway.

When Snudge had finally come to his senses, he was overcome with a sense of joy and bid them all to sit and eat at his table whilst they told him news of their adventure.

They hadn't managed to find Akeldama at the foot of the tower, but they had vowed to return when warmer weather came.

Snudge was saddened to hear of the death of so many of their group. In all, they had lost four members, and each death stung as they recalled their passing in detail. When finally it fell to Skye to tell her part in the tale, she paused for a while wondering just how much to tell.

She started by recapping the story as the other goblins already knew it, but when she got to the tower, she told them everything. She told them of Yop's betrayal and his supposed allegiance to Elflock and Jargogle and she told them of his promise to serve the queen and how she had cut him down as soon as she was finished with him. The other goblins were in uproar at this revelation, but Snudge just sat there sadly listening to the story unfold.

After Skye had finished her tale and the group had had their say on how to handle the situation, Snudge lifted his head and nodded slightly to a guard by the door.

"Collect them," he instructed, and they all knew that Elflock and Jargogle would not be able to hide for long. "Do not despair, Skye. We will defeat her," Snudge reassured her. "She has fled weakened. Without Akeldama, she is nothing. I won't wait for the spring. I will send riders out this evening to start searching for it. If it is still there, Skye, we will find it. I promise." Snudge sighed and continued, "Though we will take care of Elflock, I fear this won't end the growing anger amongst some goblins. Jargogle was just a pawn. You must have seen the scars on his back where Elflock had him flogged? He was, in his way, powerless to his actions.

"Elflock's message, however, has picked up a power of its own. They will soon find a new leader. We must be vigilant at both home and abroad in the coming months. Sometimes the greatest terror is not from those alien to us but from those we think of as our friends."

Skye mentioned that when she had picked up the orb it had seemed chipped and dented, as though pieces had been removed. She chose not to mention the shard that had broken off when she had knocked it to the floor. She didn't want to admit that she had relished the power that it had given her and that she had felt her brain fizz and fly higher than she had thought possible. She wanted to explore it more, if she ever got the chance.

"I thought that the stone couldn't be damaged by normal means," she hinted. "What could have caused it?"

"This could be very grave, indeed," offered Snudge. "It is possible that part of Akeldama has been removed and hidden away, maybe in weapons or jewellery. On their own, they would be too small to imbibe much power, but, if collected together, there could be enough to allow the queen to rise again." He shuffled nervously.

"On the other hand," he continued, more cheerfully, "it could be nothing more than damage over the thousands of years since it was created. Do not worry yourself about it, little human. Soon enough, you will go home!"

Skye allowed herself to be led upstairs to a soft bed where she fell into a deep sleep from which she didn't fully awaken for several days. When she finally roused herself, she headed downstairs to find Weard in a small, sun-filled study rolling a small, shiny object over and over in her hands.

"Yours, I believe?" she motioned to Skye.

Skye wandered over to her friend and accepted her mother's ring back. She noticed that it had been polished to a shine, but, more impressively, a small, inky black stone had been set in the clasp on top. It looked all too familiar to Skye, and she held her breath as she took it and placed it back on her middle finger.

"I found *that* in your pocket. It is certainly an *unusual* stone. I can't say I've ever seen one like it before." Weard seemed to consider something for a moment before her face relaxed once again and she continued, "I wonder where it came from?" The healer looked at Skye and winked, "Maybe we will never know."

Skye chose not to give up any more information than she had too at this point. She still felt very tired and weak and knew that there would be plenty of time for stories and conclusions in the future.

Instead, she simply asked "Am I healed now?"

"Your body is healed, yes. Your mind may take a while longer. You have rested well, though, you will be able to return home soon."

"About that, how will I get back?"

"Snudge has been meeting with some of the more

powerful druids at the Druidmotte. I must say, you made quite an impression upon them when we first visited. They foresee big things for you Skye, big things indeed. I do not think your adventures here are done."

"I certainly hope not," Skye replied earnestly. "I have only completed half of what I set out to do. The queen is still out there. She is still linked to my mother, and I can't ever forget that."

"I believe it helps to think of it more as the shadow of her image. She cannot harm your mother, and your mother will be none the wiser of her existence, I am sure."

"Either way, I...we...cannot leave her to rise to power again. I will be back as soon as I am able."

"I am sure you will, little human. We are all changed by those we meet. You, more than any, are not the same person who set out on this adventure. I hope to see you grow more yet." The healer started to tidy away the items on the desk and lifted up a thin silver necklace, no thicker than a spider's web. On it hung a small, iridescent green flake that caught the light in an intriguing manner.

"For you," Weard said, offering it to Skye. "It is the dragon scale that I removed from your shoulder. May it forever remind you of your journey."

"Thank you," gushed Skye. "It is truly beautiful.

But what is the chain? Surely it will break?"

"It is woven from the silk of the glibberig. It is incredibly rare and equally beautiful, but it is stronger than the hardest of woods. It will last you well, Skye. Use it to remember that compared to fighting off a glibberig most problems seem insignificant!"

Skye felt herself relax and laughed at Weard's comment. She knew that Keith Boggart would hold no fear for her now. Nothing would, she was sure.

"Snudge wanted to see you in his room, Skye. I fear that, for now, this is goodbye. I honestly hope to see you again. Remember us fondly."

"I will," choked Skye as she fought back tears. "I promise; I will be back."

She leant forward and gave the goblin a hug that she never wanted to end. For a moment, Skye considered staying, fighting the war and living in this world alone. But part of her knew that she had to return to Earth. She had made promises to herself throughout the adventure that she would see her family again. She had to keep her promises for herself but also for them. They deserved answers, to know where she had been. More importantly, her mother deserved an apology and an acceptance of her belief in goblins and the rest.

Reluctantly, Skye made her way up a set of thick, wooden stairs. At the top, the corridor was decorated in plain wooden panelling punctuated at irregular intervals with plinths, upon which sat various models of inventions and contraptions.

Skye didn't pay much attention to them as she slowly made her way along the well-lit passageway. Unconsciously, out of the corner of her eye, she saw something that made her stop in her tracks. She doubled back on herself and examined each model closely as a collector might study a rare stamp.

Once she was happy that she had observed every tiny detail, Skye pressed on to the end of the corridor and burst through the door that she knew led to Snudge's office.

"They are all mine!" she blurted out, far more clumsily than she had intended.

"What are?" asked Brack as he spun around at the intrusion.

Skye stumbled for a moment as she took in the fact that all of her surviving companions, minus Geldrig and Weard, were all stood around Snudge's desk. Or rather, they had been before they rushed over to Skye to give her hugs and pats on the back. They had obviously not heard that she had woken from her deep sleep and were keen to make up for lost time. Eventually, she managed to wrestle herself from their grips and found herself face to face with a beaming

Snudge.

"My inventions! My designs!" she cried. "You have copies of them all in your hallway? How is that possible?"

"The link between our world and yours," Snudge smiled, "is not so distant or weak as you might imagine. True, not many people have passed through this way and none, to my knowledge, have passed from our world to yours." He coughed politely. "Other than when we sent Weard to, shall we say, give you a little push." He had the decency to look sheepish. "However, ideas are, shall we say, more fleeting in their alliances? Your world leaves an impression on ours. You have seen the effect of your mother on the Dark Queen, have you not?"

"You knew about that?" she asked.

"Alas, no. It would have saved a lot of heartache if I had. I have been filled in on the details since you returned. Your praises have been sung very highly indeed!" The goblin gave Skye a wink. "No, there is a lot we do not know yet about the queen, but she will be back. We can count on that."

"I will fight her," Skye interrupted. "I promised to destroy her, and I will."

"Of that I have no doubt, *brave* human. I have no doubt that we will see you again. But now, we must say goodbye."

Skye made her way around the group, thanking and hugging each in turn. Eventually, with teary eyes and a heavy heart, she made her way to where Snudge was standing next to an almost identical telescope to the one that she had looked through so long ago.

"My mother's way home." Skye pointed out bluntly as she wandered over to it. "But I thought it was lost?"

"It would appear," smiled Snudge, "that is has been found. A member of the Druidmotte brought it to us this very morning. It will, of course, be returned to Landragog once it has served our purpose."

Skye couldn't believe it. She was going home!

"It will hurt," she said, matter-of-factly.

"Nothing like what you have been through," replied Snudge as he aligned the scope to a tiny blue-green dot in the sky.

With a deep breath, Skye placed her eye to the eyepiece and waited. Within seconds she felt the familiar tug within her skull and, without daring to look back at her friends, was sucked through the eyepiece and into the darkness.

Holiday

Skye landed with a thump and skidded across a hard wooden floor until she crashed, headfirst into a pile of old chairs. She sat up, a little dazed, and took stock of her bearings. The lighthouse was the same as when she had left. Outside, the storm continued to rage against the rocks.

Hesitantly, Skye got to her feet and walked over to the spyglass by the broken windows. It looked perfectly ordinary, perfectly harmless. She knew better.

Backing away from the portal, Skye edged down the stone steps made lethal by the torrential rain. At the bottom, she turned and ran across the gravel path and through the back door into the house. She didn't stop until she had thrown herself into her bed and pulled the covers over her head. Skye was suddenly overcome with emotion. She was back! What was more, it seemed like time had stood still whilst she had been away. Ron and Wilma would have had no time to worry about her. They wouldn't even have noticed that she'd disappeared had they had the desire to seek her out. Skye was relieved that her adventure would go unnoticed but more concerned than ever about what would have happened had she died on Ithilmir. For now, she put those thoughts to the back of her mind. There'd be plenty of time for that later.

Downstairs, dinner was being served and Skye was being called to take part. The contrast from her previous experiences was startling. She found herself ravenously hungry and raced down the wooden stairs of her grandparents' house and stepped back into the real world.

Over the next few days, Skye tried hard to settle back into regular life. The summer was promising to be a particularly warm one, and she spent long days sat in the gardens of Shutterly Manor reading her books or beating her grandparents at croquet.

She still had nightmares sometimes and found it difficult to get up in the morning knowing that the most exciting thing she was likely to do was to catch a trout in the stream that ran along the far end of the estate.

Part of her yearned for adventure again, to go back

immediately and seek revenge against the Dark Queen. She knew that that it would have to wait.

There would be much to consider in the coming months.

As promised, a few weeks into the holiday, her parents turned up. As a surprise to Skye, they had brought Arthur along with them. He'd only returned from his holiday to Cyprus and Skye was jealous of his walnut tan. Moreover, she was overwhelmed with emotion. The three most important people in her life were with her, and she had never missed them so much.

Skye leapt at each arrival and hugged them so hard that they were forced to glance at each to see if either of them knew what was wrong. In the end, they just put it down to one of Skye's quirks and so it was that. Over the next few weeks, local farmers' markets and quaint villages in the surrounding countryside found themselves playing host to the family.

Each time they stopped and saw a gift shop, Skye would remark on how unrealistic the garden gnomes and goblins were. This always drew funny looks from her father and Arthur. Her mother remained silent though and merely nodded her agreement.

It wasn't until they were nearly at the end of the third week that Skye's mother took her to one side on the large sun patio.

"Skye, you have never showed anything but contempt for my indulgence in Nymphology and Gnomiculture. What has gotten into you? Must you insist on mocking me?" she asked with a sad look in her eye.

"Not at all, Mother. Let's just say, I had a little adventure that changed my mind."

"Oh?" her mother asked with raised eyebrows, "And what kind of adventure would that be?"

"Do you know the spyglass in the old lighthouse?"

"I am *very* familiar with it, yes."

"So am I." Skye gave her mother a wink.

"Well, I must say, I am very intrigued to hear your story! What happened?"

"All in good time, Mother. We have the rest of the summer to talk. Just know for now, that Fen says hello and your cherry seed finally grew!"

"The spyglass *and* the cherry tree? What a tale indeed! I cannot wait to hear it!"

With that, Skye stood and went in search of her father. She had promised to take him fishing for trout and didn't want to leave him waiting. Behind her, her mother was clasping her hands together and smiling more than Skye had ever seen her smile before.

All too soon, the summer days started to shorten

and Skye and her family returned home where Skye and Arthur spent a delightful few days tinkering with various designs for a paddle boat before finally taking it out onto the river. It moved well in the water, Skye thought, though she reflected that it was nothing compared to the boat that she and her companions had rowed down the Silver River.

Like all good things, the summer holidays drew to an end, and Skye and Arthur were soon engrossed in trying to catch up on homework that they had foolishly left until the last minute. Skye knew that school was only a few days away and that she would have to wait an entire year before she could visit her grandparents again and before she could return to Ithilmir. Next time, she thought, she would have to take Arthur with her.

On the last day before the new term started, Skye spent the afternoon sitting in her garden idly playing with her mother's garden gnomes. She invented names and little lives for each one before realising that this was not the path a sensible, intelligent girl should take, even if she now knew that gnomes existed.

As evening rolled around, she lifted herself up from the dry grass and slowly, methodically made her way to her bedroom. The night before going back to school was always the worst.

As she entered her bedroom, she was met by a large present, wrapped tightly in second-hand Christmas paper. Skye quickly ripped it open and was stunned into silence. Stood in front of her was the spyglass. It had been polished and cleaned, but it was unmistakably *the* spyglass. Taped to the lens was a note.

Dear Skye,

Do not make the same mistake I did. You know what lies on the other side of this eyepiece. Make sure you live your adventures to the fullest. Be safe.

Love, Mother

Skye beamed with excitement and threw the note onto her desk. In the garden, a pair of green eyes faded into the hedgerow as the cherry tree, long since dead, burst into blossom.

Skye polished the eyepiece with the hem of her T-shirt and placed her eye eagerly to the glass.

After all, one look couldn't hurt.

About the author

Matt Beighton is a primary school teacher from the middle of England. He has two young daughters who provide a constant source of inspiration and sleepless nights.

His unfortunate classes are often the test subjects for new stories and he feels that he owes them a debt of gratitude for putting up with some of the more terrible ones over the years.

If you have enjoyed reading this book, please leave a review online. Your words really do keep authors going!

To find out more visit
www.mattbeighton.co.uk

Made in the USA
Middletown, DE
28 August 2020